REMEMBER THE KISS

LEE WOODS

SHP
Shaw Hill Publishing

Copyright © 2022 Lee Woods

Printed in the United States of America

Published by Shaw Hill Publishing, Shaw Hill Road, Sanbornton, NH 03269

www.Shawhillpublishing.com

Special mention – Nora Jones, "Come Away With Me" used with permission.

Paperback ISBN- 978-0-9989503-4-1

Digital Online ISBN-978-0-9989503-5-8

Dedicated to true love~

Cambria

ONE

Caroline sunk deep in the chair as his words settled in her mind. The room began to spin. She rested her hand on the table in front of her to keep from falling over. Her attention focused on the metallic taste on the back of her tongue, and she realized her fingers were numb. She was in shock.

She knew she needed to keep her wits about her. She couldn't crumble, or yell, or lose control of her emotions. Twenty years. It was twenty years she lived with the man she now looked at as a stranger. Who was he? She didn't want to react to the news that surely would change her life. Not yet. She needed to think, to get away from him.

With that she said, "Why? Why would you do such a thing? And for twenty plus years".

Caroline watched Tom, waiting for a reply.

He lowered his gaze to the floor as he spoke without emotion. "I don't know. At some point I should have told you, but I couldn't, I didn't want to lose all this".

Caroline stared at him, her eyes shooting daggers, yet her words wouldn't come. She sat for a moment longer, realizing he had used her. She trusted him, believed in him, sacrificed a life for nothing. He sat across from her looking as though nothing was wrong. No guilt, no shame. Caroline didn't know what to say. She couldn't look at him any longer. She pushed back the chair and stood then walked away leaving Tom to wonder what would come next.

Caroline went about her daily routine while Tom's words echoed in her ears. All day his confession festered and ate at her soul. The more time that passed, the more betrayed she felt until her mind would be silent no more.

Evening came and the two were face to face in the kitchen. It was at that moment that Caroline found she could no longer be silent. She looked across the room at him and started. "I don't understand why you would do such a thing. You tricked me into respecting you and being proud of you for a life you didn't even live".

Tom's face turned red as frustration turned to anger. "I knew you wouldn't let this go. I knew it was too good to be true. You walked away and I thought that was the end of it. But no, you must harp on it. Can't you let it go? I said I was sorry".

Caroline tried to control the tone in her voice. "Let it go! You lied to me for twenty years about who you are! You made me believe you are a big military hero, metals, badges, pins, and stories of valor, whose valor? Whose life?"

She caught her breath, attempting to control her emotions. "You weren't even in the military. You humiliated me. You lied to my family, our neighbors, and our friends. You used me. You used me so you could have that car, the garage, and God knows what else".

Caroline started to pace the floor as she attempted to make sense of Tom's confession. "Now it all makes sense. Is that why you'd never take me anywhere? Were you afraid I might find out? Our whole marriage has been a lie. We have nothing. We have less than nothing. I will never trust you again. If you can lie to me and so many others

2

for all these years, who knows what else you've lied about. I can't love a man who I don't trust. Too many bad things have happened over the years. Things you've done and said, things that I have forgiven or discounted because I thought maybe they were a result of PTSD. You have no reason to treat my children the way you have. No reason to do to me the things you've done, the lies, and pornography and gossiping about my family. More lies. You lied about the porn, but when you're caught red handed, you said you wouldn't do it anymore. Then I find pictures on your phone, and your computer. The sad thing about that is you didn't have the foresight to remove any of it before asking me to help you fix issues with either. And even worse, pictures of my daughter's friend".

She stopped pacing and turned to face her betrayer. "All of it is making sense now, the lies about why you didn't have veteran's plates, your missing graduation picture, and uniform." Caroline felt sick to her stomach as the many stories flooded her mind. "The blanket you said you got in England while you did embassy duty. And the older woman you lost your virginity to over there". Her voice was escalating. "Lies, all of it. No Paris, no Norway. No searching for POWs in Cambodia and Laos. No jump wings, no sharpshooter". Caroline walked from the room as her head began to spin. She found the nearest chair in the dining room, where she sat down and placed her head in her hands as she rested her elbows on her thighs. It's all she could think of was the wasted years of her life. The time she spent chained to a house that wasn't a home. Taking care of a man she didn't know. She would never get back those years. She would never be able to do all the things she loved to do. Things she sacrificed to live with a stranger.

She listened as Tom walked from the room. He couldn't respond to Caroline. He had no defense. Caroline sat in the silence, only listening to the tic, tic of the clock. The clock that for the last twenty years passed the time that now seemed wasted, lost, never to be recaptured.

The rush of tears was followed by weeping. Caroline cried mourning a life she tried so hard to keep together, the family she now felt like she was forced to hold together, was gone. She knew now it was all a mirage, a mirage that was quickly vanishing, as reality set in.

Caroline opened her eyes as the wave crashed against the rocks. The cool water sprayed against her face, baptizing her into a new existence. The sting of the salt water burned against her warm skin, reminding her that every pleasure is followed by pain. Her life lessons opened her eyes to this fact.

It had been three years since Caroline experienced that life altering moment. It was time to let it go. It was time to move on and make the best of what life remained. This would be the last time she would allow herself to revisit the past. It was done. He was gone and Caroline vowed to move forward with life, living it for herself. Promising she would never again let a man into her life. From this day forward she would lock away her heart and throw away the key.

Woods

TWO

Caroline stood on the boardwalk leaning on the rail that overlooked the lake. She raised her face to the bright sun inviting the warmth to wash over her skin while she took in the sounds around her.

She closed her eyes as she listened to the footsteps that echoed as people passed by, and the distant ringing of pinball machines in the arcade that survived technology, living on as a testament of a novelty that became the video age. Cars drove by slowly, some leaving the Boulevard, others hoping to pull into a rare vacant parking space. Caroline smiled while she listened to the laughing child at the water's edge as mom warned her of the dangers of getting too close. Further out she could hear the waves slapping across the hull of a boat as it rocked with the current.

It was early in the day, but time stood still as the Boulevard came to life as it did each summer. When she was a teenager, Caroline spent many a summer day walking the wooden boardwalk and visiting the shops and arcades. That was many years ago. Everything seemed new then. The arcades were built in the 1930s but the beach she now looked down on was still being formed then. The sand had been trucked in when she was a child. Over the course of time the sand had shifted and changed the shoreline to become the beach she saw today. So much had changed yet it still felt familiar to her.

Caroline didn't know why she returned to the scene she frequented in her youth. Maybe she wanted to feel young again. Maybe she wanted to forget the last thirty years of her life. The familiarity of the site somehow comforted her. It was that comfort she hoped would help her begin again.

She surely intended to put the past behind her. She agreed that coming to the Weirs would put a smile on her face and help her get back some of her youthful energy and infuse her with the positivity she desired, to continue her journey toward a better life. For the first time in her adult life, she felt free. She felt light as a feather and knew she was experiencing a renewal. She would look forward to any experience that presented itself.

Andrew jumped off the boat as it approached the dock. He quickly threw the rope around the post and secured it. He looked up at the boardwalk as he tied the final knot. Then he stood up, his attention drawn toward a curious sight. He studied her, as she stood there, her lips forming a slight smile. He was oblivious to the crowd of people passing by as he wondered what she was thinking, what would make her look so lovely and carefree. He was captivated by the innocence of the woman that he knew must be old enough that she probably couldn't be innocent.

Andrew watched her a moment longer than wiped his hands on his brown cargo shorts. He tugged at the back of his t-shirt that got caught in the waistband, all the while looking at the woman who had no idea he existed, yet he felt as though he knew her. He looked around at the people passing, walking to their destination. He was momentarily distracted by the sounds of those gathered as they waited for the Mount Washington to dock. But his attention returned to the woman on the boardwalk, and he soon forgot about the gathering crowd.

Andrew moved away from the boat and walked across the dock. He approached the steps skipping every other tread as he made his way toward the boulevard, never taking his eyes off the woman. He was embedding a picture of her in his mind, fearful she would disappear before he reached her. She was small in stature. Her hair was a brassy blond and her skin glowed in the sunlight. The slight breeze moved through her hair as the sun radiated down on her slight figure.

Andrew slowly approached her, ignoring the traffic on the boulevard, then stopped next to her. He followed her example and leaned on the rail cocking his head so he could continue to study her; small straight nose, lips of pale pink, and a slight indent above her left brow, all set in a heart shaped face. She stood motionless, unaware of his presence. Or so he thought.

Caroline opened one eye and looked to her left at the man who stood next to her. When he didn't say anything, she opened the other eye and turned to face him. She shifted her weight from one leg to the other and waited for him to speak.

He smiled at her but still didn't speak. She waited another minute that began. "Cat got your tongue?"

He shook his head and smirked at her comical question. "Oh no, no cat, just you." He stumbled over his words briefly then composed himself. "I mean, you don't have my tongue, of course. What I meant is, you are a curious woman standing there smiling at... well nothing I guess, with your eyes closed. I'm trying to figure out what has you so amused."

Caroline watched him as he tried to explain himself. She knew the man but chose not to let on. She wondered why he was here in this town. Why would a celebrity of his standard be here? Additionally, why would he be talking to her?

Remember The Kiss

She continued to smile as she watched him. His eyes were dark, darker than they looked on the screen. His black hair was shorter now than in his last picture and his face was clear of any stubble. She liked the length his hair was at now better. He was taller and broader in real life, which she thought curious because she would think a person would appear larger than life in the movies.

Andrew interrupted her rambling thoughts. "What I meant is I didn't want to speak because I didn't want to disturb you. You looked peaceful." He paused as a smile crossed his face. "Although I find it curious that you could find such peace here amid all this activity."

Caroline leaned on the rail again her attention caught briefly by the sound of the ships horn. The Mount Washington was approaching the docks, preparing for those that waited patiently to board. "I used to come here all the time when I was younger. I don't know what brought me here today, but I feel free here." She shook her head. "I can't explain it, let's just say it's been a long thirty years."

He turned and rested his elbow on the rail. "You don't have to explain to me. Sometimes we find peace amid chaos, sometimes we can't hear ourselves think in the silence. I get it."

Caroline smiled and reached out her hand. "I suppose we should introduce ourselves if we're going to continue this conversation. My name is Caroline".

He followed suit and took her small hand in his. My name is Andrew Roberts. Do you have a last name, Caroline?"

Caroline laughed out loud. "Funny you should ask. I've had a few last names. I'm trying to decide which one I want to keep."

Andrew looked at her curiously. "Which one to keep? What do you mean?"

Caroline shook her head and turned to face the water. "I don't know why I would talk to you about myself. I don't even know you, but you asked. I don't have anything to hide. To make a long story short, I've been married a couple of times in my long life. One name I've had twice as long, as the other, yet I think I'd like to be rid of both names. I don't mean that in a negative way. At this time in my life, I'm learning to let go, cut the cords so to speak. I think that by keeping either name keeps me connected to that which I'm trying to distance myself from. So, for now I'm just Caroline".

Andrew laughed as he studied the smiling face, trying to guess her age. He would have guessed thirty-five. What did a long thirty years mean? "Ok, Caroline it's nice to meet you. Do you mind my asking what captures your attention here? What brings you to stand on a boardwalk surrounded by strangers with a smile on your face?"

Caroline shrugged her shoulders. "I read somewhere that if you smile your brain will think you're happy. Eventually, if you smile enough, your brain will be convinced, and you will truly be happy." She paused to consider what she said, then continued. "I'm returning to the scene of my youth. Maybe I'm hoping I can get back a bit of what I lost for all those years."

"Is it working?" Andrew asked.

Caroline shook her head as she continued to look out at the lake."

Andrew watched her as her brown eyes focused on the sailboat a short distance from the shore. "What are you thinking?"

Caroline's expression changed only long enough for Andrew to notice the split second of sadness pass across her face. "The sailboat, I was watching the sailboat. I love to sail. Not professionally of course. When I see a sailboat, I remember as a child my father taking me sailing. Not on a boat of that size of course. We had a small boat; I think it was a Sunfish. We'd sail around the lake and sit quietly. He didn't talk much. I loved the peaceful feeling of being on the water. That was so long ago I barely remember it."

"Would you like to go sailing again, Caroline?" Andrew asked.

Caroline nodded as she listened to the waves hit the shore. "Yea, I think someday I'd like to go. Who knows, maybe someday the opportunity will present itself."

"I don't mean someday Caroline. I mean today, right now."

The smile returned to Caroline's face. "What are you talking about?"

Remember The Kiss

Andrew looked out at the boat moored at the dock. "I can take you sailing, right now." He nodded as he pointed toward the dock and repeated himself. "I can take you out. I know it might seem like a strange offer, considering we just met".

Caroline studied Andrew for a minute. Long enough to feel a connection that she knew couldn't exist. "You're right Andrew, I barely know you. You want me to go out on a boat with you. For all I know you could take me out, drown me and dice me into little pieces. I'm not sure that's a good idea."

Andrew laughed. "What's not a good idea, going sailing or me dicing you up in little pieces?"

"Funny." Caroline was now serious. "I'm only now beginning to enjoy my life. I don't want it to end because I made a stupid choice."

Andrew studied Caroline as he tried to find the words which he knew would never sound right. "Do you know who I am, Caroline? Do you really think I would do something like that?"

Caroline couldn't help but see the hurt in Andrew's face. In her heart she felt she would be safe. It was her head that kept telling her to be careful. "For my whole adult life, I've done what my head told me to do, and it hasn't turned out too well. Maybe it's time to follow my heart." She hesitated as she decided. "OK, I guess if I'm going to die, what better way to go than sailing."

Andrew scowled. "That's not funny Caroline."

Caroline shrugged her shoulders. "Ok, sailor, let's go. And by the way, yes, I know who you are. I just don't want you to think I think any more or less of you because you're a movie star."

Andrew chuckled as he stepped away from the rail and started for the boat. "Ok then, come with me."

Caroline smirked as she pushed herself away from the rail. "Said the spider to the fly".

"That's enough of that." Andrew scolded.

Andrew and Caroline walked up the boardwalk then down to the dock. He lifted his hand which Caroline took as she stepped into the white boat that loomed above her. It surely was nothing like the small *Sunfish* she remembered from her youth. She stood with one hand on the post while Andrew untied the boat. He smiled as he stepped aboard. First, he showed Caroline where the life vests were. Then he guided her to a seat next to him. He explained that he would only use the motor until they were away from the dock and out in open water.

Caroline nodded, but as soon as the wind swept across the bow of the boat Andrew's words were drowned out by her childhood memories. She closed her eyes for a moment while she remembered.

Andrew stopped talking and looked over at Caroline who sat back against the seat unmoving, eyes closed, that conspicuous smile across her pale pink lips. He turned off the engine and let the boat glide through the water feeling the momentum slow. It was quiet except for the occasional speedboat that raced by. Andrew watched Caroline while she sat peacefully as the boat rocked back and forth through the waves.

He then busied himself with the sails as he wondered where her mind had drifted to, knowing it must be somewhere in the distant past, on a small boat, on a small lake, sharing a special moment. Andrew stopped in the silence occasionally to study her face. He thought it a pretty face, yet the true beauty came from within. She somehow radiated light and he couldn't help but be attracted to her. He knew it was ridiculous to thinks such thoughts, but there was that feeling; connectedness, that he shrugged off as coincidence. He couldn't believe he even went to talk to her let alone invite her to sail with him.

Caroline opened her eyes and caught Andrew as he studied her. She offered that bright smile, which lit up her face. "What are you looking at Andrew? You're not conspiring my demise, are you?" she joked.

He smiled then spoke without breaking eye contact. "You. You captivate me. I don't know what it is about you but you're somewhat of an enigma. As Alice would say, curiouser and curiouser. How could I wish your demise?"

Caroline let out a loud laugh. "An enigma? That's funny. I think I'm the most transparent person I know. Not a thing to hide. Why would you say that?"

"I don't know. It's just that I don't generally approach strange women and invite them to go sailing." Andrew looked out at the mountains on the far side of the lake to clear his mind. He then returned to focus on Caroline. "Maybe being in a strange place, not knowing anyone has forced me to step outside my comfort zone. And you looked so peaceful. I think I was hoping if I spoke to you the peaceful feeling would rub off on me."

Andrew stood up and walked toward the ropes. It was time to sail. "In any case, here we are. Are you ready to sail across the lake in the bright light of this scorching sun?"

Caroline stood and followed Andrew. "I'm ready. I think this will be a little different though. I'm used to sitting closer to the water, able to reach the rudder and sail without moving more than an inch or two."

"Ah, you are right. This boat is nothing like the little *Sunfish* you sailed on as a child." He turned and looked at Caroline. "Do you want to learn to sail or just enjoy the ride?"

Caroline looked up at the sails as they fluttered in the wind. "I think I might like to learn."

"I thought you might say that." Andrew smiled as he tugged at the rope. "Now that you're beginning a new life, you are becoming braver and more willing to challenge yourself."

"What makes you say that, Andrew? Do you know me so well already?" Caroline joked.

"I can't claim to know you well, but I can claim to know myself, and I can see in you a sense of adventure fighting its way to the surface." His smiled faded as he continued. "Be careful, Caroline, once it's set free, there is no turning back."

"You sound like that's a bad thing, Andrew, why?"

He shook his head. "No, not bad necessarily, it's just that from what you say, you've been quietly hidden away all these years, if you lose your focus, you could get hurt. I wouldn't want that for you Caroline."

Caroline nodded. "I understand. I suppose you're right. I'll have to pace myself." She turned from Andrew and faced the wind. She smiled and spread her arms as though she would take off. She then turned back to Andrew and flashed a full smile. "I hope I can contain my enthusiasm."

Andrew threw back his head and laughed out loud. Caroline watched as he shook his head in disbelief of her response. She liked his laugh. It was bold and unguarded. She though it a sign of his carefree nature. She was surprised at how comfortable she felt in his company. She smiled inwardly as she thought this scheme to be completely out of character for her. She would mark this as the first step into her new life.

Andrew raised his hand and waved Caroline to his side. "Ok pay attention. If you want to learn, you must pay attention. Sailing is enjoyable, but it might take a while for you to think so. You have a few things to learn about sailing before you can relax and enjoy the ride."

Caroline nodded as she approached Andrew's side. "This won't be anything like the little dinghy I sailed on as a child".

Andrew shook his head and smiled. "No. It won't. As a matter of fact, you are about to embark on a lesson that will change the way you see sailing."

Caroline looked up at him as she giggled. "I don't think it can be that different. Both boats have a sail, a rudder, and move through the water by force of wind. How different can they be?"

"Well, in a way you're right, but this boat does have a motor, the wheel controls the position of the rudder through mechanical linkage, and this boat is longer, about 30 feet, considerably larger." He teased.

Andrew gently placed his hand on Caroline's waist. He could feel her tense up as he directed her to the wheel. Sensing her discomfort, he took one step back moving his hand to the wheel. "Once the boat is in motion you can direct it with the wheel by turning it left to move left, and right to move to the right. This may seem obvious because you would steer your car in a similar fashion. If you were steering the boat using a tiller you would move it left to turn right and right to turn left."

Caroline nodded as she recovered from the rush that came over her when he touched her. "I did know that."

"Andrew smiled as he continued to instruct. "Like a car, when the boat is moving faster, steering becomes more efficient, you can turn the wheel or tiller less to achieve the same arc. If you're moving slow, you would need to turn harder for a longer time to achieve the same arc." He stopped speaking and looked down at Caroline. "How are you doing? Are you lost yet?"

Caroline shook her head. "No, I'm good."

"Ok then. One of the draw backs of steering with a wheel versus a tiller, is it compromises the feel of the boat. The wheel has more internal friction due to its associated parts. Steering with a tiller allows you to feel the water as it flows beneath the boat. I prefer to steer using a tiller for that reason.

But here we are standing behind the wheel. You can stand to either side if you wish, so you can control the wheel. You want to be comfortable, but you also want to have clear visibility." He pointed forward to the sails. "The sails on this boat can obstruct your view so you'll want to move around while in motion because the sails cause blind spots that you'll need to work around.

Still good?" A motorboat sped by leaving in its wake waves that rocked the boat causing Caroline to lose her balance. Andrew reached out to balance her, then stepped closer to keep her steady until the waves subsided. Andrew smiled at her as she focused on the dark eyes that looked down at her.

Her heart skipped a beat, and she recovered her footing.

Andrew broke the silence. "Sailing can be dangerous if you don't pay attention to your surroundings. Not all boaters pay attention, so we need to be aware of what goes on around us. That leads me to mention the dangers of sailing. It's usually safer to sit forward of the skipper. On boats where there is a crew that's usually where they sit. Most of the time they sit on the windward side."

Caroline interrupted. "Windward?

"Oh yea. Sorry." Andrew smiled impressed that she was paying attention. "The windward side of the boat is the direction upwind from your point of reference, toward the wind or the side of the boat the wind hits first. The leeward side of the boat is opposite the windward side. The crew could move to that side if the wind were very light or they were sailing downwind, to help the skipper balance the boat.

Anyone on the boat should be aware of certain dangers. Even on a beautiful day like today there could be situations that rock the boat. Like that boat that sped past earlier. Some of those boats leave in their wake big waves. So, you should be aware of certain things like standing clear of the sail, the most obvious one. Stay away from the bow and stern of the boat unless necessary. If you find it necessary to go there, then hold on to the rails to keep steady."

"Why is that?" Caroline asked.

"The motion of the boat is accentuated at the ends. The movement is stronger, more forceful. You could lose your balance and get hurt, or worse still, be thrown from the boat. It sounds a little extreme, and may be is for the lake, but if you were on the ocean, it could be a real possibility.

I mentioned the leeward side of the boat a few minutes ago. It can be quite dangerous if the boat is heeling or leaning into the wind. The leeward side of the boat is closer to the water in these situations. Because the leeward side of the boat is closer to the water that makes you closer to the water. Gravity is not your friend in that situation."

Andrew looked around the boat for his next point of instruction. "You should stay away from anything shiny. Shiny means slippery. Slippery surfaces are accidents waiting to happen." He stopped and took a deep breath. "So, the safest place to be on the boat is right here." He moved even closer to Caroline and tightened his hand around her waist.

Caroline's heartbeat quickened at his touch. It wasn't the light touch of him steadying her as the boat rocked. It wasn't a suffocating one either. Caroline found Andrew's arms inviting, his hand was warm, and she could sense his strength as he helped her regain her balance. She struggled in the silence of the moment to find the words she needed to regain control of his senses, while allowing Andrew to hold her steady.

Her eyes wandered to the back of the boat, her effort to avoid eye contact with Andrew. "Earlier you mentioned the rudder.

Does it work the same way on this boat as it did on the little dinghy, I'm familiar with?"

Andrew cleared his throat and stepped back from Caroline, just enough so he could turn to face her. "Yes, the rudder. It hangs underneath the back end of the boat."

Caroline lightly laughed. "I know, Andrew."

Andrew's face grew flush. "Sorry. Of course, you do. Anyway, there is the rudder and the centerboard." He paused to confirm. "You know the keel or center board, right? It keeps the boat from skidding sideways from the force of the wind. It also provides lift so the boat can sail closer to the wind. This boat has a fixed keel."

He turned his attention to the mast. "This boat has an aluminum mast. The wires you see are called the standing rigging, and they should be inspected on a regular basis. You don't need to be concerned with that though. All of this supports the sails.

I look at the sail as the engine of the boat. It catches the wind that forces the boat to move. As you see this boat has two sails, the main sail and the headsail which is often referred to as the jib."

Andrew moved toward the mast where he took hold of the rope. "When a sailboat is ready to sail, these ropes hang loosely waiting to support the activity of sailing. We say the sailboat is rigged. There are several ropes. Some people refer to the ropes as "lines". You know, 'throw me the line'. Each rope or line has its own name." He turned and pointed upward. "The rope running up the mast is called the halyard."

Andrew reached out and grabbed the rope in front of him. "The most important rope for you to know today is the sheet. It's the primary line that adjusts the sail trim. That would be the angle of the sail to the wind. This referred to with the sail it adjusts. "

He tugged at the rope. "Pulling the mainsheet can be a tough job. Thankfully, we have a system of blocks, or pullies to make pulling the lines easier. A typical mainsheet has a cleat conveniently located to make it easier to control the rope."

Andrew stopped talking and turned to Caroline. She stood at the wheel looking as though ready to take control of the sailboat. The wind blew through her hair while it shimmered in the sun. She looked ready to take on the world. He smiled as he moved toward her. "Any questions?"

Caroline studied Andrew as he approached. "That's it?"

"That's it. Well, not really, but that's what you need to know for now."

"I didn't mean 'that's it' as in it's no big deal. What I meant is you make it sound like something I could handle. Well, maybe not on my own. Not right away anyway."

"I know what you meant Caroline. When you look at a boat of this size, it can be intimidating especially, if you don't know all the moving parts." He watched her eyes twinkle with excitement.

Andrew then reached out and took her hand. "Are you ready to feel the wind Caroline?"

Caroline looked down at Andrew's hand. It was large compared to hers. He placed his other hand over hers, waiting for a reply. Her breath caught in her throat as she forced a reply. "I'm ready and willing."

He looked into her eyes thinking about what she said. *I'm ready and willing*. He knew she meant sailing, but he was thinking about her being willing to take a different leap of faith as she had before. He caught himself as he realized there wasn't a 'before".

Caroline withdrew her hand from Andrew's as a breeze came up and moved her hair across her face. She brushed it away as she laughed. "I guess I better be ready to feel the wind. I think it's ready."

Andrew lifted his hand to Caroline's face and brushed the final few strands of hair away from her forehead. "I guess that's our signal. When I said feel the wind, I meant tracking it. The wind can shift directions quickly, so you need to remain alert."

Andrew placed his hands, on Caroline's shoulders and turned her to face the front of the boat. "Close your eyes, Caroline". He leaned closer until he was inches from her ear. "The best way to track the wind is to feel it on your face. When you close your eyes, you heighten your other senses. Move your face until the wind is blowing straight at you. Shift your face from left to right until you feel it balanced across your face and you hear the wind the same in each ear. The wind shifts so you should do this throughout your trip so ensure you stay aware when the wind changes direction."

He stepped back and watched as Caroline closed her eyes and lifted her face to the sun. She smiled while she moved her face back and forth until her hair blew back from her forehead equally on each side. The smile again. The captivating smile that caught his attention earlier, now reminded him how lonely his life was.

Caroline opened her eyes and looked at Andrew as she pointed. "The wind is blowing this way I can feel it." She then leaned forward and giggled. "I can also see it." She pointed to the flag on a drifting boat. "The flag on that boat." She then pointed to the water. "You can tell by the water too."

"Yes, you can use those stationary items as a guide, but I think feeling it is better. The flag could be moving based on the movement of the boat, even if it looks like its drifting. And the wave, well, we're on a lake that sports many boats. The water is influenced by all that movement." He watched the smile fade from Caroline's face.

"Ok, let's get out there, enough education. Now that we know the direction of the wind, we can use it to move us into the broads. We've already prepared the boat and inspected the standing rigging, you know ropes, turnbuckles, and cotter pins. Now we need to determine the wind direction." Andrew hesitated before continuing his lesson. "I believe you've taken care of that for us.

Now we point the boat into the wind. This allows for the least amount of wind resistance. We've already raised the sail and we are moving so some of what I'm telling you I've already done. We use the motor to keep the boat pointed toward the wind while we hoist the sail. I did that while we were talking earlier.

Next, we would attach the sails. We secure the bottom front of the mainsail and jib to their respective shackles on the boom and bow of the boat." He reached for the small line attached to the rear corner of the mainsail. "I pull this line, called the outhaul line taught and cleat."

He signaled for Caroline to join him, and he handed her the line. "This keeps the mainsail smooth and allows the air to flow over it. We then hoist the mainsail by pulling down on the halyard until it stops." Andrew worked the lines with Caroline. "This is tricky. You need to keep the sail tight enough to remove any fold, yet loose enough so you don't create vertical creases in the sail.

Next cleat the halyard. Using the jib halyard, raise the front of the sail and cleat the halyard off. Both sails will be moving freely now. Always raise the mainsail first then the jib because it's easier to point the boat into the wind using the main. Then we adjust our heading and sail trim for the wind."

While Andrew instructed, they both worked the sails together. They trimmed the jib sheets, then the mainsail. They watched the direction of the wind and adjusted the sails for that change. Andrew watched Caroline closely. "You're a fast learner, Caroline. Somehow, I'm not surprised."

"Well, I do like being on the water. Maybe I was a pirate in another life." Caroline joked.

Andrew laughed. "That would be something to see."

They sailed into the wind trimming the sheets tighter, so the sails were more closely in line with the boat. Caroline was keeping up with Andrew, but her hands were feeling the effects of the moving ropes. She knew she would have blisters tomorrow but wouldn't give up.

Andrew turned from the sail, "you said you had children, Caroline. Are they still local?"

Caroline rubbed her hand on her shirt. "Yes, I have children. A son and a daughter. My son lives in New York. He works for a software company out there. My daughter took a job recently in Chicago. She took a job for a big law firm out there. She interned with them, and they hired her as soon as she passed the Bar." She smiled while she thought about how hard they worked to get a good education. "I'm proud of them, but I miss having them around. I'm getting used to it though."

Their conversation was interrupted as a gust of wind came up. They continued to turn into the wind tightening the sheets as they went. They laughed as the wind challenged them to keep control of the sails.

"I don't remember hearing about you marrying. Did you ever marry?" Caroline cautiously asked.

Andrew's eyes were wide with surprise. "You've been stalking me, Caroline." He joked. "What, are you one of my groupies?"

Caroline laughed out loud. "No, Andrew. I'm not one of your groupies. But be honest, it's difficult for any celebrity to have a private life. I just don't remember hearing that you married. I'm curious, that's all."

Andrew nodded. "Yes. Curiouser and curiouser. That's Caroline."

"Seriously though. Did you ever find anyone after… well you know?" Caroline was embarrassed.

"It's ok, Caroline. No, I never did. I suppose I never took the time to look. My career took off shortly after and I never looked back. I couldn't. The memories were, well, they were too difficult to relive. Now. Sometimes I think I'm too old."

"Andrew. You're never too old to love." Caroline's eyes met Andrew's. He studied Caroline, challenging her to make an offer. "I think it would be easier for you if you weren't always on the go."

He held her gaze. "Well maybe if someone would step up, I might be willing to slow down."

Caroline looked away afraid his gaze would hypnotize her into speaking out of turn. "Andrew, I'm sure there is someone out there waiting for you. After all they say there's someone for everyone."

Andrew looked down at his feet. 'What about you, Caroline?"

Caroline dropped the rope and walked to the opposite side of the boat. "Oh no Andrew. There's nothing for me. My match must have seen me and run for the hills. I'm not meant for anything anymore. I think the safest thing for me to do is to sail into the sunset and be done with it."

Andrew followed her and stopped in front of her. "I find that difficult to believe, Caroline. I bet you have a lot to offer the right man. The challenge for you will be to open your heart and trust him when he shows up." He hesitated. "Maybe he has already shown up."

The wind shifted again saving Caroline from having to reply. They worked the sails together gliding across the lake enjoying the scenery as they continued their conversation, until eventually the wind died down.

When the wind subsided, and the sails were released Andrew moved to the wheel while Caroline found a quiet place at the front of the boat.

Andrew watched Caroline as she sat in silence. She looked out over the water as it captured the setting sun. The long day was closing and the bright rays of earlier now dimmed, and the muted light of early evening marked the end of an adventure. The shadows of early evening cast by the mountains were evidence of the closing of a day to remember.

Caroline's silent moment was interrupted by Andrew's deep voice. "Earth to Caroline." He slowly approached the front of the boat. "Have you left me for someplace better?"

Caroline turned to Andrew and smiled. "Absolutely not." She turned back to the lake and opened her arms to the fading sun. "I'm here. Look at this. It's beautiful and serene. The colors reflect off the water, the setting sun glistens in the motion of water that lulls us and comforts us, distracting us from this crazy world. There are no words."

Andrew stopped beside Caroline and placed his hand on her shoulder. "I don't know, Caroline. I think you hit the nail on the head. It's beautiful and serene. And everything else you said."

Caroline turned back to Andrew. "This was the most perfect day. I thoroughly enjoyed myself. Thank you for offering to take me sailing." She looked down at the boat rails as a slight smile emerged.

Andrew looked at her curiously. "What's so funny?"

Caroline lifted her face to Andrew's. "I'm still alive. I'm assuming there will be no drowning or dicing involved in this day."

They both broke out in laughter. "Caroline, you are a curious woman."

Caroline nodded in agreement. "Yea, well I'm still learning how to behave in public. I hope you'll forgive me."

"I'll think about it. In the meantime, were getting ready to dock." Andrew pointed at the dock in front of a house, not the docks at the boulevard.

Caroline was overcome with a moment of panic. "Where are we? I thought you were taking me back to the docks?"

Andrew read Caroline's mind. "Don't worry Caroline, everything is fine. I told you, no drowning or dicing. There is something I want you to see. I've been thinking about it for the last hour or so. I wasn't sure until I saw your reaction to the setting sun on the lake."

He pointed to a deck on the roof of the house that grew larger as they arrived at the dock. "I thought we could grab a bite to eat while we wait for it to get dark. You won't believe the rush you'll get when you look at the stars from that deck."

Caroline's face grew red, and her voice began to shake as she spoke. "I don't know why you thought I would agree, just like that. Maybe I have plans tonight. My car is probably being towed as we speak."

Andrew's eyes grew wide. "Wow, Caroline. Relax. I wasn't assuming anything. I just thought, well, the sun is already setting, and you seem to appreciate a beautiful spectacle. Plus, as I said the sun has gone down and you didn't say anything about needing to get back so I thought maybe we would have dinner before I bring you back to your car."

Caroline lowered her gaze to the deck of the boat as her face turned red, this time a result of embarrassment, not anger. She tried to smile as she responded. "I'm sorry. I don't have plans, and dinner would be fine. I guess I got a little nervous for a minute. I'm still a little stuck on drown and dice." She shrugged her shoulders.

Andrew studied her for a minute then spoke. "You really have some trust issues, don't you?"

Caroline nodded. "Most certainly. Not many good things have come out of my relationships. No drowning or loss of body parts, but I guess, mistrust is mistrust."

"Well, I know we've only known each other for one day, but you can trust that I won't hurt you." His look softened and he continued. "I've enjoyed spending the day with you. I think we have a lot in common. I bet we could be good friends." He hesitated. "If time allows."

"Time is the thing, isn't it? There's either too much of it or not enough." Caroline noticed that Andrew seemed lost in the moment. "You know we live in an age where the world has shrunk considerably. Just fifty years ago it was difficult to travel and communicate with any efficiency. Today, however, we can be thousands of miles apart and still have a real time conversation. Andrew, we can still build a friendship."

A smile flashed across her face. "We can be pen pals."

Caroline's joke drew Andrew back to her and the conversation. "Have I told you that you are a curious woman?"

She laughed as she stepped out of the boat. "Curiouser, and curiouser. So, what's for dinner?"

"Let me get the boat moored and we'll discuss it. Here." He tossed the end of the rope to Caroline. "Tie this off, will you?"

Caroline busied herself with the knot while Andrew buttoned up the boat. The sun disappeared and the dusk of evening was intruding on what remained of daylight. They finished securing the boat and walked up the dock to the house.

THREE

Caroline surveyed the house as they walked up the steps. It was a large modern house. What faced the lake was a mass of glass exposing the living space to whoever passed by. She was sure she wouldn't want to live there. The closer they got the more she could see it wasn't an inviting space. She thought it a shame that such a view wouldn't be enjoyed with warmth and love. She stiffened as they approached the door.

Andrew stopped before he reached the door then turned to Caroline. "What is it? I sense tension. You're not worried about drown and dice, again, are you?"

Caroline giggled. "No, I'm not. Forgive me. I was thinking this didn't seem like a house you would live in."

"This isn't my house, Caroline. I wouldn't buy a house like this. It's too much. Money can be better used elsewhere. This belongs to a friend of mine. He sent me out here this weekend. He said I needed to get away. I needed some quiet time." He reached for the door latch and opened the door signaling Caroline to enter.

She stepped over the threshold into a cold room. She thought the air conditioner must be working overtime.

Andrew read her mind and nodded. "Hold on, I'll see if I can turn it down."

She stood in what was probably referred to as a great room. It was large and the open concept made it seem larger. Caroline wondered who cleaned the lights that hung from the cathedral ceiling. She looked up as Andrew walked back into the room. Her heart skipped a beat as he walked toward her. She dismissed the feeling chalking it up to temporary movie star insanity. She was sure many people experienced it. It didn't mean anything.

"Ok. I turned it off. It's damn cold in here. I can't imagine what the electric bill must be in this place." He walked to the kitchen and opened the refrigerator.

Caroline snickered. "I don't imagine the person who owns this place has cause to be concerned with the expense of the electric bill."

Andrew scanned the space then chuckled. "I suppose you're right. Waste is waste." He returned his attention to the refrigerator. "Is there anything you won't eat?"

Caroline laughed. "Well, that's an open-ended question. Of course, there are things I won't eat. What are you referring to?"

"I just meant, are you a vegetarian or vegan or paleo? You know. Everyone has their thing."

"I try to eat healthy, but I'm not neurotic about it. If possible, organic is good but I wouldn't put out anyone to suit my eating habits." Caroline walked to the kitchen.

Andrew decided. "Ok then. How about grilled chicken? It's simple but I should be able to dress it up"

Caroline nodded. "Sounds good to me. How can I help?"

"You can sit right there and talk to me while I cook." Andrew removed the chicken from the refrigerator and began preparing dinner.

"You're pretty good at that. Where did you learn to cook?" Caroline joked.

"I'll never tell." He whispered.

"Ok, then I won't ask". Caroline replied.

"So Caroline, you haven't told me what you do for work. Are you a secret agent?" He joked.

Caroline snickered. "No, I'm not a secret agent. I'm working as a freelance writer."

Andrew looked up from the chicken he was marinating. "Really. You work from home then?"

Caroline looked puzzled. "Yes, I do. It's convenient and allows me to work independently."

"I see." Andrew dropped the subject.

Caroline watched as he finished dicing the pepper. He tossed the salad then placed it in front of Caroline. "Would you mind putting this on the table please?"

"Of course not."

Andrew walked around the counter and placed the chicken on the table. He went to the cupboard and returned with plates, silverware, and glasses. Then directed Caroline to the table where they enjoyed their dinner.

They finished the meal with little conversation. It was a comfortable silence that was interrupted with only a few questions.

"Andrew, I'm curious. What's it like to live as a 'movie star'?"

Andrew set down his fork. "It has its ups and downs. I get to travel a lot. Some movie roles allow me to be a hero. That's fun." He joked.

"It's great that you've played a variety of characters. You haven't gotten stuck in the situation where you only act in one type of movie. You really get to showcase your talent."

"Really? Wow. And how many of my movies have you seen? You are a groupie." He teased.

Woods

"No, Andrew. I'm not a groupie. Be real. There aren't that many good movies. You've acted in some of the good ones. That's all. You're pretty talented."

"Wow. Thanks."

"Don't let it go to your head. There are some good actors out there." Caroline paused to think. "To me there is something about you more impressive than the acting."

"And what's that?"

"Your charitable contributions, and your down to earth outlook on life. I'm impressed with you as a role model for young people. Your charitable work shows me and others that you know what's truly important." Caroline watched him, waiting for him to respond.

"Hmm. I'm not the only celebrity to be charitable."

"True. But your one of the few that finds it more comfortable to live is a small home than the Taj Mahal."

"I like to live simply."

"I see that. I think that shows good character. That's all."

Andrew watched Caroline while she finished her salad. There was something familiar about her. He felt like he knew her from somewhere. He knew it was impossible, but he couldn't shake the feeling that he knew her.

The remainder of the meal was littered with small talk and an occasional question about Andrew's work. Tonight, would not be the night he learned anything more about Caroline beyond her having two adult children, and a lack of trust in men.

They cleaned up the remnants of dinner and Andrew turned off the lights in the kitchen. Caroline followed him into the great space where he stopped in front of the large windows. She followed his example and looked out at the lake. He turned to her and smiled. "Are you ready?"

Caroline nodded hesitantly. "I'm not sure. But I hear whatever it is I should be ready for is quite spectacular."

He placed his hand on her elbow and led her to a set of spiral stairs. They stopped at the bottom where Andrew instructed her to follow him. "The lighting isn't too good leading to the roof, but once we get there you should be fine. Watch your step."

27

Remember The Kiss

She followed him up the stairs and waited while he opened the door that led to the deck on the roof. She stepped out into the night air and a light breeze caressed her face. She caught her breath as her gaze followed Andrew's hand as he pointed to the dark night sky, littered with millions of stars. Caroline caught her breath as she looked into his eyes. The stars were amazing, but the eyes were even more dazzling.

She was familiar with the depth of darkness that displayed the explosion of light millions, maybe billions of miles away. But those eyes were as dark as the night sky. And while he looked up the stars they were reflected in those deep pools. She reigned in the thoughts as she reminded herself, he was only a man. His celebrity didn't make him more so. After tonight, she would never see him again. She would not get attached.

They stood in the night air studying the stars and talking about the possibilities that might exist in deep space. They shared similar beliefs and ideas related to the topic, yet somehow mocked each other when an outlandish idea was shared.

Andrew led Caroline to a chair at the edge of the deck. "Caroline, please sit."

She followed his instruction as he disappeared. He soon returned with a second chair which he placed next to her. She watched him unfold the chair, then he pushed it close to hers. They each sat reclined in their chair looking up at the sky. They shared an intimate silence that was neither uncomfortable, nor irritating.

Andrew was the first to break the silence. "You know, when I was a kid, I had a telescope. I loved to look at the stars. This is different though. Yes, you can see minute details in one star through the telescope, but this, you can see millions of stars all at once. Each star is set in a different place in the universe. By the time we see them they could be burnt out."

"I know. It's almost sad to think we're looking at something that has already happened. A star is born, a star dies, it's beautiful but at the same time I wonder what I'm really seeing." Caroline pulled her legs up and rested her feet on the chair.

Andrew studied Caroline while she spoke. She looked out into the night sky as though she was searching for something, long ago lost. The brief flash of sadness passed across her face, then disappeared. He wondered what brought on the temporary sadness. For the second time today, those eyes captured his heart. He couldn't explain why, but he liked the feeling, even if the eyes were sad. "Where are you, Caroline? What world have you deserted me to? What are you thinking Caroline?"

She looked away from the stars and focused on the face next to her. She liked the face and was beginning to feel a connection with the person it belonged to. Caroline smiled shyly. "Nothing really."

Andrew sat up in the chair and dropped his legs one to each side of the lounge. "Your eyes say otherwise. I was watching you look out into that vast dark universe. I think if you looked out there much longer you might have been transported beyond the stars. You can talk to me. I'm beginning to feel like we've known each other a very long time. I know it's not possible, we only met today after all. But I feel a connection to you." He leaned back again. "Maybe we were close friends in another life." He shifted his gaze from Caroline to the star filled sky.

Caroline followed his example and looked out into the night. "Friends". She paused. 'I'm not sure I really know what that's like. I mean to have a friend."

Andrew laughed lightly. "Come on Caroline, everyone has friends."

Caroline shook her head. "Not everyone. Not true friends, maybe acquaintances but not friends". She turned her head to see the look on Andrew's face. "That surprises you?"

She shifted on the chair, stretching her legs out in front of herself. "Earlier today you came up to me and said you were curious about the smile. It was real if that's what you're wondering. I was smiling because I was thinking about how I've lived the last thirty years in the shadows. I felt as though I was the shadow of the man I married, both times. I always did what I thought they would want me to do. I spent all my energy trying to create a family." Caroline snickered. "I thought if I could create this family environment, everyone would get along and we'd live happily ever after".

Andrew interrupted. "And it didn't happen".

Caroline shook her head. "No. It didn't. The only thing that happened is I wasted my whole adult life forcing something that never happened. In the end, I think I was the only one who was disappointed". She let out a sigh.

"But now, I'm free from all that. My kids are grown and have families of their own, and I'm on my own again, and I can finally truly be me." She turned to Andrew. "I think the sadness you see in my eyes on occasion is me mourning for all those lost years, all the time wasted for nothing".

Andrew lifted his left leg over the chair and turned to face Caroline. "Caroline. Nothing is ever wasted. No, you can never get back the time that passed. But in each moment of all that time, you learned something. You took away from each experience, something that made you stronger, wiser, and happier. If not right now, eventually."

"I know that. I think that's why I smile. I still have time to enjoy life." Caroline stopped to think for a minute. "I think the biggest challenge will be to trust that the people I meet will want to truly be friends."

Andrew leaned his elbows on his knees as he began to speak. "Everything in time, Caroline". He reached out his hand and placed it on her knee. "You will learn to trust again. And any person who is truly worth calling friend is worth being patient with. That includes being patient with yourself".

"Oh my God… time. What time is it?" Caroline sat up straight in the chair.

Andrew shrugged his shoulders. "Time? You're worried about the time?"

"My car has been sitting for hours. It's probably been towed by now. Oh no. Can you bring me back?"

"Now?" Andrew asked surprised. "Caroline your car is about a half mile from here. I can drive you out there if you want. Wouldn't you rather sit here under the stars though?"

Caroline noticed the disappointed look on Andrew's face. "It's getting late anyway. I should probably go home. You must be getting tired of my company by now."

"No. I'm not getting tired of your company. Actually, I was hoping we could spend the day together tomorrow."

A surprised look passed across Caroline's face. "Why?"

Andrew threw back his head and laughed out loud. "Why? Because I enjoy your company, that's why. I'm only here at the lake a few days and well, I don't know anyone. I know I came here to rest but I don't want to be in seclusion. I like you. You're good company. I think we have a lot in common and we should spend tomorrow together. Let's do something. What would you like to do?"

Caroline watched Andrew as he struggled to come up with an idea. "Do you like to hike?"

"What?" He looked up, surprised.

"Do you like to hike? You know up mountains."

He smiled as he began to laugh. "Yes, I hike. I haven't been hiking in years. That's a good idea."

Caroline interrupted him. "But my car. I wonder if it's still parked where I left it? I really should go."

Andrew shook his head as he stood up. "Ok. We'll go get the car. I would have rather spent the night under the stars, but if you want to get the car, we'll get the car".

Caroline rose to her feet to come face to face with Andrew who stopped talking as they stood in front of each other. "Wouldn't you rather lounge here with the stars, Caroline?" He looked into her eyes tempting her to defy him".

She caught her breath as his twinkling dark eyes held her gaze. She stumbled over her words as she looked in his eyes. "I… well yes, the stars are beautiful, and who would want to leave such a place if they didn't have too." She placed her hand on Andrew's chest and smiled. "But my car. If I'm lucky I'll only have a ticket. Hopefully, it wasn't towed or worse still, stolen."

He placed his hand over hers and teased. "My, my, aren't you all gloom and doom". He leaned a little closer as he took her hand in his and whispered. "It's just a car".

Caroline laughed as she pulled away her hand and stepped back. "Maybe to you. But to me it's my ride, my independence. And if it's not there when we get back, you're going to have to stay here and chauffer me around until I can replace it".

Andrew took a step toward her. "Ok. I'll call the studio and tell them I can't finish the film until we find a car for you".

Caroline shook her head while smiling ear to ear. "I think this has become a sparing competition. Well, you win. Take me to my car please".

"Yes, ma'am." Andrew mocked. "Your wish is my command."

When they reached the door, Caroline turned and took one last look at the black velvet sky littered with millions of twinkling lights. She looked back at the chairs placed close to each other on the deck. She hadn't realized how close they were while they sat next to one another. She could see now that they sat close enough to touch. She looked up at Andrew as he stood next to her ready to depart from their quiet evening oasis.

Andrew smiled down at Caroline, wishing they could have sat a bit longer. He wanted to get to know her better. But he didn't want to make her uncomfortable. He didn't want her to think he wouldn't let her go.

They walked in silence down the spiral stairs one in front of the other. Andrew left the room briefly and returned lifting his hand to display keys to her freedom.

They rode in silence for the half a mile it took to arrive at the boulevard. They drove down the strip where they saw the flashing lights of the arcades and signs that welcomed patrons in for a drink. Andrew drove slow, stopping occasionally to passing pedestrians. The scene was a complete contrast to the quiet star filled sky they enjoyed moments ago.

The night was young on the boulevard, and the people were still willing to experience what it had to offer. Caroline remembered enjoying the excitement in her younger years, but tonight she was ready to hand in the towel. As much as she wanted to feel and be free in her life, she knew when her body was tired, and wasn't too proud to admit it.

She turned to Andrew and smiled. He looked out the window beyond Caroline, then focused on her face briefly, before returning his attention to the road in front of him. Andrew nodded in silent agreement. He too, was fond of rest now-a-days. He still played hard, but when it was time to rest, he knew when to quit.

Caroline pointed to the car as soon as it came into view. "There it is. It's still there".

Andrew sarcastically replied. "Did you have any doubts? And look someone left a space just for me." He pulled into the parking space next to Caroline's car, then turned off the engine. "It must be fate." He mocked.

They sat in silence for a moment listening to the activity around them. Andrew looked at Caroline and smiled. "Well, here we are." He took the keys out of the ignition and opened his door. Caroline followed his lead. She opened her door and stepped into the humid night air. A slight breeze brushed against her neck as she turned and closed the door.

She walked around the front of the truck and approached the car. As she thought, underneath the driver's windshield wiper rested a yellow envelope, a parking ticket. She walked up to the window and pulled the ticket from beneath the wiper and lifted it for Andrew to see. "I told you so. A ticket."

Andrew walked up to Caroline and reached for the yellow envelope. "I'll take care of it."

Caroline quickly pulled back her hand. "No Andrew. I can get it. It's my car and my ticket. I should have thought about it before taking off."

"I don't mind. After all I'm the one who kidnapped you today." Andrew joked. "Notice I didn't mention drown and dice."

Caroline shook her head and started laughing. The night was catching up with her and she knew she was over tired. "I'll never live that down, will I? Drown and dice... sounds like some kind of infomercial." She stood to face Andrew. "I can take care of the ticket. It's worth it. I had a wonderful time today. It was a nice way to begin my new life."

Andrew stepped a little closer and interjected. "Well, the fun isn't over yet. What time should I pick you up in the morning? We still have a hiking date."

Caroline lifted her eyebrows. "Date? I think it's more like an adventure. Hiking is adventure, dinner is dating."

Andrew reached out and took Caroline's hand. "Well maybe after adventure we can have dating... I mean maybe after hiking we can have dinner." He teased.

Caroline gently pulled back her hand as she looked, into the deep dark pools that earlier reflected every star in the heavens. Andrew smiled as he stepped back and reached for the door handle. He opened the door to Caroline's car, and she slowly ducked under his arm and slipped in behind the steering wheel.

Andrew closed the door and stepped back from the car.

Caroline turned down the window and smiled. "Thank you for the memorable day. It's been a long time since I've been out on the water. I'd forgotten how therapeutic it is."

Andrew observed her twinkling eyes. "Is that what today was, therapeutic? I would probably consider it more fun than therapeutic. But if it works for you... I'll pick you up around eight tomorrow. I'll need your address though."

Caroline turned and removed a small pad of paper from the center console and wrote down her address and handed it to Andrew. "I hope I don't regret this". She joked as she pulled the seatbelt around her waist.

Andrew watched as Caroline nodded then backed out of the space. He looked after her, watching her taillights disappear into the merging traffic.

Woods

FOUR

Andrew walked up the path that led to Caroline's front door. He knocked then turned to survey the front yard. The house was situated on a quiet country lot. There were no neighbors, at least none he could observe from her front door. He listened while the birds sang as the sun crept through the trees. He could smell fresh cut grass and wondered who would have mowed this early in the day.

The door opened and Andrew turned to face a smiling Caroline. "I'm ready if you are." She scooted out the door and closed it before Andrew had a chance to invite himself in. She raised a backpack to display. "Water for the hike. And a first aid kit."

The early morning sun cut through the trees and reflected off Caroline's golden hair. Her smile was genuine and lit up her face.

Andrew knew she was ready for the hike. It was evident by the emerald-green t shirt, kaki capris and heavy soled hiking boots that she wore. He was temporarily distracted as his eyes moved from Caroline to the front door which she had closed and locked before he had a chance to step inside.

He was curious about the space she occupied but soon realized that now was not the time he would find out. He quickly turned and followed Caroline to the truck. "What's your hurry, Caroline? I'm a little early we don't have to run off right away." He looked back to the front door and pointed. "I thought I might be able to observe you in your natural habitat before leaving."

Caroline shook her head. "Maybe another time." She looked up at the bright blue sky. "It's a beautiful morning. I don't want to waste a minute of it. I know the perfect trail to hike today. It won't be difficult for you I'm sure, but it will be a beautiful walk."

Andrew lightly laughed, ignoring Caroline's recommendation. "What do you have to hide, Caroline? There aren't any dead bodies behind that door are there? "He teased.

Caroline laughed out loud. "Why Andrew, you caught me. I have a pool in the back yard where I drown before dicing up my victims." She joked as she studied the expression on Andrew's face. She wondered why he was intent on seeing what was behind her front door.

The smile left Andrew's face. "You are joking, right?"

Caroline looked across the hood of the truck as she approached the door. "Wouldn't you like to know?" She flashed him a smile as she slid across the seat then reached for the seat belt.

"I guess I better watch my back today." Andrew placed the key in the ignition. "As far as the trail is concerned, what do you have in mind?" He paused for a moment. "I hope there is no water where we're going."

They both laughed as Andrew backed out of the driveway.

When they were on their way, Andrew looked at Caroline quickly then returned his attention to the road.

Caroline focused on programing the GPS then inquired. "What are you looking at Andrew?"

"I'm not sure. I thought I was looking at an innocent woman, but that quick get-away makes me wonder what you're hiding. Why wouldn't you invite me in?"

"I make it a habit never to invite strange men into my home." Caroline said jokingly.

"Since when am I strange? We spent the whole day together yesterday. I invited you to my home."

Caroline interrupted. "Correction. That isn't your home. That is a hotel for the rich and famous, a revolving door of privilege and excess."

Andrew snickered. "Well, I guess you're right about that. I could never live there. It's ok to spend a few nights there, but you're right." He looked over the hood and focused on the yellow center line on the road. "All joking aside Caroline, why didn't you invite me in?"

Caroline was silently contemplating her answer. "It's not that I didn't want you to see my home. I felt that if I invited you in, you'd want to look around and, well, to be honest, I wanted to enjoy the hike."

Andrew looked confused. "What does looking around have to do with enjoying the hike?"

Caroline smiled as she began to speak. "I was afraid if I let you in you would look around and see how I live and what I do, and then you'd start asking questions and we'd never leave. Or we'd leave and I'd be distracted while hiking, wondering what you were thinking. This way we go hiking, enjoy the view and the day and I don't have to obsess about what's going on in that pretty little head of yours."

"Pretty little head of mine? Wow. I don't think I like that reference. I'm more than a pretty face you know. I have a brain… and feelings." He was trying not to laugh.

Caroline started laughing at his attempt to be serious. "Ok. Let's call a truce. You can see the house when you bring me home. Maybe that can be your incentive to bring me home. Now, don't you want to know where we're going?"

Andrew shook his head as he focused on the road. "I suppose it would be a good idea. Am I traveling in the right direction?"

Caroline nodded. Yes, but you're going to want to head north on the highway so take a left once you pass under the bridge." She paused and smiled. "And by the way, there is water where we're going. Lots of water."

Andrew raised his eyebrows. "Oh really? Will I be safe with you? Or maybe it's you who should be worried." He turned on his directional then took a left. "So, where are we going?"

Caroline tugged on the seat belt and turned to face Andrew. "The Basin. It's a little over an hour drive. The hike itself isn't difficult and only a few miles, but it's beautiful." She sighed then continued. "It's serene and peaceful and, well, you'll see."

Andrew nodded as he watched the expression on Caroline's face. "You look like a child in a candy shop, almost like you're describing the sweetest treat."

"Andrew, that's ridiculous. I don't look like that." She sat back against the seat and thought for a moment. "It is beautiful though. You'll see. The rocks, and waterfalls, streams, and trees."

Caroline stopped talking and gazed out the window listening to the tires against the pavement until Andrew broke the silence.

"Caroline, where are you this time? There aren't any sailboats where we're going are there?"

"No, of course not. Why would you ask that question?"

"Well, for one thing, you have that look on your face." Andrew explained. "The same look you had yesterday when you were thinking about sailing. Is there a connection or memory to this hike?"

Caroline smiled. "No, there isn't any connection. I love the water. This hike is, I don't know, it's like the water sings to me." She stopped talking long enough to compose her thoughts.

"Andrew, do you enjoy being outside? I love to walk through the trees and listen to nature going about its business without caring about human intrusion. Anyway, you'll see. I hope you won't be disappointed."

38

Woods

"I'm sure I won't be. If it's half as beautiful as you make it sound, I won't be." Andrew fiddled with the vent on the dash then opened his window about an inch. "Do you hike often?"

"No. I haven't been on a hike in years. I used to love to hike." She stopped to think carefully about her response. "One thing I've learned over the years, actually, not that I learned over the years, but I've realized recently. I lost myself in those I surrounded myself with. Now I know that is wrong. I think that's why I was unhappy for so long. I guess you could say I gave away my power. I allowed myself to conform to what others wanted." Caroline looked to Andrew and smiled. "I won't let that happen again. I'm too old for that. If I do it again, I'll never enjoy who I'm supposed to be."

Andrew shook his head. "I get that. It's too bad you felt stifled in your life. I look at you and see someone full of life and scratching at the lid of adventure. I know what it's like to lose yourself. Although I don't believe I was lost in the same way you were. "

Caroline looked puzzled. "What do mean?"

Andrew sighed then sat quietly for a moment before continuing. "I lost the woman I love. She died and it left a gaping hole in my heart. I don't know if I've ever truly recovered. Sometimes I think I'm on the mend, then something reminds me of a moment we shared, or a place we visited. Those experiences open old wounds." A sad smile crossed his face. "Then I have to start to heal all over again."

"That's sad Andrew." Caroline said. "You never found anyone who could help you get beyond the pain?" She took a deep breath preparing to expose her wounds with what she said next. "I can't imagine anyone could get over losing someone they truly love, to death. To have your second self, ripped from your soul at a time when you are most connected. That would be the worst".

She looked at Andrew while he focused on the road in front of him. "I hope someday you find the person that can help you heal. You need someone who will love you and, in a way love the one you lost. I think when two people find that connection, they become one; two halves of the same soul." She smiled briefly at Andrew when he looked at her. "It's difficult to love half of a person."

39

Andrew sat quietly waiting to see if Caroline was finished speaking. "Is that true? Do you believe that? I don't know a person who would be that open to love."

"We must be that open if we want to be free. When we take that control from our ego, we can love to that degree." Caroline dropped her head and focused on the floor mat beneath her feet. "It's funny, isn't it? That we spend a good portion of our lives forcing love, controlling our emotions, and brainwashing ourselves to believe that love is basically egotistical. Then when everything goes to hell, we finally throw our hands in the air and yell 'I give up', we finally see that true love has nothing to do with any of that." She looked out the window as they passed trees and rocks that jetted out of the hillside then spoke in a soft voice. "Then it's too late."

They drove in silence for a few miles. It wasn't an uncomfortable silence Caroline noted.

Andrew interrupted her thoughts. "I don't think it's ever too late to love, Caroline. I think a person must be willing to open up the heart to the possibility that it exists, and they can experience it."

"That may be true for some, but I vowed that I would spend the remainder of my life in peace. I intend to experience the beauty of life, nature, and people. I want to finally get out in the world and meet people and go places and do things."

"Caroline, are you telling me that you've never done any of those things?" Andrew asked surprised.

Caroline shrugged her shoulders. "Basically."

"That's ridiculous. You must be exaggerating." He continued.

"No, I'm not. "Caroline shook her head. "It's not for me. For the last twenty years, at least, my life consisted of going to work, going home, making dinner, going to bed, getting up and doing it again. Grocery shop on weekends. Dig in the dirt in the garden to keep busy. And sometimes go to Wendy's or the diner for a quick bite on a Thursday or Friday."

Andrew's voice cracked as he spoke. "That can't be true. If it is, I'm not surprised you feel the way you do."

Caroline swallowed as she tried not to let her emotions get the best of her. "It's quite true."

"Well then I'm sorry for you." He sounded determined. "We must do something about that. I can't imagine you in such a boring existence. You seem so happy, most of the time."

"I am happy, Andrew. I finally have the chance to do all the things I mentioned. Sometimes I feel sorry that I will be doing them alone, but at least alone, I don't have to worry about things."

"What kind of things?" Andrew was curious.

Caroline snickered. "It's not important. Let's just say that trust is not something that I have experienced a lot of in my life." She hesitated then looked up wide eyed. "Hey, I'm not looking for pity. I'm happy now. I still have plenty of life left in these old bones. I've already started living. I checked of the first thing on my 'bucket list' yesterday." She joked.

"Oh really, and what was that?" Andrew smiled wondering if he had anything to do with her first milestone.

"Well sailing of course. I have wanted to get out there on the lake and feel the breeze blow through my hair and smell that lake smell that I've missed. Maybe someday I'll get brave and sail on the ocean." Again, her eyes grew wide as her expression became animated.

Andrew laughed at her expression. "I hope I can see that. If you're this excited about imagining it, I wonder what will happen when the experience finally materializes."

"Anyway, everything is much better now. I'm happy." Caroline sounded convincing.

Andrew nodded. "Good, I'm glad." He was interrupted by the voice of his GPS. "It looks like this is our exit."

Caroline sat up straight. "Yes, it is. It won't be much longer now."

They drove the remainder of the way in silence. Andrew watched the signs and dodged traffic. "Wow it gets quite busy through here, huh?"

Caroline nodded. "Yea it does. It's crazy in the summer, especially on weekends. I was hoping it wouldn't be too bad today. We're early so the trails should be somewhat quiet. Either way it will be beautiful."

FIVE

Andrew signaled than turned off the main road. He noticed the sign *The Basin.* He pulled into the parking lot and found a space. He turned off the ignition then turned to Caroline. He studied her for a moment as she sat looking back at him smiling. He reached over and slowly brushed away the hair that had fallen across her cheek. He looked into her sparkling eyes as he guided the stray hair behind her ear.

Caroline shivered as his hand grazed her ear. She interrupted the moment by reaching for the door handle and exiting the vehicle. "Come on Andrew. The sooner we start the sooner you can see why I'm excited to begin the hike." She grabbed the backpack then closed the door.

Woods

Andrew followed Caroline's example and stepped out of the truck. He took a deep breath as he stretched then stood to survey the area. He heard what he thought to be the murmur of voices in the distance. He looked over the hood of the truck at Caroline, a questioning look, on his face.

Caroline nodded her head. "You can hear it can't you?"

He nodded as his face silently questioned her.

"You hear running water. I thought I was the only one who heard it from here. I guess I've met my match." She lifted her hand to Andrew. "Come on. Let's walk."

Andrew methodically walked toward Caroline as he reached for her hand. When she took his, he smiled to himself as his thoughts were diverted to the sensation of his hand in hers. He made no attempt to speak for fear he would break the spell. Caroline didn't flee from his touch so Andrew tread lightly as they left the parking lot and walked toward the Basin, past the sign at the beginning of the trail then stepped onto the paved path that he hoped would show him the world, or at least this little part of the world through her eyes.

The walk began slowly, and the terrain was easy to navigate. The path was surrounded diversely by trees; the silver gray of the gentle birch, the majestic oak that spread its canopy and showered the forest floor with acorns, and the beautiful maple that would produce its show in fall when leaves changed from the green of summer to the bright vibrant reds, oranges, and golds of autumn.

The silence wasn't intrusive in the woods of the Basin. It was welcoming, calming. Andrew forgot how peaceful nature could be. He listened as they continued, to the birds singing high above the trail.

Caroline looked over at Andrew as they walked on, to see if he felt what she felt. She could see a gentle smile forming as the corners of his lips formed a slight smile. She didn't speak, but gently pulled back her hand to release the hold Andrew had on her, both physically and emotionally. She knew better than to allow an attachment to form, especially with someone who would be gone in a day or so. Besides, she was only beginning to enjoy the freedom she had recently acquired. It would be enough to make a new friend. She would be ready to say goodbye when the time came.

Soon they crossed the bridge that passed over the river, their steps echoing as their boots connected with the wooden floor of the bridge. They stopped on the bridge and watched the water rush below their feet, the white water forcing its way through the bed of rocks and sand beneath it.

"I love the sound of the running water of the river. It helps me to relax, how about you?"

Andrew smiled and nodded. "It does have a calming effect. It's been a long time since I've had the opportunity to walk like this, to hear this." He turned to face Caroline. "To feel this way."

Caroline looked intently at Andrew long enough to sense the danger in the exchange. She turned away and began to walk on. "I'm glad you are able to take the time to experience this." She looked back prompting Andrew to follow. "It's not the most challenging hike, but there I so much beauty to see out here. "

Andrew smiled as he tried to hide his disappointment. He didn't want her to be intimidated by his desire to stay close. He enjoyed her company. He liked the way she looked at life, the positive spin she put on everything, even if she didn't believe what she was saying.

The sound of running water was louder now. Andrew looked out over the landscape as the rocks appeared, immediately followed by cascading water. It ran across the rocks over the surface that, polished by time, created smooth surfaced stone, stones absent of any sharp edges.

Caroline's voice was soon drowned out by the increasing sound of rushing water. Andrew 's pace now matched Caroline's, step for step. Not far from the bridge they came upon a powerful cascade of water. Caroline urged Andrew on then directed him along the path beyond a beautiful aqua-tinted pool. He stopped as they approached the bright blue water.

Caroline giggled in response to the look of surprise on Andrew's face. He turned from the bubbling sound of water to Caroline then spoke. "It's beautiful and sounds so peaceful".

Woods

"I love to come out here. It's really quiet in early spring, although you have to be prepared for snow at that time of year." Caroline picked up the pace and Andrew followed.

He looked across the pool to see a sandy beach. His eyes followed the river's edge to see more cascades which had, over time worn down the rock until the water ran freely across the smooth surface. He turned back to witness the cascade they passed to arrive at the place where he stood.

Andrew turned to Caroline in awe. "This place is beautiful. You are right, it's amazing. No wonder it's so popular." He looked around at those that shared the view he presently enjoyed. "I can't believe this. I'm speechless."

Caroline approached him then guided him to a place in the sun and prompted him to follow her lead and sit down on the warm smooth surface of the rock, carved out by the water over time. He sat next to her in the sun and watched her as she leaned back on the rock to soak up the heat stored in the stone below her.

She lay motionless as the rays penetrated her skin. Andrew sat still as her body relaxed. He watched as she lay there smiling, the same smile that drew him to her the day before. He looked at her wondering what it was about her that entranced him. Over the years he'd met many women, but only one had ever touched his heart in a way that moved him. She was gone. He never thought he would feel for another the way he felt for she he had lost.

But now he sat looking at Caroline, resting peacefully in the sun, wondering if she could fill that void. He tried to force the thought from his mind, knowing that time and space would make it difficult to near impossible for anything to come of their meeting. Friendship may be what he'd have to settle for.

Caroline sensed his eyes on her, and she opened hers as he turned to the aqua pool beyond the smooth rocks. She sat up in time so see a fleeting look of pain pass over Andrew's face.

"Andrew, what were you thinking about? Are you sad? Maybe this wasn't a good idea." She started to stand but Andrew lifted his hand to stop her.

"No, Caroline. Please sit back down." He scanned the area, taking in the scene of rocks and water, and the sounds of that around him. "I'm not sad. I was just thinking that I would like to get to know you better. I would like to spend some quality time with you. You intrigue me."

Caroline laughed. "Wow, yesterday I was an enigma, today I'm intriguing. Be careful Andrew, my ego doesn't need any help from you. I'm trying to keep it under wraps so I can hear myself think."

"I'm serious Caroline. We spent the day together yesterday and today we're enjoying this hike. All this conversation leads me to see that we have a lot in common, similar views, and a love of nature. The more time we spend together, the more I feel like we have some supernatural connection." He studied her, waiting for a reply.

"Yes, Andrew. But you're forgetting something. You live on the other side of the country. Your work keeps you on the go, and you have very little time for a relationship. Don't you think those things would keep any relationship from succeeding?" She watched as Andrew looked away. "Plus, you don't really know me. I've never had a successful relationship. I might not be the best person to consider getting involved with."

He turned to face her. "I hear what you're saying Caroline. I don't agree with you, but I hear you. Let's just forget I said anything. Let's spend this time together. If nothing else, we can be friends. Pen pals remember?"

Caroline smiled and nodded as she stood up stooping to pick up the backpack. "Ok, it's time to move on. We have more to see."

"Hey, wait up, why the hurry?" He said as he stood up to meet her.

"No hurry. Not really. I'd like to enjoy the park before it gets busy, though." Caroline smiled as she pointed toward the couple that approached slowly.

Andrew followed her lead and brushed off his pants as he stood to face her. "You're the guide, where to next?" He reached out to take the backpack from Caroline. "Here, let me carry that."

The smile returned to Caroline's face as she released the pack. "The main attraction. The Basin. Come with me."

Woods

Andrew followed her taking in the sound of water as it cascaded over the falls and rushed into the rock basin and collected before continuing down the stream. Andrew placed his hands on the rail as he scanned the area. He turned to Caroline as she approached his side and leaned against the wood rail.

"It's beautiful, isn't it?" She raised her face to the sun momentarily, then focused on the water as is rushed into the basin.

Andrew shook his head as he spoke. "Beautiful, amazing, awesome. What a jewel hidden here in the little state of New Hampshire."

Caroline nodded in response. "It is amazing. There are many amazing places in this little state. Unfortunately, not many of them are secret anymore. Each year there's more and more traffic passing through the parks, it makes it difficult to visit when it's quiet. That's why I wanted to get an early start. I wanted you to see it before it got too busy."

"Well, you succeeded. It's something else." Andrew studied the face of the woman that looked back at him. In another lifetime he would have pursued her. He would have taken her in his arms and never let her go. But today was not a day for that kind of passion.

Caroline looked into his eyes trying to read his thoughts. What she saw made her redirect her gaze. She looked down into the pool of water to refocus and collect her thoughts. The pool of water was a much safer place to focus her attention than the deep pools she knew she would drown in if she kept looking at him. She thought it a shame that she didn't meet him years earlier, before the trials she faced throughout the years.

Andrew cleared his throat. "I agree, yet I believe people come into our lives when we are ready for them. Not sooner. Not later." He reached out and placed his hand over hers which rested on the rail. "You may not believe that, but I do. I don't know why we were brought together this weekend, but I'd like to find out."

Caroline lightly laughed. "I thought we agreed it was because you needed a pen pal." She looked down at the hand resting over hers as a confused look crossed her face. "How did you know what I was thinking?"

"It's obvious Caroline. There's an energy passing between us that I know you must sense. I don't think it's the energy of a pen pal though." He smiled at her as her confused look was replaced by one of embarrassment.

"I thought we agreed pen pals to be the safe option." Caroline took a deep breath before she rushed on. "Anything more would be foolish. We live in different worlds."

Andrew interrupted. "Not different worlds, Caroline, different coast of the same country maybe but not different worlds. Plus, you said last night that the world is shrinking, and that technology has made it easier for people to keep in touch."

"I remember what I said." Caroline paused as she searched for words that would convince Andrew that it was a bad idea to get involved with one another. "Andrew, I'm a bad relationship risk. I've never been good at it. They always end badly. I'd hate to include you in my track record. Plus, how many long distant relationships do you know of that work out in the long run?"

He nodded. "I agree with what you say."

"Then it's settled." She pulled back her hand as she straightened her shoulders.

"Let me finish Caroline." Andrew stood to face her. "I agree that long distant relationships are difficult. But they're not impossible. I will continue to argue a point you made under the stars last night. The world is getting smaller, travel is easier and takes less time. And finally, if a person wants something bad enough, they can make it work."

Caroline's stomach began to turn, a reaction to the words that had yet to pass over her lips. "What if only one person wants it bad enough?" It was out there. She said it and couldn't take it back.

A look of disappointment crossed Andrew's face. "If I believed that, I never would have considered mentioning it." Andrew rested his hand on Caroline's elbow to reassure her. "Look Caroline, I make a habit of listening to the energy around me and watching for signs that might lead me to make certain choices. I think that you can do that too. I remember yesterday, you told me that you spent your life listening to your head and those voices hadn't been too reliable. If you would just listen to your heart, you may find it tells you something different."

He moved his hand from her elbow to her wrist then took her hand in his. "I really think there is something here, between us but I'm going to let it go. I want to enjoy the remainder of the weekend and if it means we make a pact to be pen pals or just friends then that's what I will settle for." He lifted his free hand to her chin briefly then released her and turned back to the Basin.

Caroline felt strangely disappointed, but she knew in her mind it was the right thing to do. "Thank you, Andrew."

He smiled at her as she returned to the rail. "I find it hard to believe that anything can top this view, do I dare ask what's next?"

The smile returned to Caroline's face. "There is more. Probably nothing to top this, but you never know. Beauty is in the eye of the beholder."

Andrew nodded. "True."

"Well, we should continue before the area becomes infested with people." Caroline stepped away from the rail. Andrew followed. They walked along the path and crossed over a bridge and took a right where they stepped onto Basin-Cascade Trail. The path took them through the woods and toward Cascade Brook. Once they arrived at the brook, they followed it, passing many sets of cascades.

Caroline walked ahead to explore the rocky brook bed. She signaled to Andrew as she pointed out the fall that spanned the width of the brook, falling into a huge pool. They stopped and watched the water pass over the falls and listened to the soft rush of water as it met the pool below.

Caroline turned from the running water and continued the walk. She smiled at Andrew as she turned off the path. She waited for him to catch up then descended to Kinsman Falls. She pointed below to a straight, narrow plunge, over a small cliff.

Andrew looked down as they passed by the top of the waterfall then returned to their guide, Cascade Brook. They walked the trail, passing rocks as they climbed further until they reached a steep pitch on the opposite side. They passed many cascades before the trail leveled a bit before it continued up hill to overlook Rocky Glen Falls.

Caroline reached out to take Andrew's hand as she guided him down into a gorge so he could get a better look at the falls. They stopped in front of the running water briefly. Caroline closed her eyes as the sound penetrated her thoughts. Andrew tightened his grip as he sensed Caroline preparing to pull away.

"No. Just wait, stand here a bit longer. Can you feel it?"

Caroline stopped to listen. "Feel what?"

"Come on Caroline. I know you feel the power behind the water."

"Andrew. We agreed." Caroline's guard went up.

He squeezed her hand gently. "I know we agreed. This isn't about that. Close your eyes and listen. I forgot how powerful nature can be. Coming here is almost like coming home."

Caroline smiled. "You feel that way too?"

"You see, we're on the same wave-length." Andrew teased.

"Funny. We may be on the same wave-length, but I think you've gone over the edge." She joked.

Shall we continue? She prodded.

They walked on until they reached the turn to Cascade Brook Trail. Caroline pointed out that it was also the Appalachian Trail. They continued to explore the trail as it crossed the brook and ascended gently. They could see the brook from a distance until the junction at Kinsman Pond Trail, where it eventually met a rock filled outlet brook of Lonesome Lake. The closer they got to the lake the steeper the rock stairs became. They crossed a few bog bridges and passed a marsh as they walked their way to Lonesome Lake.

Caroline looked out over the placid lake. The air was still, and the lake was like glass. On the far side of the water the tree line set the stage for Franconia Notch that spanned as far as she could see. It was still early enough that she could commune with nature without additional human interaction.

Andrew walked up behind her and stood as still as the water in front of her. He stood close enough to touch her but resisted the urge out of respect for Caroline's wishes. A slight breeze passed over her head and Andrew recognized the scent of lavender and rosemary that would haunt his mind once he returned home. He looked out over the lake, but it didn't hold his attention. Lavender and rosemary hair brought him to imagine holding Caroline in his arms.

Caroline caught her breath as Andrew approached and stopped behind her. The hair on the back of her neck went up. She swore she could feel the warmth of his breath through her hair. She wanted to turn to him but remained steadfast and focused on the waters' edge until she saw movement out of the corner of her eye.

She looked in the direction of the movement to see a large moose on the shoreline. She was about to signal to Andrew when she felt his hand on her waist. He slowly leaned forward and whispered. "I see him. Don't move. He's beautiful."

The two stood motionless watching the moose graze, moving occasionally when he depleted his food source. The blood running through Caroline's veins was burning, the result of Andrew's touch. She wanted to stand there forever but knew it wouldn't last. Nothing good in her life lasted. This time however, she decided she would enjoy the moment. She wouldn't sabotage something that would never happen again.

Andrew leaned in closer. His hand still rested on Caroline's waist. He didn't dare move too much, fearing she would pull away. Her body was warm beneath his hand. He thought they fit together nicely, his hand resting just above her hip, nestled in the curve of her waist. He fought against the desire to place his other hand on the opposite side and pull her closer. He knew better, so accepted the pleasure of being near her.

They silently watched the moose continue to graze until he moved to the edge of the water and turned and disappeared into the woods. Leaving the two of them to decide what should happen next. Caroline looked out over the lake to distract her from the warm feeling of Andrew's breath on the back of her neck. Andrew focused on the moving trees, while he stood still a moment longer taking in the scent of lavender and rosemary, memorizing the feeling he was afraid he'd never experience again.

The spell was broken by the sound of laughter coming up the trail. Caroline turned and looked up at Andrew as he smiled down at her, his hand still resting on her waist. She could feel the beat of her heart in her throat. Her ears were pounding, and her mind raced as she anticipated something, she knew she wasn't ready for.

Andrew removed his hand from Caroline's waist, though he wasn't ready to let go of her. He lifted his hand to her face and brushed away that stray hair that kept finding its way to cover her brown eyes. He slowly stepped back and took a deep breath. "That's the first moose I've seen that close. He was beautiful. They're so big and awkward, I never imagined they could be so graceful."

He smiled and shook his head. "This is amazing. The lake, the moose, the falls. I know it's been here since the beginning, but for someone like me who rarely has the opportunity to experience nature, this is amazing."

Andrew turned to the lake and inhaled, then focused on Caroline. "Thank you for bringing me here. I feel like I've been here before. I know that's not possible, but I feel a connection to this place."

"It's beautiful, and peaceful. I feel the same way when I'm out here." Caroline followed Andrew's lead and turned to the water. She took a deep breath and sighed, not wanting the morning to end.

The trail was becoming more active now and the serene feeling was disappearing. "Do you want to go on to the hut? The view is nice. We could stop here for a break if you like. Or we can head back. The morning is gone. It's going to get busy around here. If there weren't so many people it might be nice to continue the hike, but I prefer to hike the trail when it's quiet and I can commune with nature. What do you think?"

Andrew watched Caroline as she spoke, the curve of her lips, the creases on either side that appeared when she smiled, the eyes that sparkled as the water reflected in them. He would never get tired of looking at that face.

"I don't know. Why don't we head back? Maybe we can find a place to stop for lunch on the way." He turned back to the water to take one last look at the 12-acre lake, set in the hills. He scanned the mountains beyond the trees, noting the contrast between the dark hills and the bright morning sky.

Caroline watched Andrew as he focused on the mountains in the distance. "Franconia Notch State Park." She took a step closer and pointed to the hills as she spoke. "That's the Franconia Notch State Park beyond those hills. There's much more to explore in the little State."

"If the rest of its anything like this place, I'm sorry not to have the chance to see it all." He turned his head toward Caroline as he continued. "Maybe I'll have opportunity another time."

"That would be nice." Caroline replied in a low voice.

Andrew bravely looked deep into her eyes. "It would be nice. I would enjoy nothing better than to spend time with you."

Caroline interrupted him before he could say too much. "Well, I guess we should head back now. It's getting crowded here. Too many people."

Andrew leaned toward Caroline and smiled. "I agree. Let's go."

SIX

Caroline stepped back on the trail and walked along the bog bridges and Andrew followed. They passed the many falls along the way, following the path along the brook, until they walked over the bridge. They stopped at the Basin for a few minutes to watch the water tumble over the falls and into the aqua pool. Caroline leaned against the rail and rested her hands there while she listened to the rushing water.

Andrew stood two steps behind her, looking into the pool, and listening to the chatter and laughter of many voices. He studied Caroline, noting the way her hair fell over her shoulders. His gaze moved down her back and stopped at her waist, where he recalled the pleasure of a perfect fit experienced earlier. He stepped forward and silently stood next to Caroline.

Woods

Caroline looked up at Andrew and smiled. "It's too bad it couldn't always be quiet here." She turned back to the path and shrugged her shoulders. "But I guess, everyone wants to enjoy the beauty."

She then addressed Andrew. "Are you ready to continue?"

Andrew nodded and met Caroline on the path that led back through the trees, rocks, and water to the parking lot. They arrived at the lot and approached the vehicle as the sun was reaching its noon time position.

Andrew unlocked Caroline's door and held it open while she slid across the seat. She watched him as he passed in front of the truck and moved to the driver's door. She noticed the unsettled look come and go in his face. She smiled when he opened the door and tucked the backpack behind the seat.

He smiled as he placed the key in the ignition. "This morning was amazing. I enjoyed the walk, and the falls, they're beautiful. And that moose, well, there's only one thing that would make the morning perfect." He looked intently at Caroline. He wanted to hold her and tell her she was beautiful. He wanted to stay close. More than that, he wanted Caroline to be comfortable, happy, maybe even experience love again. The present moment wasn't that time, and he knew it. So, he turned his attention to his next question.

"So, how about lunch? Where might there be a good place to stop?"

Caroline, silently relieved, responded. "There are quite a few places around here, but I think you might enjoy Black Mountain Burger Co." She shifted on the seat to face Andrew. "It's about 20 minutes south of here. What do you think?"

Andrew nodded and handed her the phone. "Program it in, we're on our way."

Caroline turned to face the windshield and shifted the seat belt. "I'm not sure we really need to. Just head south on the highway and take exit 32. We head toward Loon Mountain on Route 112 and it's on the right." She paused and looked over at Andrew. "I can program it if you prefer."

He shook his head. "If you know the way I guess it's not necessary." He placed the car in reverse and backed out of the space. "Lead on, Caroline. Where you lead, I will follow." He joked.

The twenty-minute drive to Black Mountain Burger Co. passed quickly. Andrew used the travel time to continue his interview. He cautiously questioned Caroline. "I'm curious, Caroline. You don't have to answer if you don't want to, but how did you end up with such trust issues? Who did that to you?"

Caroline focused on the road in front of her, taking time to decide whether she wanted to answer. "I don't like to talk about my marriages. It no longer hurts to discuss them I just choose not to relive the past." She paused. "Plus, I don't want to talk bad about people. We all have issues."

Andrew nodded. "I understand. I feel the same way. Focus on the positive. But in this case, you wouldn't be bad mouthing anyone. You're just communicating facts. Only to help me better understand you. You know, get to know you."

"Ok, I suppose. It's not like you're going to see any of them. Plus, you don't appear to be the type of person who would judge others or gossip." She sighed before continuing. "We were young, me and my first husband. We didn't even know each other, not really. What we thought was love was probably romantic infatuation. The marriage ended somewhat amicably. The children were the result of that marriage. He's since remarried and is happy, I believe.

The second marriage lasted longer, but it wasn't because we were blissfully happy. It was because I am stubborn. I spent my time and energy trying to force a family situation. You know the Norman Rockwell painting version of what is seen as family. It didn't work. He was fine with the children when they were young, but as soon as they were old enough to have an opinion, he ignored them or worse yet, was condescending toward them."

A sad smile passed across Caroline's face, then disappeared. "It's difficult to be a family when no one talks to each other. Then there were the lies. We were married for almost twenty years when I found out my whole marriage was a lie. He lied about who he was, where he'd been, what he'd done, and who he'd been with. He lived two lives."

She shrugged her shoulders and continued. "I tried to get past the lies, but when nothing changed, I decided it was time to cut the cord. I couldn't let go while he was there. I finally got up the nerve to tell him he needed to go. He's gone, I'm here, and my life has improved greatly since his departure.

I don't know why he did what he did, and he could never give me a reason. Now every time I think about considering the idea of dating, I talk myself out of it. I don't know that I will ever trust anyone again."

Andrew shook his head. "That's sad. But Caroline, not all men are like that. Some of us are good guys." He chuckled. "And we pay the price of loneliness, because of those that lie and cheat. There are some really, good guys out there that would love to be with someone they could share their lives with. Me included." He stopped talking and focused on the road sign coming up. Exit 32. He signaled and slowed down as he prepared to exit the highway.

"You know, Caroline, you've twice mentioned that you have always listened to your head when making choices. Yesterday you made a choice to follow your heart when deciding to go sailing. Did you enjoy yourself?"

Caroline's face lit up as a full smile crossed her face. "I did. I haven't had that much fun in years." She hesitated. "That is, except for today."

"Well, maybe you should listen to your heart more."

"Yea, well that is easier said than done." Caroline said as she pointed to the sign at the roadside. "There it is. Black Mountain Burger Co."

Andrew signaled and turned into the parking lot. "Sometimes you have to take a chance, Caroline."

Caroline exited the vehicle without responding. She walked toward the entrance. Andrew moved quickly to match her stride.

Inside the hostess directed them to a table and placed their menus in front of them. "Your server will be with you in just a moment." She smiled then left the table.

Remember The Kiss

Andrew looked at Caroline who sat with the menu open on the table. She focused on the page in front of her to avoid eye contact with him. He smiled while he watched her attempt at avoiding the comment he made when they pulled into the lot.

"You know Caroline, yesterday you said you were embarking on a new life. That you were going to experience adventure and throw caution to the wind. I hope someday that includes sharing your life with someone. Life is too short to waste it alone." He turned to look out the window and sighed before returning his attention to Caroline. "I should know."

"Andrew, unlike you, I haven't spent my life alone. I've spent it trying to please everyone that I become involved with. I think people sense my desire to please, and they take advantage of it. I'm trying to avoid being a doormat again. I'm protecting myself from the pain and disappointment that seems to result from relationships." Caroline closed the menu as the server approached.

Andrew smiled. "Saved by the server." He joked.

They placed their order and the server smiled and left the table, leaving Andrew to decide whether he wanted to continue the conversation, or change the subject.

"Caroline, I'm not going to try to talk you in to believing not all men are created equal. I believe the right person is out there for you, maybe even closer than you think. But I'm not going to badger you about it. I hope someday you have the experience of knowing and loving someone, and that you will be able to trust that person. Go with your gut, you know. I'd like to spend the remainder of my stay enjoying your company in a relaxing fashion, so, no more talk about relationships."

The server returned to the table placing in front of Caroline a turkey siracha BLT and sweet potato waffle fries. And in front of Andrew, a bison burger, and fries. "Can I get you anything else?"

Caroline spoke up. "I'd like a sparkling water, please."

Andrew chimed in. "Make that two, please."

"No problem. I'll be right back."

"Thank you, Andrew. I've had enough relationship talk for today. Like you, I'd like to enjoy the company of my new friend without further friction.

Woods

The ride home ended when Andrew signaled and pulled into the driveway. He turned off the ignition and turned to face Caroline. "Well, that was a great hike. There is a lot of beauty hidden in those hills. I truly enjoyed myself today."

Caroline nodded. "Yes, it was wonderful. I never get tired of that hike. It's the same, yet somehow, I always take away something different each time I go out there." She paused and smiled. "I know you're dying to go inside. I don't know why, but for whatever reason. Would you like to come in for a while?"

Remember The Kiss

Andrew placed his hand on the door handle and flashed her a broad smile. "I thought you'd never ask. Yes, I'd love to go in."

Caroline chuckled. "I figured you'd say that. Could you hand me the backpack please?" He opened the door and reached behind the seat to pull out the bag that belonged to Caroline.

Caroline took the bag and rummaged through it searching for her key. She pulled out the key and closed the door. Andrew followed her to the house and looked around the yard while he waited for her to unlock the door.

"After you." Caroline pushed open the door and let Andrew enter first. "I know you've been chomping at the bit all day, waiting for this moment." She snickered. "I'm surprised you were able to enjoy the Basin."

Andrew laughed at her comment. "Caroline, That's not true. I didn't think about it at all while we were out there." His eyes met hers and held her gaze. "I had better things to focus on."

Caroline brushed off his comment. "Well, here we are. Home sweet home. Come in and have a seat."

Andrew stepped into the space and looked around. "Sit? Why would I want to sit? I want to explore." He smiled and looked at Caroline. "Exactly as I pictured it in my mind."

"Really?"

"Yes. Neat and uncluttered yet littered with touches that make the space unique to you." He moved to the living room and turned a circle taking in the energy. He focused on the fireplace in front of him. Then to the picture above it. He walked toward the picture that hung on the wall. "This is beautiful. Is this what I think it is?"

He turned and looked at Caroline waiting for a response. She smiled and nodded.

"It is. A visit to the lake. I take pictures when I hike then, when its quiet and I have free time, I paint what I see."

"You painted this?" Andrew looked surprised.

"I did." She then apologized. "I know it's not the best. I'm not a professional artist. It's only a hobby."

"Are you kidding." Andrew interrupted. "This is great. I'm surprised this isn't your career choice."

"You're very kind Andrew, but my painting isn't artist worthy. It's only something I do when I'm in the mood."

He looked at Caroline as she fidgeted under his observation. "Caroline. You don't give yourself enough credit."

Andrew turned back to the picture and studied it for a moment longer before turning his attention to his desired exploration. The living room wasn't large, but the space was warm and cozy. The furnishings were clean cut, and the sofa was plush and inviting. The sofa and matching love seat were a deep brown, accented with pastel throws and pillows. Andrew noted the plants strategically placed throughout the room. The windows faced south allowing the sunlight to shine through most of the day, making the room bright and cheerful.

He walked across the wood floor the sound of his shoes muffled when he stepped on the area rug in the center of the room. He looked up at Caroline before continuing.

Caroline laughed as she recalled their earlier conversation. "Go ahead. I have nothing to hide. Not in the house anyway. The bodies are buried in the back yard." She joked.

Andrew's eyes grew wide, and his eyebrows lifted. "Very funny, Caroline."

He moved to the short hallway where he noticed four doorways. One led to the main bathroom. Not of interest to Andrew. Another to what appeared to be a spare room. It was decorated conservatively and didn't hold his attention.

He walked to the next door and stood in the doorway looking into the room. The room was larger and brighter than the other room. He smiled as he stepped over the threshold. "This is so you."

Caroline walked down the hall when she heard his exclamation. She stood in the doorway watching his expression change as he moved throughout the room.

He stopped at the desk in the center of the room which faced the windows. "You spend a lot of time at this desk."

He walked around the desk observing the items that lay on its top. Three pads of paper, all top pages covered with notes or writing of sorts. There were pens and highlighters and a laptop

61

closed to any intruder. Finally, pictures of Caroline's children at different stages in their lives.

He ran his hand along the edge of the desk as he walked around it. He placed his hand on one of the notepads, focusing on the words on the page.

Caroline walked toward the desk and placed her hand over the words that captured his interest. He smiled at her as she quickly protected her secrets. "Awe, come on Caroline. I'm curious, that's all."

She shook her head. "No. I draw the line here."

He smiled and nodded. "Fair enough. For now."

He reached out and picked up the frame that stood next to the paper that he, moments ago, attempted to read.

"These must be your children?" He focused on two young children playing in the sand.

Caroline stood at Andrew's side. "Yes. Obviously when they were young." She looked over his shoulder at the picture of a moment lost to time. "They don't look like that anymore. I miss them at that age."

Caroline's voice sounded sad, maybe melancholy. She sighed as she remembered the day years gone by. She then chuckled. "I'm pretty sure they wouldn't play in the sand like that today."

Andrew continued looking at the smiling faces in the picture. "They look happy."

"Wouldn't you look happy if you could be carefree and not have to worry about the things, we adults have to concern ourselves with?" She thought back to the day when she took the picture. "They were happy children."

Andrew returned the picture to its place on the desk and focused on another. He reached out and picked it up to get a closer look. "I like this one. You look happy too."

What he saw was a picture of two young adults, one at either side of Caroline. The young lady in a cap and gown, the young man stood a foot taller than Caroline in a polo shirt and kakis.

"That picture was taken at Danielle's college graduation. That was years ago. They've both changed so much." She spoke softly. "They're all grown up and on their own."

Andrew placed the picture on the desk and turned to Caroline. "You must be proud of them."

Caroline nodded as she continued to look at picture of the three smiling faces. She focused on her smiling face, remembering that day. She remembered how she forced the smile knowing it would be the last time the three of them would be together for a while. Her smile told one story her eyes told another. She always hoped only she saw the sadness behind those eyes.

"I'm very proud of them. They've both done well. I guess I always knew they would pursue their dreams and move away." She swallowed her sadness then continued speaking. "I miss them, but the reality is children grow up and move on, leaving their parents, to adjust to adult lives. I guess that's where the term 'empty nester' come from. A parent gets used to doing everything for their kids. Over the years they require less and less attention, until one day they're gone."

"I've always been torn when it comes to children. Part of me wishes I'd had them. Another part of me..." Andrew hesitated before deciding to finish his thought. "Well, I'm sure you know about my girlfriend losing a child at birth. That experience was tough to get over. Sometimes I think it will stay with me forever. Having an experience like that makes one think twice about starting a family."

Caroline studied Andrew, seeing for the second time during their visit sadness in his face. "I do remember hearing about your loss. It's terrible." She looked out the window and focused on the black-eyed Susan's waving in the breeze. "Losing a part of oneself isn't something one gets over."

Andrew looked to Caroline who still stared out the window. "Caroline. Caroline."

"Huh?"

"Where were you? What were you thinking?" He stepped closer to Caroline, with a confused look on his face. "You know, don't you?"

Caroline turned away. "Know what?"

Andrew pursued her. "You know what." He watched Caroline as her discomfort became too much for him to bare. "Look. Forget it. You don't have to tell me anything you don't want to." He reached up and wiped the tear that escaped down her cheek then changed the subject.

"I like this room. It's bright and airy. Do you do all your writing here?" He looked to the wall of books that each told their own story.

Caroline cleared her throat. "Most of the time. It depends on the assignment. Sometimes I work in the living room or the dining table." She paused as she thought about his question. "Come to think of It if it's nice outside, I will sit on the deck with the laptop."

"I don't blame you. Why stay inside when you can be out of doors." He looked from the books to the floor where a painting leaned against the shelf. He approached it and picked it up to examine it. "Another one of yours?"

Caroline approached Andrew's side and looked at Squam Lake. She painted that one after returning from a hike up Rattlesnake. "Yes, it is. It's Squam Lake."

He studied the picture a moment longer then placed it on the floor where he found it. "You know Caroline, you really should sell these."

She turned toward the door. "Yea, maybe someday. After I've practiced, and the paintings are good enough."

Andrew followed her to the door. "I don't know what you're waiting for. They're very good. How much practice do you think you need?"

Caroline looked back at Andrew as he followed her out the door. "More, than I've had."

He stepped into the hallway and looked at the final door, which was closed. He was confident that it must be her bedroom but didn't approach it. He waited a moment for her to offer but when she didn't, he followed her to the living room.

"What's behind door number four?" He joked.

"You, never mine what's behind door number four." She giggled.

"Oh, I get it. I thought you said the bodies were buried in the back yard."

Woods

Caroline laughed. "If anyone were to overhear this conversation, they'd have me arrested. We shouldn't joke about that anymore."

Andrew was laughing with Caroline. He stopped next to her as she stood near the dining table. "You're probably right. I think we've pretty well worn out that joke anyway."

Caroline agreed. She looked at the clock on the stove. "You must be getting hungry. It's supper time."

Andrew looked surprised. "Really? Already? It seems like we just arrived. How long have we been talking?"

"Wow, we've been here over three hours, exploring and talking. That doesn't seem possible." Caroline looked disappointed.

Andrew shared her feeling. "Time flies when you're having fun. This weekend is a blur. I feel as though we've known each other for ever. Yet it's been only two short days."

"Yes." Caroline agreed then repeated her question. "Are you hungry?"

He shrugged his shoulders. "I could eat, I suppose. Do you want to go grab a bite?"

"I thought I could reciprocate. You cooked last night. I'll cook tonight." She walked into the kitchen and opened the refrigerator.

"Well, I don't know. Is it safe?" He smiled broadly.

"Is what safe?" Caroline paused letting the question digest. "Funny, Andrew. Yes, it's safe. Are you insinuating that I might not know how to cook?" She closed the door and faced Andrew with her question.

"Of course not." He joined her in the kitchen. "I could help you know."

"The way you let me help last night." She paused. "No thank you. You can sit at the table and keep me company, though." She mimicked the comment he made the evening before.

"I guess I'll have to settle for good company then. We can talk while you cook. What are we having?"

"Well, we had chicken last night so we should do something different. Do you like fish?" She turned to the freezer and pulled out a sealed container.

"I do."

65

Caroline stood with the freezer door open sealed container in hand. "Next question." She hesitated. "Do you like salmon?"

"I do like salmon. Is it pacific salmon?"

Caroline set the container in the sink and turned to Andrew. She smiled as she responded. "Yes, it is. That's the only salmon to eat. Most other salmon is full of mercury. Or if it's farmed, antibiotics and pesticides."

"We really do think alike." Andrew turned the chair to face Caroline. "It's almost scary."

Caroline turned her attention to preparing the salmon for the grill. "This is Alaskan King Salmon. My brother caught it, had it freeze dried and sent it to me. It's a treat I receive once a year."

"And you're going to share it with me?" Andrew watched Caroline open the door and step out to the deck.

Caroline called from the other side of the door while she lit the grill. "Of course, I will. A special treat is more special when you can share it."

Andrew agreed. "Especially if the someone is as special as the treat."

"If you say so, Andrew." Caroline returned to the kitchen and worked on the salad while the salmon thawed.

Andrew watched her move around the kitchen. He could tell she enjoyed her task. "Do you like to cook, Caroline?"

"I do. Well, I used to. I don't have anyone to cook for anymore so it's not as enjoyable as it once was." She moved to the sink to rinse the spinach. "I don't cook much anymore. It's nice to have a reason to prepare a meal for someone else."

She wiped her hands on the towel hanging from the oven door then removed the salmon from the sink and prepared to season it. The summer air helped it defrost and it wasn't long before she was able to take it out and place it on the grill.

"Watch the time, it only needs to be out there for 10 to 12 minutes." Caroline returned to the salad. "In case I get distracted. You know, while talking to you."

"How long has it been since you cooked for someone, Caroline." Caroline looked up at Andrew who was watching her closely.

"I don't know. Long enough that I don't remember, I guess."

"That's too bad. I can tell you enjoy cooking."

Caroline looked at Andrew and smiled. "I do. I really like entertaining. Which is strange because I rarely had the opportunity to do so for years. Now, well I don't know many people, so I don't cook." She stopped herself in mid-sentence. "That's going to change. Part of the new me. I'm going to go out and meet people, make friends, and eventually, I'll have friends to entertain."

"You can entertain me anytime, Caroline." Andrew looked intently at Caroline willing her to come to him. When she didn't move, he stood up and approached her.

Caroline stopped what she was doing and watched Andrew approach. Her heart, beat faster, she could feel it beating in her throat. He stopped in front of her and took the knife from her and set it on the counter. She could feel the blood burning as it coursed through her veins. She looked at her wet hands hoping he would return to his chair. He placed his hand on her chin and lifted her face to his. He leaned closer, brushing back her hair from her face, he gently kissed her.

Caroline froze, she couldn't move. His lips touched hers and she lost all sense of herself. She wanted him to kiss her, but she fought against the tides that brought her to the point in her life that made her step back.

"Andrew, I don't think this is a good idea." She wiped her hands on her capris and turned her face from Andrew's.

He gently touched her arm. "Caroline, is it your heart or your head that causes you to react? I know I said I wouldn't push you. I won't. But I think you need to give yourself a chance. I don't know what happened to you, but I hope you don't let, whatever it is, keep you from taking a chance on love. You deserve to be loved."

"Andrew, I don't want to go there. Every time I do, I get hurt. I can't go through that again. The lies, the manipulation. I'd rather be alone." She shook her head as she stepped back. "I can't."

Andrew released his hold on Caroline's arm. "I hear what you're saying Caroline. But I can't help but think that we were brought together this weekend for a reason. I've been alone for a long time. Part of me had given up on finding my soul mate. Then I saw you standing there on the boardwalk. I couldn't stop myself from approaching you. It was like some outside force pushed me toward you.

Don't you believe in fate, Caroline?"

"Andrew, I don't know if I believe in anything anymore. I've been disappointed too many times to think that Mr. Right is out there waiting for me."

"But Caroline, you can't deny there is something going on here. You must admit there is an attraction."

Caroline turned to Andrew. "Ok. I admit it. There is an attraction. But that doesn't mean it's good." Caroline shook her head focusing on the meal. "The grill. I need to bring in the salmon." She brushed past Andrew and went to the grill. She returned with the plate and placed it on the table.

"Let me get plates." She busied herself with collecting that which they needed for the meal, plates, silver ware, the salad, and condiments.

She stood in front of her chair. "There. Everything is ready. We should eat before it gets cold."

Andrew stood looking at Caroline, wondering how he could get through to her. For the time being he set aside his desire to convince her and pulled back the chair and sat down. "It smells wonderful."

Caroline took Andrew's plate and placed a serving of salmon on its center. While she served herself, Andrew found the salad and busied himself with the condiments.

"Oh, I almost forgot." Caroline stood up and went to the cabinet where she pulled out two wine glasses. She then went to the pantry and returned with a bottle of white wine. She placed it on the table. "Would you like to do the honors?"

Andrew smiled. "Sure."

They ate their salad in silence. Andrew took a bite of the salmon. "Caroline, this is good. It's seasoned just right. Very good."

"Thank you, Andrew. I'm glad you like it."

"You'd never know it was frozen." He savored the taste.

When the meal was complete, Caroline placed the dishes in the dish washer and cleaned up the sink while Andrew sat at the table enjoying his wine. He looked out the door into the evening sky where he saw what he believed to be the first evening star.

Caroline noticed he was quiet after she shot him down. She felt bad for him. He was trying so hard to convince her that she should give in to love. She couldn't. She didn't trust herself any more than she could trust a man. She didn't believe she knew what love felt like. Any time she let down her guard, she would be disappointed by the outcome. She watched Andrew looking out into the evening sky. What was love? How could she trust herself, believe in herself?

Andrew turned to her once more. "It's getting dark."

Caroline nodded. "Yes." She felt disappointed as the words passed through her lips. "Is it time to go?"

Andrew could hear it in her words. Hope. He sensed that she wanted him to stay longer. "No. That is only if you want me to."

Caroline shook her head. "No." she couldn't stop her words. "Andrew, I enjoy your company. I'm not ready to trust myself let alone a man. We agreed. Friends. You are supposed to be my first friend. The first friend as I pass from the old me to the new me."

Andrew scooted the chair back and stood up. "I know, Caroline. I know what we agreed. I'm sorry. You're right. Let's start over. He picked up the bottle of wine and refilled her glass then his. He picked up the glasses and handed one to Caroline.

He pointed to the door. It looks inviting out there. I see the first star of the evening. Last night we enjoyed the stars without incident." Smiling. "Shall we return to a familiar place?"

Caroline smiled, nodded, and handed her glass to Andrew. "Wait here."

She left the room and minutes later returned with a large blanket. "I don't have a deck on my roof so we can't climb the stairway to heaven and view the stars from that pristine location. Sometimes when the night is clear, I take this blanket out and spread it on the lawn and spend hours out there gazing up at the stars. How about it?"

"I think that would be perfect."

She shifted the blanket to one arm and opened the door allowing Andrew to pass. She closed the door and watched Andrew as he walked into the evening air. He was tall and carried himself well. He wasn't lanky but neither was he stocky. His form was graceful in a masculine way. She felt he was a good man but wasn't ready to trust. She followed him to the lawn, found the perfect place then spread the blanket.

Andrew watched her, waiting for her to make the first move. She stepped onto the blanket then sat down. Andrew followed. He handed her the wine glass, then sat next to her, careful not to sit too close.

"I know this is nothing compared to the deck on the lake, but it's peaceful. And sometimes when I lay out here and look up at the stars, I almost feel like I'm out there with them."

Andrew looked up at the night sky, watching as the stars came into view. What started with one evening star, ended with billions of shiny sparks littering the heavens. He sat next to Caroline watching her get lost in the night. She looked at him and smiled then returned her attention to the stars.

He waited until she set down her glass on the grass. She hesitated, but eventually gave in and leaned back on her elbows and finally dropped to the blanket on her back and watched the twinkling lights.

Andrew waited a little longer, then slowly, attempting not to disturb her, he lowered himself to the blanket and looked out into the heavens. He lay still and avoided any contact, being conscious of their agreement. He wouldn't make the same mistake a second time. He would be her friend.

He knew now she needed a friend first. He would be that friend, win her trust, then eventually, hopefully, more. For now, he wouldn't pressure her. Maybe she was right. Maybe he had been alone so long that what he thought he felt was nothing more than wishful thinking.

They lay on the blanket staring into the heavens sharing their knowledge of it. They discussed the constellations and the legends that grew out of lore as the night grew darker.

"It's so peaceful out here at night. Sometimes I can hear the owls, but it's usually quiet. Like it is tonight."

Woods

"It is quiet. And the night sky is perfect for star gazing." Andrew turned his head to see Caroline looking into the night sky. "How well do you know your stars, Caroline?"

"I don't know, I'm no astronomer, but I know the circumpolar constellations. You can see them year-round, and they are easy to find by looking to the brightest stars." She pointed into the night air.

"Ursa Major is the largest of all northern constellations. When you see the big dipper, you're looking at Usra Major. And there, is Ursa Minor or what many refer to as the little dipper. Then there is Cassiopeia."

Caroline paused and moved her hand across the night sky and pointed to the flat 'W' that was Cassiopeia. She then pointed to Cepheus. "And her husband Cepheus."

She laughed as she considered the legend. "Poor man. Set in the heavens for all eternity to listen to his wife boast of her beauty." She laughed. "That can't be fun."

"Why is he a poor man. If he loved his wife, wouldn't he want to be at her side forever?" Andrew pondered.

"Well, maybe, but legend has it, according to Greek mythology, that Cepheus, the legendary king of Ethiopia was considered a weak king because he allowed Cassiopeia to continually boast of her beauty. He allowed his daughter to be sacrificed to the sea monsters as punishment for Cassiopeia's boasting that she was more beautiful than the gods. So, because he couldn't keep his wife quiet, and he allowed his daughter to be sacrificed he was punished by having to listen to her forever."

Caroline moved her pointed finger back to Ursa Minor. "Draco, the large serpentine is wrapped around Ursa Minor. His tail is between Ursa Minor and Ursa Major." She pointed to the head of Draco. "And his head points to Hercules. It's not real bright, but if you look long enough, you can see it." She stopped to consider the large constellation. "Did you know Draco is the eighth largest constellation in the sky?"

"Wow." Andrew was surprised. "I'm impressed. I recognize Ursa Major and Minor, and I know Cassiopeia, but I don't remember

Cepheus. Nor do I remember hearing the legend. And the daughter, what was her name?"

"Andromeda – The Chained Lady."

"Andromeda. I know that constellation, but again, I didn't realize there was a story behind the name."

Caroline smiled as she focused on the stars. "Poseidon took offense to Cassiopeia's claims of beauty. She wouldn't take back her words, claiming she was more beautiful than the gods. So, Poseidon created a great sea monster and chained Andromeda to a large rock in the sea where she waited for Cetus the sea monster to take her."

Andrew interrupted. "That's terrible."

"Well, the story had a happy ending. Perseus arrived as Cetus was about to claim his victim. Perseus had killed Medusa before arriving to see The Chained Lady, and he carried her head in a special bag. He drew the head from the bag and held it so the sea monster could see it. The sea monster turned to stone and Perseus took Andromeda for his bride and queen. After his death Zeus gave Perseus a place next to Andromeda in the heavens."

"Well, that's comforting to know." Andrew looked out at the stars while he considered the stories associated with them.

"Well, they're only legend. Not reality." Caroline lifted herself to a sitting position.

Andrew stayed for a moment longer before following Caroline's lead. When he sat up his hand grazed Caroline's and she reacted by pulling her arms to her lap.

"Caroline, your hands are cold." He wanted to reach out and take her hands in his, only to warm them. But he knew better. He wasn't going to risk scaring her off.

Caroline rubbed her hands together. "Yea, they're always cold, even in the summer. I'm used to it."

"It's getting late, we've been out here for quite a while. Maybe it's time to go inside." Andrew slowly stood up, allowing his legs to adjust after laying stationary for so long.

Caroline stood up and stretched. "It is cooling off out here. Maybe you're right." She reached down and picked up the blanket, then her glass.

Woods

They stood in silence as they took a final look into space. Andrew focused on the stars that made up the Andromeda constellation remembering her story had a happy ending. A woman chained to a rock was saved from her demon by a good-hearted man. He looked at Caroline as she stared out into the velvety night that sprinkled with light made up the vastness of space. He wondered if Caroline might share the same fate as Andromeda. Could a good man rescue her from her demons and unchain her heart?

Caroline shifted the blanket.

"May I take that for you?" Andrew stepped forward and reached out his arms.

She shook her head and smiled. "No. That's ok, I got it. I guess it's time to go in."

They walked toward the house together in silence. Andrew hoping Caroline would open her heart, trust, and love again. Even if he couldn't be the one. He knew what it was like to live shut up in his mind. It was a lonely existence and getting lonelier.

Caroline approached the door not wanting the evening to end. Yet she wasn't ready to let him in to her heart. She wondered if she was fooling herself. Could she be free and live a full life? Could she experience all that she desired without sharing it with someone?

Caroline opened the door and stepped over the threshold with Andrew at her heels. She looked at the clock on the stove. Ten-thirty.

Andrew looked at the glass he held, then at the bottle on the table. "What do you say we sit a while longer? Maybe we can finish off this bottle before we call it a night."

Caroline watched as Andrew picked up the bottle. She shrugged her shoulders. "I guess that would be alright. How about we take it to the living room?"

"Sounds good." Andrew moved around the table in front of the couch, placed the bottle and his glass on the table then sat down. Caroline started for the chair adjacent the couch, but Andrew protested.

73

"Caroline. Come sit over here on the couch. I won't bite you. I promise to keep my hands to myself." He joked.

She hesitated, then gave in. "Ok." She walked past the chair and sat on the couch far enough from Andrew so as not to encourage him.

"So, when did you learn so much about the stars?" Andrew shifted so he could look directly at Caroline.

She chuckled. "Well, it's silly, but when I was a kid, I was fascinated with Greek mythology. In junior high then high school when we studied history, we briefly touched on mythology. You know, as much as how it related to the way people during the time, we were studying, viewed God or the gods. It amazed me that intelligent people could base their life decision on such nonsense.

Once I started reading, I got drawn in and became fascinated with the stories. The more I learned the more I realized the correlation between mythology and astronomy. That's how I learned about the stories related to the constellations we saw tonight."

"Well, you certainly did your homework."

"I think I just got sucked in, like the Ancients did." She thought for a moment. "The stories were cruel, yet romantic."

She snickered. "I guess some things don't change. Anyway, there's more to life than romance."

Andrew nodded his head, not wanting to start a debate. "So, tell me more about your work. It appears you know everything about me. What do you write?"

Caroline got comfortable on the couch while she organized her thoughts. "I write pretty much anything. I write articles for magazines and newspapers. I've expanded to blogs and website content. I've ghostwritten a couple books for clients, and I have a few clients that I provide editing services for. That's basically it."

Andrew remembered the pages on the desk in her office. The pages he briefly saw before she stopped him. "Hmm. I thought maybe you were a writer of fiction or something."

Caroline shook her head and smiled. "No. I'm not that good. I don't know that I could come up with a complete story."

"I see." He studied her while she brushed off the possibility that she had a novel in her. "Well, it doesn't matter what you write, I'm sure you're good at it."

"I'm good enough to make a living at it."

"I should have you ghostwrite my story." He waited for a reaction.

"Your story? Are you planning on writing a memoir or something?"

He shook his head. "I don't think I need to. The media has already taken care of that. I'm an open book. My life story has no cover, and the pages are spread across the globe, my life circumstances exposed for everyone to judge."

Caroline felt his pain. "I think the media is terrible. It's all they care about is the money they'll make when they exploit people. I suppose if people didn't buy it, they would stop invading the privacy of others."

"Yea, well, it's like you said, no one cares about the feelings of others. Especially when something bad happens." Andrew looked down at the glass in his hand.

"Ah, yes. You have experienced your share of pain." Caroline recalled. "There's nothing like the pain of losing a child. Even one you haven't had the chance to know."

Andrew shrugged his shoulders. "I don't think you ever get over it." He studied Caroline's face, watching while she attempted to smile. "Do you, Caroline?"

Caroline tried to call his bluff. "How would I know? My children may have grown up and are now living lives of their own, but I'm still able to see them if I chose."

Andrew took a risk. He knew something wasn't right. His senses were telling him whatever it was it was something that kept that chain wrapped tight around her heart and locked up to protect from further heartbreak. "Is that true, Caroline? Something tells me you aren't being honest. Not with me, but more importantly, not with yourself."

Caroline placed her glass on the table and attempted to change the subject. "I miss them, but like every parent I have to let go. They are great kids, but time waits for no one. It's passed and they must live their lives the way they see fit."

"That's not what I'm talking about. How long ago was it?"

Caroline looked surprised. "Was what? I don't know what you're talking about."

"I think otherwise." He scooted closer to her and took her right hand in his. He held it tight enough so she couldn't pull away, but not so tight that he would hurt her." You're going to have to tell someone eventually, Caroline. It will be the most painful thing you will ever do, but it will be the thing that sets you free."

Caroline continued the deception that kept her sane for many years. She locked horns with Andrew insisting she didn't know what he was talking about.

Andrew went out on a limb, sharing his pain. "When we lost our baby girl my heart broke. I know I never met her, but I had nine months to prepare the introduction. I imagined how our first meeting would transpire. I would hold her, wrapped tight in the pink plush blanket. I would protect her and keep her warm. I imagined looking down at her smiling face while she looked up at me with her big blue eyes." He stopped to explain. "Amanda had blue eyes. I imagined the baby with her mother's eyes. Bright blue and sparkling, full of life. From there I imagined her taking her first steps, experiencing new foods. Then there would be her first day of school".

Caroline watched Andrew's face. She noticed his eyes misting over as he continued. "I dreamt about her fist date, our first fight, and bursting with pride as she went off to college. I thought about walking her down the aisle at her wedding and eventually, holding my grandchildren."

He looked into Caroline's eyes, not hiding his tears. He let her see his pain. His suffering. "I imagined and dreamt about all the experiences a father has when he is gifted with a daughter." Andrew continued to stare into Caroline's eyes. "But it was taken away from me before I had even one of those experiences."

He took a breath and continued. "I held her once. I held my lifeless daughter in my arms. I couldn't see the bright blue eyes, or the smile. She didn't look up at me memorizing her daddy's features. She was already gone."

Caroline lifted her free hand to her lips as tears streamed down her face. Her heart broke for the man sitting next to her. Why would he do this? Why would he share such sorrow with her? Why would he let her see such vulnerability?

Andrew reached out and placed his free hand over Caroline's hand that he held securely during his confession. "Caroline. Let it go. You need to speak the words so you can let it go."

Caroline pulled her hand from his and stood to face him. Her heart was breaking for him but more than that it was breaking for her loss. The loss she had pushed into the dark recesses of her heart and locked up so tight she might forget about it.

She spent a lifetime trying to forget. She forced it from her mind, but her heart couldn't let go. The memory was as clear today as it ever would be or ever was. "No!"

She lifted her hands to her face, covering her eyes from the truth. She turned from him and shook her head forcing the memory from her mind. Willing it to die as she felt she had all those years ago. "No! I can't let it go."

She then turned back to Andrew while he sat quietly listening to her unburden herself. "I can't let go of the little boy who will never have a chance to grow up. I can't let go of the guilt I feel. I should have protected him beyond anything else, including my own life."

Andrew watched, confused, as the tears streamed down her face. The tears returned to his eyes as he realized the consequence of her words. He waited for her to continue, watching her without judgement. He watched as she struggled to reign in her emotions. She searched for words that would explain her pain and the reality she lived with.

Caroline began to convulse in tears. "He forced me." Tears. "He made me do it." Sobbing. "I didn't know what to do. I let him control my better judgement. I should have killed him before I let anyone hurt my child!" She was yelling at the top of her lungs forcing the words to pass over her trembling lips.

Andrew stood up and walked toward her. He wrapped his arms around her as she sobbed into his chest. He held her close while she released years of pain, anguish, and tears. When the sobbing subsided, Andrew stepped back and looked down at Caroline. "I had no idea. I'm sorrier than you know for forcing you."

Caroline shook her head. "It doesn't matter now. It's out there. Now you know."

Andrew took Caroline's hands in his and he led her to the couch and directed her to sit. He kneeled on the floor in front of her. "Caroline. I know it's difficult, but please talk to me about this. I know our circumstances are different, but not so very different that we can't help each other. Will you tell me what happened?"

Caroline stared at the man in front of her. He looked back at her with tears in his eyes. He earlier shed tears for his child, but now was mourning the loss of hers.

"It was so long ago. I thought I forgot about it. I thought I had it under control. It happened so long ago. I figured it didn't matter anymore."

Andrew lifted his hand to her cheek and brushed away the tears that stained her face. "Caroline, it's affecting your ability to move on. This is what's keeping you stuck. We need to work through it."

Caroline looked confused. "We?"

"Yes, we. Caroline, the last two days have been a blessing to me. I feel a connection to you that is so strong, that I can't stop thinking about you. We were brought together for a reason. You said you wanted us to be friends. You said our lives are too different to be able to share a life together. I think you're wrong."

Caroline started to argue. "Andrew."

Andrew interrupted. "I think you're wrong, Caroline, but I'm not going to push you, or argue with you about it. I'm going to stand here with you and help you finally work through this as your friend."

He stood from where he knelt and moved to the couch. He sat next to Caroline. He sat close enough that he put his arms around her shoulder and pulled her to him. "Now. I want you to sit here and relax. Don't read into anything. Don't let your mind tell you

I'm putting the moves on you. I'm not. I'm comforting a friend who need to be comforted.

When you're ready, I'd like you to start from the beginning. I'm not going to judge you, Caroline. I want to help you.

Caroline stopped fighting with herself and relaxed against Andrew's chest. She closed her eyes and tried to calm herself. She lifted her hand to wipe away tears that continued to stream down her face. Caroline took a deep breath as she listened to the gentle beat of Andrew's heart. He sat, motionless, waiting for her begin.

Caroline fought with her conscience to sort through the suffering that she endured throughout her life. So much had happened. She wondered if talking about it would make a difference. She had lived this long without talking, maybe it wouldn't help. Maybe she would spill her guts and Andrew would get up and walk out, disgusted with her reality. Her head told her to push her pain to the back recesses of her mind where they had been hiding all these years. Her heart, well, her heart was beating in her chest, keeping rhythm with the heart of the man who now comforted her. Her heart told her to talk.

Andrew sat patiently holding Caroline while she collected herself. The silence was deafening. The night grew darker as the tension subsided. He felt her relax in his arms and wondered if she fell asleep. He leaned his head back and closed his eyes while he waited. Never releasing his hold on Caroline.

Caroline was surprised she felt safe in his arms. She didn't feel the need to run and no longer felt like hiding. She swallowed as she wiped her tears one last time. She lifted her head and looked at Andrew as he tried to read her. She nodded her head and sat up.

"I had a disturbing childhood." She began. "For years I struggled with it. I was in counseling when I started seeing my second husband. He moved in and we married before I realized what happened. I thought he was a good guy. And maybe in some ways, he was.

I wasn't supposed to be able to have more children. But somehow, I ended up pregnant. When I told him, he went crazy, he said I had to get rid of it. I protested. I told him I couldn't. I begged him to either let me have it and put it up for adoption or let me raise it myself." The tears returned and Caroline began to sob.

Andrew reached for Caroline's hand. "It's ok. Take your time."

"When I asked him why he was so adamant about it he said he already had a son. He didn't want his son to have to share him. He didn't want to have to be responsible for another child. We fought about it for hours. I cried about it for days. He told me I had no choice. He would pay for it, but I had to end it.

I became depressed and couldn't focus on anything. I felt like I was losing a part of me. In a way I guess I was. It was terrible. I went through my life in a daze. I was shocked that anyone would make another person do such a thing. The day came and he killed my baby. I don't remember the procedure. I don't think I can bring myself to remember.

When it was over, I had to go to Jonathan's concert. Everything was so surreal. I remember listening to the children singing but feeling like I wasn't really there. I was numb. I think I've been numb since then.

Many years have passed since then. And throughout the years I've experienced disappointment and been lied to. I feel like I've missed the boat. My life passed me by, and I didn't get to experience anything good."

Andrew squeezed Caroline's hand. "I'm sure it was difficult to speak the words. Let them settle now. You'll never forget, but you will be able let go of the pain. At least most of it. There will be days when you feel vulnerable, but it will be tolerable." He hesitated before asking the next question. "Caroline, is that why you split with him?"

"Not the only reason. There were many things that happened during the marriage that caused me great pain, but the final straw was when I found out he lied to me about who he was for over twenty years."

Andrew looked surprised. "Twenty years? What was the lie?"

"He lied to me about his whole existence. Where he'd been, who he'd been with, who he was as a man. I think I've succeeded in forgiving him, and I tried to let it go. I tried for three years. In the end I couldn't trust him. I didn't love him. I couldn't live with him anymore. Now he's gone.

"Do you mind if I ask what was disturbing about your childhood? You don't have to tell me if you don't want to."

"My parents divorced when I was young. My mother remarried and we moved out of state. We moved away from my father, all my aunts and uncles, cousins. We left my entire family behind. We settled in a small town out west. One where there were few people and those that lived there lived far enough apart that we didn't see our neighbors. It wasn't long before I realized my stepfather was an alcoholic. He'd come home from work drunk. He'd yell and throw things. He was demeaning and degrading at first. Shortly after we arrived, he started making, lewd comments, sexual ones. That led to his sneaking around. I caught him many times watching me dress. I was still young and didn't understand what was happening.

Soon after, he would sneak into my bed. He would 'accidently' come into the bathroom when I was showering, which of course, led to further advances. The abuse continued for years. I had no one to turn to, nowhere to go. We were thousands of miles away from anyone. I didn't have access to a phone, and we were too far from anywhere for me to run away. Plus, he threatened me. He said if it wasn't me, it would be my sisters. There were other threats as well. It still makes my skin crawl when I talk about it. Counseling helped me come to terms with the abuse. I realize now that it wasn't my fault, but it certainly affects the way I see myself and the world.

For years I let men take advantage of me, in one way or another. When you saw me smiling on the boardwalk, I was smiling because I know no longer had an attachment to any of that. No one can hurt me anymore. I thought I had come to terms with all of it and let it go."

Caroline sat quietly, looking over Andrew's shoulder and out the window at the stars suspended in the night sky. She was wishing she could be out there among them. Far from the conversation that brought back memories she thought were long ago buried.

"I've done a good job of moving on. I'm starting to enjoy life finally. I'm happy. I have momentary relapses on occasion, but I'm starting to enjoy life." She repeated.

"Caroline, I don't doubt that you are moving on, and that you are happy. But don't you feel that something's missing? I'm not asking you to answer me. I only want you to think about it. I've spent many years alone. The older I get, the more I realize I'm missing out on something very important. Spending the weekend with you has shown me that I want to find that special someone to share my life with."

A sad smile crossed his face. "I know you don't want to hear it, but when I saw you standing on the boardwalk smiling, then watched you enjoying the wind and water, and finally when I shared a quiet moment at the lake watching the moose, I thought I found her. I believed you could be my soul mate."

Caroline sat silently next to Andrew listening to him confess his realization. "I know that you believe I'm that person. But what if you're wrong? What if you find out I'm psychotic?"

Andrew chuckled. "Caroline, we're all a little crazy. In the end I think we're all looking for someone to share our lives with, flaws and all. We all need someone with whom we can unburden ourselves and I've waited a long time to consider the possibility. You are she that has opened my eyes to my desires.

I'm not asking for anything, beyond you considering the possibility. I want us to get to know each other better. We have many things in common and yet we are both independent of the commonalities. We've both suffered a great loss, many losses, I'm sure. I've learned to get past the pain and find a way to live a good life." He paused to consider. "Maybe our meeting is intentional. Maybe I came to you to help you heal. And then share with you as you experience all the things you've wanted for many years of your life."

"I've tried to let it go. The guilt has been eating at me for years." Caroline looked up at Andrew from where she sat leaning against his chest. "What if I never get over it? What if I let down my guard and let you in. What if we spend time; months, getting to know each other and you end up hating me?"

Andrew smiled and tightened his hold on Caroline's hand. "I could never hate you. If we aren't meant to be together, we can at least be friends. Isn't that what we are now. We are learning to be friends. Anything beyond that will be that which grows out of a beautiful friendship."

The two sat in silence contemplating their conversation. Caroline suffered for many years in her guilt. She felt lost and depressed at times and didn't know if she wanted to let anyone see her like that. She wanted to be strong, yet there were days when she felt weak and vulnerable. She wasn't sure she could trust Andrew enough to let him see her like that. It was done now. The conversation was out there. He knew the darkest secrets. One's she hadn't shared with anyone. As she thought about it, she realized that in her heart she trusted Andrew enough to share those secrets. Now she had to let go of the consequences.

Andrew held Caroline's hand as she silently sat next to him. He knew she was suffering and wanted to free her from the years of pain that kept her from enjoying life. He wanted to be with her more now than when he first saw her standing on the boardwalk.

Caroline straightened her shoulders and intently looked at him. "Andrew, I've been on my own for three years now, and am enjoying my freedom. I can do what I want, when I want and I don't have to worry about someone pulling the wool over my eyes, making me look foolish, and keeping me from realizing the dreams I have that I've repressed these many years. I'm only now starting to live and enjoy my experiences. I'm not ready to give up the opportunities I have."

Andrew sat up to face Caroline. He took both her hands in his. "Caroline. I wouldn't ask you to give up anything. Plus, pleasure is twice as nice if it can be experienced with someone close to you." He gave her hands a squeeze. "I'm not asking you to give up on any of your dreams. I would never stifle you. I want to support you as you spread your wings and take flight. I want to see your face light up when you realize a dream. I want to watch you laugh and share with you the joy you experience." He searched her eyes looking for some sign of hope.

He waited for her to respond, when she didn't, he continued. "Caroline, I know you have trust issues. I know you've been disappointed and hurt in the past. I wouldn't do that to you. There is an advantage to becoming involved with me, even as friends." He joked. "I'm an open book. The paparazzi have exposed my whole life to you. No investigation necessary."

Caroline smiled in response to his comment.

"You know a hundred times more about me than I know about you. You know my flaws and weaknesses. You know who I've been involved with and why those relationships didn't last. You know all the stupid things I've ever done. And I've done some pretty stupid things." He snickered at those memories. "I'm not perfect Caroline. But neither, am I a terrible person. I've never intentionally hurt anyone. I never would."

Caroline watched Andrew's expression as he defended his honor. "Andrew, I know you're a good person. You've done many good things with your time and money. I think that is what I like about you."

Andrew interrupted. "What, you mean it wasn't my good looks and charming personality that caught your eye?"

Caroline drew her hands from Andrew's and placed them in her lap. "Funny Andrew. No, it wasn't. Not that your bad to look at. I find the heart more important than physical beauty."

Andrew smiled as he heard Caroline's familiar wit sneaking back into the conversation. "I see. Well, then I guess it's a good thing I have a giving heart then." He paused while he waited for Caroline's reaction.

"Look Caroline, I don't want to spend the remainder of my visit debating with you or trying to convince you that I'm a great guy. I'd like to spend it with you, enjoying your company. How about we put aside the debate and visit. Talk. Build our friendship. We'll leave anything else to chance. What do you say?"

Caroline smiled and nodded her head. Andrew watched as her shoulders dropped and she relaxed a little. "I'd say that's a good idea. Maybe we can shift the focus of the conversation to something more interesting, something less, me."

Woods

Andrew sat back against the couch challenging her. "And what might that be?"

"Well, you've exposed my demons so there is little left to learn about me. I bet you're far more entertaining."

"I hardly think I've learned everything there is to know about you. You're a complex woman Caroline. I believe it will take more than two days to know everything about you. I'm sure there are many quirks I have yet to learn."

Caroline followed Andrew's example and sunk back into the couch cushions. "That may be, but I bet you have secrets that even the media hasn't unraveled."

"I don't know how that can be." Andrew replied sarcastically.

"Even if it isn't true, I'm sure I haven't read all the dirt. I don't subscribe to gossip media." Caroline then spoke more seriously. "But even if it isn't true, there must be somethings you 've been able to keep to yourself, ideas, dreams. What do you think of your work? You've made many movies. How does your life affect your work? Better yet how does your life spill over into the roles you portray?"

"Well, I think to do a job well, you need to have some skin in the game. In the case of acting, you need to relate to the role you're playing."

Caroline interjected. "I remember reading somewhere that you said when you're in character, you try to remember a time in your life where you may have been in a similar situation."

"Yes, that's true."

"You've had your share of pain and heartache. That must be what makes you successful as an actor."

Andrew chuckled. "I guess that's one way to look at it. If I hadn't experienced pain and discontent in my life, I wouldn't be able to imagine myself as the characters I play."

"You've acted in some pretty challenging roles. Diverse."

Andrew laughed. "I feel like I'm being interviewed here."

Caroline shook her head. "Sorry. I don't mean to. I think you're good at what you do, and it fascinates me to think you can harness true personal pain and funnel it into a fictious character. It would be one thing if you only played one type of role. Some actors only play in action movies, or drama. Some only play sappy roles. You, however, can act anything." Caroline stopped talking as the words she spoke registered.

"Maybe I should be concerned. What if you're acting right now?"

Andrew looked surprised. "What? Never."

Caroline looked grave for a moment, before a smile crossed her face. "Just kidding."

She sat up and faced him. "I'm curious. You've played in many action movies as the disconnected hero where you're masked and mysterious. Unwavering. What about *Finding Time*? That movie is completely different from that action role. In *Finding Time*, you are vulnerable. Not in the way most people would be portrayed in film. You somehow make the character natural. Real. When I watch the movie, the scene where you meet Sara for the first time. I look at your face and try to imagine what memory, you are conjuring up to make the character real."

Andrew moved to the edge of the couch and leaned his elbows on his thighs. He brought his hands to meet and rubbed them together as though trying to warm them. "Well, that role was a challenge. My character was living a life that I couldn't relate to. For the first time, I didn't draw on personal experience. Alan was living a life that I couldn't place. Not at any time during my life.

So, I had to go deeper. Alan was feeling a connection to Sara that neither time nor space could affect. He wanted to be with her, but the obstacle was one he had no control over. Somehow, I feel in meeting you, I am reliving a similar situation."

"What did you do? How were you able to overcome the situation?" Caroline was curious.

"I turned my thoughts inward. I put myself in Alan's position."

"Really? I don't know if I could imagine myself that way."

"I went into the deep recesses of my heart, a place that doesn't often see the light of day. I went to that place and drew from there a desire I would love to experience. You must have that same way of bringing to life something you want?"

Caroline shook her head. Not relating to what he said.

"Never? You've never wanted something so bad that you imagined it as you would have it be?" Andrew sounded surprised.

"Well, no. I mean I tried for years to make a family situation, but it didn't work."

Andrew nodded. "Maybe it's because you were trying with this." He pointed to his head. "Instead of your heart. Whatever you desire, must be a desire of love, not control."

"Wow. I never thought of it that way. So, I was trying to control the people in my life by forcing 'family' instead of loving them." She paused for a moment as what she said settled. "I don't think that can be right. I loved my family. So much so, that I wanted us to live happily ever after."

She snickered. "Maybe it didn't work, because happily ever after doesn't exist."

"Caroline. It exists. You need to imagine it through love though. I'm thinking you had trouble with that because of the way you were raised. You said you wanted that "Norman Rockwell" family. But maybe your brain, your conditioned body fought what you imagined, and won. It's not your fault."

Caroline grew impatient. "Yea, yea. I get it. We're not shrinking right now though. We're talking about your role in *Finding Time*."

Andrew sat up and turned to face Caroline while he thought about his response. He took her hands in his again and looked into her eyes. "I imagined what I'm experiencing these last couple of days. I imagined seeing a beautiful woman in a crowd. And being taken with what I see to the point that I must approach her. I imagined a feeling of closeness that is natural and responsive. I brought to life the feeling of commonality, connection, and an unbreakable bond.

I imagined standing close enough to touch her and feeling a burning desire to reach out to her. But holding back for fear that she wasn't real. Or that she'd disappear when I reached out to her.

In my mind I pulled her close and gently kiss her. I felt the heat of her breath on my face as I looked into her eyes and drown in the deep pools of her bright eyes. I imagined that I was returning to my true self. My soul. My soulmate."

They sat in silence while Andrew's words hung in the air. Caroline sat motionless, waiting for his next move. She felt the pulse in her neck, her ears were ringing as blood flowed to her temples. She caught her breath as she was overcome with a lightheaded feeling.

He listened as the words he spoke vibrated in his mind. He sat holding Caroline's hands waiting for her to pull away like she had done so many times during their two-day adventure.

Caroline sat motionless, not wanting to break whatever spell she was under. She was torn between pulling away or giving in to the energy that passed between the two of them.

When she composed herself, she smiled at Andrew who sat patiently waiting for her reaction. "Wow, you are a good actor. You also have a great imagination. What a beautiful image you paint of that first meeting."

Andrew knew he wouldn't win, at least not yet. Caroline protected herself with a tough outer shell that she wasn't ready to let anyone penetrate. And he didn't want to force his way through, only to risk her running away. He smiled, squeezed her hands one more time then released them. He then sat back against the couch cushion.

"You talk about my movies as though you're an expert. Did I stumble on a stalker?" He teased.

"No, Andrew, I'm not a stalker. I'm sure I haven't seen all your movies. I lean more toward the legendary movies. The movies that relate, even on a broad level, to a real-life experience or myth. I've seen a few of your action movies. They're good, but they don't hold my interest as well. And some of your early work, the comedy's, well, they were interesting. They appealed to the younger crowd. Which I suppose I was part of when the movies were made."

"Yes, we were all young at one time. Those days were fun. I lived a carefree life full of adventure."

Caroline nodded in agreement. They were all young once and life was there for the taking. Experiences existed that each of them could take. Both Caroline and Andrew chose a path and now

Woods

sat across from each other wondering if the road traveled was the best choice. In the end it didn't matter because they traveled a road that brought them to where they sat at that moment, having the conversation that brought them closer together.

EIGHT

They talked and shared stories of past experiences until the early morning sun peeked through the trees as the deep orange hue washed over the house and into the front window. When the first rays hit the living room floor Andrew realized they talked through the night.

Time passed quickly, the night turned to morning and Caroline knew they were one moment closer to saying goodbye. She yawned and stretched, sending life giving energy through her body, her attempt to focus her mind and prepare for goodbyes.

"We stayed up all night Caroline." Andrew chuckled. "I haven't done that in years. I can't believe I was able to stay awake."

Caroline nodded in agreement. "I know. I guess the conversation was engaging enough that neither one of us was paying attention to the time." She paused then looked toward the kitchen.

"Do you have time for breakfast, or do you need to leave?" Caroline stood up while she waited for Andrew's reply.

"Well, I do have a party to attend later, but I have plenty of time for breakfast."

Caroline fought to keep her disappointment hidden. "Oh. Ok. Of course, you have a party to go to. I wouldn't expect that you would be free for another day." She laughed lightly as she opened the refrigerator. "How about an omelet?"

Andrew followed her to the kitchen. "That sounds great." He watched Caroline while she moved around the kitchen. "May I help?"

She shook her head. "I can handle it. If you'd like you can set the table." Caroline pointed to the shelf where Andrew would find the plates.

He watched her as he removed the plates from the shelf. "I'd like you to come with me?" He cautiously waited for a response.

Caroline looked up at him, her eyes grew wide. "Me? No. I don't think so. I wouldn't fit in. I don't know anyone."

Andrew laughed out loud as he set the plates on the counter. "Caroline, you should see your face. You're as white as a sheet. I asked you to go to a party, not take a trip through outer space. Although come to think of it, you'd probably like that."

He walked toward her, and stopped in front of her, placing his hands on her shoulders. He smiled as he looked into her eyes. "You are a new woman, who needs new friends. I'm going to propel you in the direction of people who could fit the bill."

Caroline looked up at Andrew. "No. No Andrew. These are your people. I'm sure, rich, and famous and calculating."

Again, Andrew laughed out loud as he lowered his arms. "Caroline, what kind of person do you think I am? Just because someone has money, and is well known, doesn't mean they are devious and calculating." He stopped laughing and looked at Caroline seriously. "Do you think I'm cold and calculating?"

"Of course not, Andrew. I didn't mean…well I don't know what I meant. Except, I'm not like them. What if I have nothing to talk about?"

He returned the task of setting the table, removing the plates from the counter he walked to the table while he continued his conversation. "Caroline. We talked all night. You can't tell me you have nothing to say."

That's different Andrew. You're…well you're…you're my friend. I can't spill my guts to just anyone."

"Let's have breakfast. We'll clean up and then you can shower and get ready. Once you have a chance to take a shower, you'll see things clearer. These people are my friends. They will be happy to meet you and get to know you because you are a wonderful person."

Caroline snickered while she brought the eggs to the table. "That's going a little far, isn't it? I wouldn't describe myself as wonderful. I have many flaws and haven't always made the right choices. I'd hardly say I'm wonderful."

"Ok then, you're a decent person who's had some tough breaks, but survived." He took a bite of his omelet then pointed his fork at Caroline. "Now eat."

"Yes, sir." She giggled.

They finished breakfast and Andrew helped Caroline clean up the kitchen. Andrew removed the dishes to the dishwasher while Caroline returned the eggs to the refrigerator and placed the herbs and spices back on the shelf. Andrew wiped off the counter then turned to Caroline.

"Ok, I'll finish up here. Go take your shower. Or do you need help with that too?" He joked.

"Very funny Andrew. I think I can take care of that myself." She was afraid she was being thrown to the wolves but knew arguing with Andrew about it would serve no purpose. His mind was set, and he was on a mission to bring Caroline into the light and provide the push she needed to start her new life.

"Well hop to it. An audience awaits. I'm sure I can find something to entertain myself while I wait."

Woods

Caroline headed for the shower leaving Andrew to himself. Left alone, Andrew further explored Caroline's world, He moved around the house stopping in the living room to study pictures of her children at different ages. He focused on their smiling faces, imagining Caroline as the parent who interacted with such beautiful children.

He moved past the photographs and stopped in front of one of her paintings. He thought the painting was good. It had depth and it depicted a real presentation of Squam Lake. In his travels he saw many photographs of the lake that became famous in the 1980s. He was satisfied her painting did the lake justice.

Andrew turned from the painting and walked down the hall and studied other paintings Caroline had created. The further he explored, the more convinced he was that she should be selling her work. He made a mental note to address this with Caroline soon.

He stood outside her office door looking into the well-lit room. The sun shone through the large windows offering warmth and light that brought comfort to the space. He stepped inside and stood to look around the room. He moved to the bookcase that spanned the back wall of the space. He walked along the wall and noticed familiar authors from years gone by, Steinbeck, Dickens, Austen, Shakespeare. He then came upon the Greek tragedies, The Iliad, Antigone, and The Odyssey. He smiled as he recalled the conversation between him and Caroline the night before. He continued to peruse more recent titles before turning his attention to the center of the room.

He once again looked at the desk that was littered with Caroline's inspiration. He moved to the desk and looked down at the pictures he and Caroline studied together the day before. His eyes were then drawn to the pages strewn across the top of the desk. He looked down on words scrawled across pages that caught his eyes. Curiosity gnawed at him, tempting him to investigate. He stared at the pages from where he stood then turned away.

He recalled Caroline, a day earlier, covering the work so he wouldn't read what was displayed. His desire to know what she was writing was intense, but not as great as his desire for her to trust him. He stepped away from the desk and returned to the hallway.

He stepped out of the room and listened as he heard the gentle rush of water from the shower only a room away. He looked to the door that he was forbidden to see the day before. He placed his hand on the door that was slightly open. His curiosity, again, was snuffed out by his desire to be true. He stepped back at the same moment the shower became quiet.

Andrew moved back through the living room and the kitchen as he returned to the task of exploration. He passed through the kitchen and stood at a closed door. It was a door that he hadn't seen the day before. It was a door that he hadn't been forbidden to open, so he decided to risk it.

He reached out and turned the knob and pushed open the door. He looked to the space that was bare of furnishings, and the light was dim. To his left he noticed a window. In the window hung a blind that remained closed. In front of him on the far side of the room was an exterior door. In the window of the door also hung a blind. The room was clean. He walked across the wood floor and stood in the center of a large open space.

To his amazement he saw, hanging on the white walls, painting, after painting. He stood amazed at the artwork that hung in the isolated space. He returned to his senses and looked back to the door he, moments ago, passed through. He saw a light switch on the wall next to the door. He retraced his steps and flipped the switch that lit up the room. He turned around to face three walls covered with artwork.

He walked around the room looking at the paintings that hung in the forgotten space. He stopped to study each piece then continued until he heard Caroline call from the main part of the house.

"Andrew. Andrew. Andrew, where are you?"

He looked up to find Caroline standing in the doorway, a guilty look on her face. "What are you doing out here?" She asked cautiously.

"What do you mean what am I doing out here? I've stumbled on a gold mine." He approached Caroline, a surprised expression across his face. "Caroline. Why are you hiding these paintings? They're beautiful. You should be sharing these with the world."

Woods

Caroline stepped over the threshold into the room that archived the works she produced through many years. She shrugged her shoulders as she turned around to look at paintings she hid away. "I don't know. They're not very good. Some of them are awful. But I can't throw them out. They're like children to me. I put a lot of time and effort on the canvas. I've spent hours with each piece. I think throwing out the bad ones would be like disregarding a child that didn't turn out the way a parent would want."

She walked around the room and looked at the artwork on the walls. "Some of these I haven't looked at in years. I suppose if I continue, I will have to remove some of them to make room for the newer ones."

"Are you crazy Caroline? These are really good." Andrew followed Caroline as she walked across the floor. "You should be selling them. They should be on display somewhere. It's a shame to have them hanging in this space where no one can enjoy them."

He reached for her hand to stop her from moving to the next picture. "Caroline. You have a gift, here. I don't understand. Why won't you do something with them?"

Caroline let out a deep sigh. "I don't know. I guess I don't believe they're good enough."

"You should let the experts decide. We need to have someone look at these, someone with experience with this sort of thing." He stood in front of Caroline holding her hand. He stepped closer to her and drew her hand to his chest drawing her closer to him. "Caroline these paintings show a side of you that I'm sure you rarely expose. Please. Let me find someone to look at your work. This could be another way you move into your new life."

Caroline looked into Andrew's pleading eyes, fighting to maintain composure. She could feel the beat of his heart beneath her hand while willing hers to remain steady. She smiled as she replied. "Well, how can I say no to such a plea." She gently pulled her hand back from Andrew and turned to face the wall of art.

"Good. You need to have more faith in yourself if you're going to start the new life you keep speaking about. You need to be brave Caroline."

"I know." Caroline replied impatiently. "I know. But right now, is not the time for this discussion. You have a party to attend. Remember?"

Andrew smiled and nodded. "We. We have a party to attend." He stepped back and looked at Caroline. "Hmm. You look nice."

"I'm probably underdressed. I have no style…"

"Caroline, stop worrying. They're normal people, like you." Andrew guided her through the door to the kitchen. He stopped briefly and looked one last time at the artwork that hung in isolation, before he turned off the light.

Woods

NINE

Andrew opened the door and stepped into the room that two days earlier, Caroline had visited. She followed Andrew into the space and stopped to look around. She watched as people buzzed around preparing for the afternoon.

A young woman looked up and smiled at Caroline as she scanned the

He leaned closer and spoke softly. "Caroline, I'm going to shower. Why don't you explore the place while you wait?"

Caroline snickered. "God knows there is enough to explore. I hope I don't get lost."

"Funny Caroline. Will you be ok while I'm gone?" Andrew removed his hand and stepped back so he could see Caroline's face.

She nodded. "I think I'll live. There are so many people here working. What kind of party is this anyway?"

Andrew shook his head. "It's just a group of friends getting together. Honestly, I'm not sure how many Sean invited."

Caroline nodded as she looked around the room one more time. "I see. Well, you better make yourself presentable, before someone important shows up."

Andrew quickly agreed and turned to the staircase. Caroline followed him with her eyes as he ran up the stairs, skipping every other step. She watched him until he disappeared down the long hallway.

Caroline looked back at the woman who worked diligently in the kitchen. They smiled at each other one more time than Caroline turned her attention to the large glass windows that looked out toward the lake.

The sun cast its bright light across the water as it rose in the morning sky. Caroline focused on the water as ripples formed, a result of the passing watercraft. She could feel the warmth radiating off the glass as it penetrated her face. She closed her eyes momentarily as she listened to the buzz of activity around her; the shuffle of tables, the clanging of pans and plates, and the chatter of excited voices as instructions were given.

Caroline opened her eyes and turned as a plate hit the floor, crashing, and sending shards of glass everywhere. She turned to see a young man scurrying to clean up the pieces while others worked around him. A smile crossed her face as she decided to retreat to the silence of the deck.

She opened the door and stepped outside into the sunshine. The deck was inviting, and Caroline took up the offer and walked the length of the space until she stood at the corner that overlooked the lake. Slight waves teased the shoreline tapping against the sand then receded.

Caroline moved to the steps, her escape to the beach below. She stopped on the final tread and removed her shoes before beginning her trek across the warm sand. She stopped at the water's edge and closed her eyes. She could hear the familiar sound of water hitting the hull of the boat. The rhythm keeping time with her heart that beat slow and steady as the cool waves tickled her toes. The water moved away taking the sand beneath her feet with it.

Caroline wiggled her toes and smiled, recalling an early childhood memory, a memory experienced on the very lake she stood in front of at that moment. The smile left her face while she remembered it as the final family get together before her parents split. She opened her eyes as she thought about early life disappointments and how they had affected her as an adult. None of them mattered anymore, but she couldn't help thinking those events caused her much pain throughout her life.

Caroline sighed as she opened her eyes, the smile returned to her face, as she reminded herself that she had complete control of her life now. Nothing, no one could change that. No blame, no worry. She turned and walked along the beach, lifting her face to the sun that warmed her shoulders. She turned and followed the speedboat with her eyes as it raced down the lake.

"Caroline."

She turned to face Andrew as he approached.

"I see you found a way out." He joked.

"I did. It's nice down here. I think I'll stay here while you socialize with your peeps". Caroline smiled waiting for a reaction.

"I don't think so, Caroline. I'm going to introduce you to your future".

Caroline was struck with curiosity. "Oh, really"?

"That's right". He paused as he cautiously chose his words. "Those paintings, Caroline. They're beautiful. You need to do something with them".

"Andrew, I already told you…"

"Caroline, listen to me". He spoke softly, not wanting to agitate her. "I think you should have someone look at your work. Let them decide if it's good enough. We're all our own worst critic. This could be another step taken in your new life. You could have new experiences, meet new people, and share a gift that you're hiding away I that dark room".

"I'm not ready, Andrew".

"Caroline. If you wait until you're ready, you'll never take the leap." He reached out and placed his hand on her shoulder.

"Close your eyes, Caroline, and jump. It could be the best experience of your life".

Caroline turned from Andrew to face the water. "Yes". She paused. "Or it could be the biggest disaster of my life".

"I wouldn't do that to you Caroline. If I didn't believe you had talent, I wouldn't push you." Andrew walked around Caroline and stopped in front of her, blocking her view of the water. "At least try." He stepped closer and lifted his hand to brush the hair from her eyes as he pleaded with her. "For me"?

Caroline studied Andrew while he waited for her response. She gazed into the deep pools that bore into her soul. Her heart raced. Her eyes mentally traced the strong jaw then stopped just above the chin where she focused on the pale lips that displayed a slight smile. She then turned her attention to the eyes again, unable to look away.

Andrew moved closer and put his hands on her waist. "Come on Caroline. Think how amazing it would be to share your gift with the world". He leaned in and in almost a whisper said. "You're being selfish, Caroline, and you don't even know it."

Caroline caught her breath as she felt Andrew's breath on her neck. He didn't retreat but remained close enough that Caroline could smell the mixture of cologne and soap still present on his skin. She didn't know how to respond. She looked away as she smiled, focusing on the white sail of a passing boat. "You make it sound like I'm a terrible person. It's just art". She stopped talking, taking a breath as she decided. "If it means that much to you. Okay".

In his excitement Andrew lifted Caroline off her feet and spun her around. He set her down and wrapped his arms around her as he spoke. "I know you won't regret it".

He stepped back but kept his hands on her waist. "Caroline. I don't think you know how wonderful you are. You have been living under a dark cloud long enough. The sun is about to shine on you with a brilliance that will keep you glowing for the rest of your life".

Caroline stood, her hands still on Andrew's shoulders as the smile disappeared from her face. "I think you're exaggerating, Andrew".

Woods

Andrew smiled down at Caroline. His dark eyes twinkling, a slight smile on his face. Caroline was conscious of Andrew's hands as he drew her close. "Caroline, I've never been more serious about anything in my life". He spoke barely above a whisper as he moved his hand to her chin and lifted her face to his. "It's time for you to shine. Like a nebula waiting to burst into the bright star it's meant to be". He leaned closer and Caroline froze. She wanted to turn away, but she stood captivated, entranced by the eyes that she couldn't resist.

Caroline stood in agony struggling between wanting Andrew, and not being able to stop his advance. His lips met hers, a gentle kiss. Caroline's senses heightened by the warmth of his breath mingling with his cologne and she relented.

They stood on the beach in the sun, arm in arm. Caroline lost herself in Andrew's embrace. She began to panic as she could feel herself drowning in his kiss. She was right where she wanted to be, yet she wanted to run from him, escape his touch. Andrew consumed her and was consumed with her. Caroline was weak in the knees and her breath drew short, knowing all the while that Andrew was destroying her with each passing moment.

Caroline drew on years of past disappointment and hurt, finding the strength to take control of her emotions. She pulled back from him and stood determined not to be weak. "Andrew, didn't you come down her to tell me people were arriving?"

Caroline noticed the look of disappointment on Andrew's face. "I guess I did". He lowered his gaze and smiled meekly, not wanting Caroline to realize she had hurt him. He cleared his throat, looked up and smiled. "Yes. I wanted to let you know that Peter Carlton arrived. He is the person we need to talk to about your paintings".

Caroline stood stunned. She didn't think he was serious about searching out anyone to consider her work. "Really, Andrew. I thought you were only saying that to make me feel good about the art. Maybe we should wait for another time. I don't want to take advantage".

"It's already done, Caroline. When he came in, I told him I found his next gold mine. He can't wait to talk to you." He reached for her hand and drew it to his chest and gently spoke. "You can deny this all you want, Caroline. But it's real. You can deny it all you want, but one day you'll realize that not all men are out to get you". He smiled at her but didn't release his grip. He turned and walked toward the stairs, guiding Caroline up the steps to return to the deck.

Caroline stopped and turned to the lake. She rested her elbows on the rail, stalling for time. "The view is spectacular from here, isn't it?'

Andrew laughed. "Caroline, stop stalling. I'm not bringing you to the racks, I'm introducing you to your future. You should be excited. Come on".

She turned from the rail to face Andrew. "You can't blame a girl for trying."

"It will be fine, Caroline".

"You sound so sure of yourself. There are no guarantees in life, Andrew".

He took her hand and led her to the door. "Except in this case. This is a sure thing. Let's go."

Caroline followed Andrew through the sliding glass door and into the living space where Caroline looked upon many people talking in small groups. There was laughter, and music played quietly in the background while private conversation kept everyone occupied. Caroline was glad that no one looked up when they entered the room. She was self-conscious and didn't want to make the feeling worse by prying eyes.

Andrew looked around the room, his eyes studying each small group until he saw Peter Carlton. Peter looked up and waved when he saw Andrew walking toward him. Caroline followed behind Andrew. Her stomach began to turn at the prospect of not only disappointing herself, but Andrew too, when this art expert told Caroline her work was mediocre at best. Caroline thought the one consolation was that Mr. Carlton wouldn't be viewing her work today. So, she could relax for the present moment.

Peter stepped away from the conversation as Andrew made the introduction. "Peter, this is Caroline..." Andrew looked at

Caroline curiously, remembering he didn't know her last name. "This is Caroline. Caroline, meet Peter Carlton".

Peter looked up at Caroline as he lifted his hand to shake hers. "It's nice to meet you, Caroline. I understand you are an artist".

Caroline shyly shook her head as she attempted to discount what Andrew said to Peter earlier. "I don't know Mr. Carlton..."

"Call me Peter. Please".

"Very well. Peter, I don't know how much of an artist I am. I know Andrew insists you see my work, but I don't want to waste your time. I don't have a degree in any type of art. Painting is a hobby. I don't know that any of my paintings are good enough to be wasting your time on".

Andrew interrupted. "Caroline, you have a gift. Gifts are not learned they are part of who you are. They come from within the soul. What you have is special".

Peter turned to Caroline. "He's right you know. There are many artists who didn't have formal training. Take Henri Rousseau for example. He lacked any formal training. As a matter of fact, he was 40 years old before he started to take himself seriously. He worked as a clerk for most of his adult life. Ultimately, his work was exhibited alongside van Gogh, Paul Gauguin, and Henri Matisse. Heck, Pablo Picasso collected Rousseau's work. Picasso thought enough of Rousseau's work that he bequeathed several of Rousseau's paintings to the Louvre".

Andrew stood next to Caroline smiling. He knew Caroline couldn't argue with Peter's statement. "See Caroline, you don't have to have a formal education to be successful. You should at least let Peter see your work before you discount your abilities".

Peter agreed. "Caroline, you won't be wasting my time. Even if I don't agree with Andrew, you should feel fortunate that he believes in you enough to stand here and fight for you". Peter studied Andrew as he smiled down at Caroline. Peter sensed something in Andrew's glance. Something more than simply wanting to help her get recognized for her work. He dismissed the feeling for the moment.

"Caroline, I'm going to be here for a few days. Why don't we schedule a time to meet...do you have time tomorrow? I can come to you. I'll be completely honest with you." He paused while he thought of Caroline and what she must be feeling, torn between the excitement of being discovered and the disappointment of not being good enough.

He'd seen it many times in his career. He looked at Andrew and smiled before focusing his attention on Caroline again. "It's never easy to expose yourself and your work to critique. But what do you have to lose? Only me, you, and Andrew will ever know this conversation took place. One of two things will happen. You could remain as you are today, unknown, or you could end up being famous for your work. Neither option is bad. It is what it is. You will be who you were meant to be...one way or another".

"I guess you're right. It's not like I'm ten years old and my feelings will be hurt. I'm an adult. I can take it". The conversation stopped momentarily while Caroline considered her options. "Okay. I'll do it. You can see the paintings tomorrow. I'll prepare myself for my fate and that will be the end of it".

Peter smiled at Caroline as he offered his hand to her. "Wonderful. It was nice to meet you. I look forward to seeing you tomorrow". He shook Caroline's hand then addressed Andrew. "I'll talk to you later."

"Great. I'll talk to you later. Enjoy the party".

Caroline and Andrew watched as Peter returned to his earlier conversation. "See Caroline, that wasn't so bad, was it"?

"No. I suppose not". Caroline looked up at Andrew. "Do you really believe my paintings are worth taking Peter's time?"

"You know what, Caroline? We'll find out tomorrow. Until then let's just enjoy the day".

Andrew and Caroline spent the afternoon mingling with guests. Caroline was surprised how down to earth many of them were. It made her nervous when Andrew left her side, but slowly she learned to trust herself.

Caroline watched as Andrew went to get drinks for them, then was sidetracked when someone stopped him to talk.

"He is something, isn't he?" Caroline was startled by the voice behind her. She turned to see a young woman smiling as she looked in Andrew's direction. Caroline guessed her to be in her late twenties, maybe early thirties. She became tense as she watched the young lady standing next to her. She looked familiar, but Caroline couldn't place her. She carried herself with confidence yet projected a friendly manner. Why wouldn't she be confident, she was young and beautiful.

"He is a good man, I believe." Caroline responded.

The young woman looked at Caroline and smiled. "I've been watching you today. I don't recognize you. Have we met?" She paused, looked at Andrew, then focused on Caroline again. "No, I'm sure we haven't met. I think I'd remember you."

Caroline looked puzzled. "Why would you remember me?"

Well, for one, you're pretty, maybe even beautiful. Beyond that you are beautiful inside. I can see it in your eyes. Secondly, I'd remember any woman who has the attention of Andrew Roberts. He's in love. It's written all over him."

Caroline looked from the young woman to Andrew who was engrossed in conversation, then she focused on the young lady again. "What? With whom?"

The woman laughed out loud. "I'm sorry I should introduce myself. I'm Amanda. And you are...?"

"Caroline..." She said.

"Caroline. What a practical name. He's in love with you, Caroline." She looked intently at Caroline, waiting for a response. "Any woman would love to be in your shoes. To have Andrew Roberts pay a complement like that would be beyond anything any woman could hope. I have to say I never thought I'd see it."

"That's crazy. I only met him two days ago. He can't be in love with me."

"Caroline, look at him. You may have only met him recently, but I've known him for years. Ask anyone here and they'll tell you. He's in love. I hope you don't plan to break his heart."

"Absolutely not. I hope you don't think I've encouraged this. I keep telling him I'm not ready for that kind of relationship. I mean, I enjoy his company, but I can't think of anything beyond that."

"Caroline, you may not be ready for him, but he's clearly ready for you. He's been alone for a long time. He isn't a man to fall easily. He's a good judge of character and has a heart of gold. If you're even considering the possibility of a relationship with him, you better not wait too long. I mean, I can't imagine anyone would come along right away, but you know how things work. When you least expect it, expect it."

Amanda studied Caroline momentarily. "I think you must be a good person. He sees something of value in you worth his time and energy. Don't take that lightly."

She smiled as she moved her focus to Andrew then back to Caroline. "I like seeing him in this light. Every man should fall deeply and passionately in love. Not just infatuation, but pure, true, deep, and passionate burning love. I think this is it for him." She looked into Caroline's eyes, as though she was looking for a deep secret. What did you do to him?"

Caroline became uncomfortable as she watched Amanda's eyes searching her own for a secret that Caroline didn't have knowledge of. "You know, now that I have a moment to focus on it, I look at him, then I look at you, it's almost as if you two share an energy field."

Caroline looked confused and couldn't find words to respond to Amanda's observation.

Amanda nodded as though she read Caroline's mind. "I know. I'm freaking you out. A lot of people tell me that when I tell them what I see. But I sense something between you two, some unresolved force or energy. Maybe you're soulmates. Maybe you were lovers in another life and share a bond that even time can't break."

A chill went down Caroline's spine as Amanda's words echoed in her ears. She looked at Andrew who stood across the room in deep conversation. He looked up and smiled at her before refocusing on the conversation. Amanda's words reverberated in her head. Caroline's heart began to beat faster as she heard Amanda's words in her head, *maybe you are soulmates. Maybe you were lovers in another life and share a bond that even time can't break.*

Caroline turned and Amanda was gone. She scanned the room for signs of the young lady that, seconds before cautioned

Caroline about toying with Andrew's heart. She looked around for a few more minutes, until Andrew returned to her.

"Are you having a good time, Caroline?" Caroline was conscious of how close he stood, and now more than ever she was completely aware of his presence.

Caroline nodded." Yes, It's a wonderful party. I have to say, I'm surprised by how down to earth everyone seems. You're right. They're no different than me." She took a deep breath attempting to brush off her conversation with Amanda.

Andrew was concerned by Caroline's demeaner. "Caroline. Are you okay? You look like you've seen a ghost."

Caroline closed her eyes and shook her head to dismiss the feeling of discontent that wouldn't leave her.

"No, I'm fine. Maybe it's getting a little warm in here."

Andrew placed his hand on Caroline's elbow and guided her toward the door. "Let's step outside and get some air. You'll feel better after you get some fresh air." He looked around the room as he navigated his way through the dwindling crowd bringing Caroline to the door. They stepped outside and Caroline took a deep refreshing breath.

"There. Do you feel better?"

Caroline leaned on the rail and nodded. "Yes, thank you."

Andrew looked back toward the door, noticing there were only a few people remaining at the party. "Wow, the day certainly passed quickly. I hope I didn't leave you alone too long."

Caroline shook her head. "No. actually, I had a conversation with a nice young lady. She gave me a lesson in unrequited love."

He looked intrigued. "Really? Who's breaking whose heart? He joked.

Caroline shook her head not wanting to share the details of the conversation. "No one. Really. It was only a general conversation."

"Who were you talking to?"

"Her name was Amanda. I didn't get her last name. She claims to know you though."

"Hmm. I can't say without a last name."

Andrew shrugged his shoulders. "Well, it's not important. What do you say, are you ready to go?"

Caroline's heart sunk as she replied. "Sure". Her confirmation would be the catalyst for her return home. A place she wasn't sure she wanted to return to tonight. Not alone, anyway. It was inevitable though. Her Cinderella hour would end soon, and she would return to the real world; the world she was creating for herself.

Andrew smiled as Caroline nodded. 'I have an idea. Do you want to go home or are you up for a bit more adventure?"

Caroline laughed. "More adventure? I'm not sure I can take much more. But why not?"

"Good, let's go." He took her hand, and they walked along the deck and down the steps toward his truck. He opened the passenger door and guided her into the truck.

Caroline looked at Andrew and giggled. "What, just like that? No explanation. Nothing?"

Andrew closed the door and walked around the front of the truck and slid in behind the wheel. He grinned at Caroline as he fastened his seatbelt, then started the engine.

Caroline spoke as he backed out of the driveway. "Do you care to tell me where we're going?

"For a ride."

Woods

TEN

Caroline laughed at Andrew as he headed southeast. She found his spontaneity refreshing. "Don't you have something else to do besides drag me across the state?"

"Absolutely not. You're mine until tomorrow." Andrew announced.

"Until tomorrow? What's tomorrow?" She chuckled

"How soon you forget. Tomorrow is your debut as a painter. Artist extraordinaire." He smiled at Caroline then turned his attention to the road.

"How can you be so sure?" Caroline looked puzzled.

Andrew maintained focus on the road, while responding. "I don't know. I have a feeling. I can't explain it. I see you as a painter. I see you doing great things. Somehow, I feel almost as though this moment for you, is a Deja vu moment for me. Almost as if I've experienced it before. This whole weekend has been like that for me. I feel like I've known you all my life. I don't know."

They left town and headed south, driving along the lake for miles before Andrew spoke. "I think I know the answer to this question, but I'm going to ask it anyway. Do you like the ocean, Caroline?"

Caroline's face lit up. "I love the ocean." She leaned her head back against the seat and closed her eyes as she smiled. "It's one of the most peaceful places on earth. I love to walk in the warm sand, to feel the grains of sand working their way through my toes spilling over the tops of the feet, until I can't see them. To hear the waves, pound against the shore and splash along the rocks, keeping perfect rhythm with the moon, it's the best form of therapy."

Andrew laughed. "Then we're headed in the right direction. I'm taking you to the ocean."

Caroline turned in her seat to face Andrew. "How did you know I like the ocean?"

He shrugged his shoulders. "Just another feeling."

Caroline studied Andrew as he watched the road. How did he know her so well? What made him so in tune with her desires? She hadn't even tried to read him. She spent the last two days putting up walls, fences to keep out the intruders, to keep Andrew from breaking in and steeling her heart.

She turned to face forward while her mind continued to reel. How did he know her so well? She thought for a moment longer before abandoning the self-sabotaging conversation. She decided not to read into the coincidences that couldn't be explained. Maybe he was just good at reading people.

They drove for another hour enjoying occasional conversation. Caroline looked out over the lake taking note of the shadows while they grew shorter, an indication that the sun was working its way west. The summers were long now and while the sun was no longer high in the sky, the air remained warm. The day had been humid. Caroline was glad to be removed from the earlier crowd. She leaned against the door while the wind tossed her hair into disarray. The breeze was refreshing.

Andrew turned to watch Caroline occasionally. There was something about her that made him want to draw her close and not let go. The more time that passed, the more he felt he needed to protect himself and her. Somehow, he was becoming attached to her. The more time he spent with her, the greater the connection he felt.

Andrew moved his elbow to the door as he returned his attention to the road in front of him. A content feeling washed over him as he drove on. He was approaching the rotary and was cautious, making sure he paid attention to merging traffic.

Caroline was familiar with this route. She knew where she was and took a deep breath allowing the smell of the salt air to consume her. It wouldn't be long now. She turned to Andrew and smiled. "We're almost there."

He nodded in agreement as he maneuvered his way through traffic. He wasn't surprised at the amount of traffic still on the road. The long summer days kept people near the ocean. The roads were narrow now. The sand dunes were evidence of the approaching coastline.

Caroline could hear the waves in the distance, crashing along the shoreline. She smiled at the familiar sound that for years was absent from her existence. She checked herself as she thought *I'm coming home. Curious*, she thought. What would make her say she's coming home. She never lived near the coast. Only visited when she was young. She felt sad as she realized she had missed it for the last twenty years.

She missed out on many things. She again checked her thoughts. None of that mattered anymore. She would begin again. A new life. New experiences.

Andrew drove through what he would describe as the neighborhood, where houses were close and makeshift parking lots popped up. He nodded as a young man waved and signaled to Andrew, letting him know there were vacancies. Andrew turned on his directional and stopped to hand the young man ten dollars.

The wind blew through Andrew's window and across the cab of the truck. Caroline could taste the sea air as it moved past her face. Andrew smiled at her as he pulled into a parking space and turned off the ignition. They simultaneously stepped out of the truck and closed their doors.

Andrew walked to the back of the truck where he met Caroline. They stopped to look at each other, a moment of uncomfortable silence that was soon carried off by the breeze. He smiled as he reached out and took Caroline's hand in his.

She hesitated, systematically wanting to pull back. This time however, she allowed him his way. They walked along the side of the road observing the traffic, both pedestrian and motorized. Andrew stayed close, using the excuse of avoiding traffic that passed them. Caroline smiled to herself as she thought of his subtle excuse to remain nearby.

They walked in the dirt removed from the heat of the pavement. They still had shoes on, but both could feel, beneath their feet, the burn of the tar. Caroline smiled as she shared a memory. "The heat of the pavement brings back a memory from when the children were young."

Andrew was attentive. "I hope it was a good one."

Caroline snickered. "Well, it wasn't at the time. We, the children, and I were on the beach playing in the sand when Jonathan decided he needed to use the bathroom. They were both quite young. He may have been three years old. We, none of us had shoes on. I don't know what I was thinking but I carried the two of them to the bathroom, across the hot sand and burning pavement." She shook her head as she relived the memory.

"By the time we got back to the blanket, my feet were burning. We stayed for a couple more hours then went home. That night I was in so much pain, I couldn't walk. Blisters formed on my feet and I wasn't able to walk for days." Caroline shook her head as she continued. "I crawled around the house like a baby for a week. How foolish was I not to put on my shoes? I never did that again."

Andrew looked down at Caroline, concerned. "You were alone with them?"

Caroline laughed. "You sound surprised. You make it sound like I wasn't capable to be alone with them."

"That's not what I meant. I only meant it's sad that their dad wasn't with you."

Caroline shook he head. "By that time, I was alone with them. The three of us did everything together. Until Tom came along anyway. Then we didn't do anything." She paused while her mind sorted through her memories. "Hmm, what a shame that we often see things too late."

Andrew watched Caroline while she thought about time lost to a past that wasn't pleasant.

She shrugged her shoulders. "Well, none of that matters anymore. The children turned out fine, so, all is good."

They stopped and looked both ways before crossing the busy street. Caroline noticed the road remained mostly unchanged. The businesses along the boulevard may have changed over the years, but the arcades and small gift shops remained as they were.

She smiled as they crossed the road, catching a glimpse of the public restrooms that years ago were the scene of her earlier recollection. Andrew released Caroline's hand as they approached the steps that descended to the sandy beach.

They stopped at the stone wall that separated street from sand. They each leaned against the wall and removed their shoes before venturing down onto the sand.

Caroline moved first. She couldn't wait to feel the sand between her toes. She closed her eyes as her feet met the sand. It was warm and tickled her toes. Andrew watched her face with pleasure, Caroline's expression as she returned to another time. He could sense it. She truly was home.

They walked across the beach being careful not to disturb those that rested as they passed. They each walked in silence carrying their shoes which would be needed eventually. Caroline headed for the water with Andrew at her heels.

The people on the sand grew sparse as Andrew and Caroline got closer to the water. They moved from deep warm soft sand to the cool, wet, compact ground at the water's edge. Together they walked in and out of the water as the waves met the shore, then retraced their path until they disappeared into the vast ocean, only to return, again.

The sound of the ocean comforted Caroline. She felt a sense of peace at the beach that she rarely felt anywhere else. Andrew moved closer and took her hand sensing the ease with which she moved. He knew it was possible she would withdraw, but he knew he couldn't resist the opportunity to be close to her.

To his surprise, she didn't dismiss his advance. She leaned in and walked close, lifting her free hand to rest on Andrew's arm. They walked in silence for a while. Each lost in thoughts or memories that were long ago lost. Neither able to shake the feeling of belonging that they felt, at that moment.

The water was cold as it teased their feet, but it was a refreshing change from the humid land locked air they experienced earlier. The waves splashed up against bare legs as they made their way down the beach. They were walking away from the crowd that congregated at the main beach. Caroline had her eyes on the sea breaker that jetted out from the coastline. She remembered walking among the rocks, removed from the people that, she felt, didn't understand the need for temporary isolation.

Caroline drew back her hand from Andrew's grasp as her pace quickened. The distance grew between them and Andrew watched her with curiosity as she made her way to the massive wall of rocks near the waters' edge. She looked back and smiled at Andrew as he continued to follow Caroline.

Andrew smiled as he watched Caroline, who by now had let go of any worries. The wind blew up the coastline and passed through Caroline's hair leaving in its wake a tossed mass of golden locks that she brushed from her face. She laughed and began to run across the hard, wet sand. Lifting her hands and turning in circles celebrating the free feeling that the wind offered.

Caroline waved her hand, inviting Andrew to join her. He laughed out loud at her juvenile carefree attitude as he picked up the pace and ran to meet her. He came up on her quickly and surprised her when he reached out and lifted her off the ground. She squealed as her feet left the sand, and she rested her hands, on Andrew's shoulders as she looked down at him.

He turned her around until he began to feel dizzy, then released his grasp enough that she slid down the front of his chest until her feet were on solid ground. Andrew looked down at

Caroline who was still laughing. He wasn't ready to release his hold on her and surprisingly, she didn't run away.

Caroline looked into Andrew's eyes as a confused look crossed her face. Her hands remained on Andrew's shoulders. She stood still, as she sorted through feelings of a deep connection. She composed herself while she dealt with feelings of love and loss and the possibility of being torn from Andrew. No not Andrew, someone else. She shook her head as she lowered her hands and turned from Andrew, not knowing if what she felt was real or her only getting caught up in the moment.

The smile left Andrew's face and he moved around to face Caroline. "What's wrong, Caroline?"

She shook her head as she addressed Andrew. "I don't know." Shrugging off the confused state. "Maybe it was all that spinning around. I guess it made me dizzy." Caroline turned her attention to the rocks jetting out into the water. That's where she was headed before she started to act so, juvenile. "Come on, I wanted to spend some time on the breaker over there." She pointed to the rocks surrounded by the foam created by the force of waves hitting the immobile surface.

Andrew nodded and followed her as she headed toward the breaker. He walked quickly until his stride matched Caroline's. "You seem focused on the breaker. Is there a specific reason?"

"No. Not really. I enjoy sitting in the sun out there. It's warm and quiet. Plus, it's a great place to find sea-shells when the tide is out."

Andrew stepped up on to the rock first. He reached out his hand to Caroline, which she ignored as she climbed her way to the top and stood facing the breeze. She watched as the sun's reflection on the water, faded. The bright light of the day had turned orange and mingled with the waves as they broke and crashed along the rocks, sending spray into the air. Caroline closed her eyes as drops of water sprinkled across her cheeks. Her nose tingled when she breathed in the sea air.

Andrew followed her to the far edge of the rocks where she stood. He stopped next to her and smiled down at her as she filled her lungs with the sea air. "Don't you think you might be kind of close to the edge here? The tide is coming in. The waves appear to be gathering strength. There must be a storm brewing somewhere out there."

They looked across the water noticing the dark clouds as they moved closer. The wind was increasing, and the temperature dropped. Caroline wasn't concerned though.

"I don't think so. I'm not that close. I would like to get a closer look at that spot on that rock." She pointed. "I think that might be a sea star or star fish as they are commonly called."

"Hmm. I don't think I've heard anyone else refer to them as sea stars, besides me, I mean." He paused to consider the term. "I think it's an old term. One remembered from another lifetime."

Caroline giggled. "I don't know. I've referred to them as sea stars for as long as I remember." She shifted her weight to get a better look what she noticed to be more ivory than white.

She continued to focus on the sea star for another minute until she realized the wind was increasing in strength. Andrew cautiously stepped across the rocks to stand next to Caroline. She took a step to her right and was about to turn to face Andrew when she lost her balance. A gust of wind carried with it a wave that crashed into the rocks and caught Caroline as it receded into the vastness of the ocean.

Caroline screamed as she went over the edge of the breaker. She reached out, feeling for anything that would keep her from falling into the water. She dropped quickly, unable to catch her breath. Her heart raced as she heard Andrew call out to her. She could hear him screaming above the crash of the waves. "Caroline! Caroline!"

The wind blew through Caroline's hair as she continued to fall. She could hear the wind whistling as she moved closer to darkness. Her arms were flailing, reaching out hoping to grab on to anything she could as she continued to fall. She knew only seconds had passed since she left solid ground, but it seemed like she'd been suspended in air for ages.

She picked up speed, grazing her shoulder against a rock as she went down. The burning sensation on her shoulder distracted her momentarily until she hit the cold water. She coughed and thrashed around kicking as she forced herself to stay afloat. Caroline fought against the waves that forced her further from the rocks. She kept thinking, *I'm a good swimmer, I need to focus. Why is this so difficult?* She bobbed above the waves long enough to take a breath before being pulled under. Her lungs took in water as the ocean took control.

Caroline tried to catch her breath as she continued to cough. She was losing consciousness. Her mind was playing tricks on her as she fought against the waves. She heard a splash in the distance and someone calling out. "Julia, Julia. Don't leave me. Julia. Where are you?"

Confusion was all she knew now. She struggled to look around her and was stunned to realize she saw a ship being tossed in the waves. Further confused to notice the ship was a wooden ship, the sails were torn from the halyard and there was debris floating in the water. Again, she heard the words "Julia, Julia" as she went down for the last time. Her body weighted down and exhausted, gave way to the sea and she dropped deeper into the abyss. Her limbs became numb, and she was surrounded in darkness. This was a familiar end, one she experienced before but she couldn't think how it could be. Her heart was barely beating now. She gave herself up to the sea, no longer needing to fight. It was over…

"Caroline… Caroline". She came to as Andrew put his arm around her waist. He grabbed her and pulled her to the surface then dragged her, coughing to the beach where he dropped down next to her on solid ground.

He hovered over her a familiar feeling of remorse enveloping him as foreign words intruded on his thoughts. Julia, Julia. Don't die. This can't be happening again. I only recently found you again. Please, don't leave me.

"Andrew?" Caroline's voice invaded thoughts that confused and concerned him. "Andrew, what happened?" She was coughing as she struggled to pull herself to a sitting position. She took a deep breath as she focused on Andrew's face.

"Caroline. Thank God. What happened out there? You really scared me." I tried to catch you when you lost your balance, but it happened so fast, and the waves, well, your hands were wet, and you slipped from my grasp."

"I don't know what happened. I mean, I remember falling, but the drop isn't that far, and the water wasn't that deep. I should have been able to stand up and walk to shore"

Andrew nodded. "Yes, I know. I could see that. But as I watched you it was as though you panicked or forgot where you were." He reached up and brushed the sand from her shoulder to find the abrasion left by her earlier fall. "One would have thought you were drowning the way you were flailing about." He looked toward the ocean trying to see what Caroline might have seen in her despair. "And Caroline you were screaming and calling out to Daniel." He hesitated before deciding to ask the question, which in his heart he believed he knew the answer to. "Who is Daniel?"

A chill went down Caroline's spine as she realized her panic had been more lifelike than she thought. "I don't know, Andrew." She proceeded cautiously not wanting Andrew to think she was crazy. "What was a short fall somehow turned into a panic attack. I don't know why. I'm not afraid of the water."

Andrew moved closer to Caroline and took her hand. "Well, you scared me half to death. I think you might have drowned if I hadn't jumped in and pulled you out." He lowered his voice as he took her hand in his. "I don't think I could bear that, Caroline." He stopped long enough to give Caroline an opportunity to object. "I feel like I've finally found someone who really sees me, and one who I feel a connection with."

He looked passed Caroline and watched the seagull pulling at the seaweed that lay on the wet sand. "I know you don't want a relationship, Caroline. And I get it. I'll wait. I'll wait because I feel that we are meant to be together. We know each other. I can feel it.

Caroline's thoughts returned to her earlier fight in the water. The memory flashed through her mind once again as the words "Daniel" crossed her lips with such force, she knew who ever he was he must have been someone important to her. Why she couldn't remember who, was beyond her. She knew one thing. The scene that she experienced earlier was familiar to her. For now, she would let it go.

Woods

"What if you wait and I never feel what you feel?"

Andrew looked into Caroline's eyes, hoping the answer would jump out at him. "Caroline, I know that won't happen. Somewhere deep inside, you feel it too. I'm not sure what it is, but something is happening here, between us. I can feel it. I think you can too. Only you're not ready to admit it."

Caroline stared back at Andrew fighting to remain neutral. There was something in his eyes that held her, captivated her. He lifted his hand to her face and ran it across her chin, then along her jaw until he reached her ear where he found the familiar strand of hair falling across her cheek. He brushed it back until it was securely behind her ear. Her pulse beat wildly in her throat and her skin burned beneath the hand that caressed her skin. She closed her eyes, to imagine what it would be like to surrender to his touch.

Somehow it was a familiar touch. Her thoughts returned to her struggle in the water. The hand that reached out to her as she went down into the black abyss of unknowing, was more than familiar. She, now, felt the same energy pulsing through her that she felt a lifetime ago, in Andrew's touch. Caroline began to panic. Andrew's hands, that were meant to comfort her, left her feeling confused. Caroline took a deep breath as she opened her eyes and gazed into the dark pools that she was learning to trust.

She drew back from Andrew's touch as her head began to spin while she heard her own voice calling out the name "Daniel, Daniel." She reached up and put her hand on Andrew's, guiding his hand away from her face and bringing it to rest on the cold wet sand.

"Maybe you're right Andrew. Maybe I'm not ready to admit it. Maybe there's nothing to admit." She looked down at his hand resting next to hers. "I don't know what's going on here. Whatever it is, is unsettling to me. At least right now".

Caroline stared out at the waves as they rolled to the shore. When they broke on the sand, she returned her attention to Andrew. "I don't know what happened, or why I panicked. But I'm not ready to talk about it. Can we just let this go, forget about it for now, until I sort out all this, figure out what it means?" She tried to laugh of the feeling of discomfort. "Maybe I'm crazy".

Andrew shook his head and smiled. "No, you're not crazy, Caroline. I have a feeling I know what's going on. But you're right. Let's forget about it for now. It's always better to let things flow naturally. Forcing anything is never a good thing." He looked up and the sky which reminded them the day had faded and the early evening hours were their reality.

"It's getting late, and the air has cooled a bit. At least it feels cool in these wet clothes." He looked toward the shore at the lights on the boardwalk. Let's see if we can find some dry clothes." He then looked down the beach. "Then we should see if there might be a room available so we can shower and get out of these wet things".

Caroline started to object but Andrew anticipated her thoughts. "No, Caroline. We're only going to shower, rinse clean of the sticky salt-water residue, and get into some dry things, then we're going to find a place to eat. I'm starving. I've worked up an appetite playing the hero". He joked.

She hesitated for a moment then nodded her consent. Andrew stood up and offered his hand to Caroline. "How are you feeling? You didn't hit your head did you"?

Caroline reached for the hand offered as she replied. "No, I caught my shoulder on the rocks as I went over, but I didn't hit my head. At least I don't think I did. There's no pain to indicate I did. I feel fine, outside of being embarrassed".

"Good". Andrew slipped his hand around Caroline's waist. "This is to keep you steady. Don't get any bright ideas". He winked as he picked up his shoes and they began to walk toward the road.

"I think I'm fine, Andrew. I don't think that's necessary". Caroline fumbled for her sandals as he adjusted his arm. They continued walking, up the cold wet sand that became warmer, until they were walking through the soft deep sand.

"I know you're fine. Humor me please." Caroline stumbled in the deep sand but caught her balance before Andrew was finished speaking. "See. Just walk with me".

Caroline gave in and brought her hand around Andrew's waist. They walked the remainder of the way arm in arm in silence. At the road they slipped on their shoes and crossed the street. They looked at storefronts as they walked north on Route 3, until they came upon a clothing store.

Andrew slowed and looked at Caroline. "Do you think we'll both find something here"?

Caroline nodded, then panicked as a thought came to mind.

"What? Caroline, what's wrong?"

"Andrew, I left my bag in the car. My wallet…"

"Don't worry about it, Caroline".

"Andrew, I won't have you buying clothes for me". A short answer.

Andrew laughed at Caroline as he led her to the door. "Caroline, stop it. You can pay me back later. You must get out of those wet sticky clothes".

The sales associate looked up as they walked through the door. She was a young woman, maybe in her mid-twenties. She was a pretty girl. Caroline noticed a spark in her bright blue eyes as she recognized Andrew. He looked down at Caroline and shyly smiled. "I'm sorry. This happens a lot".

Caroline looked up at him and grinned. "I bet".

The cashier excitedly approached them. "I'm sorry, I don't mean to pry, but are you Andrew Roberts?"

He nodded.

"I thought so. I won't bother you. I just wanted to tell you how much I love your work. You're amazing." She stepped back and looked at Caroline, who stood at Andrew's side smiling.

The woman nodded at Caroline. "I'm sorry I didn't mean to intrude. I'll let you get back to shopping".

Caroline smiled at the young woman who went back to her work. She then looked back to Andrew who by now was looking through a rack of cargo shorts. She watched him for a moment until he looked up at her and smiled. He lifted two hangers to display his find. "I think I'm all set. How about you"? He looked at Caroline's empty hands. "Come on Caroline find something so we can get going".

She turned from Andrew and walked to a round rack that displayed women's capri's and shorts. She flipped through the rack, becoming agitated when she realized they didn't have any in her size.

"Excuse me, miss". The starstruck young woman came up behind Caroline. May I help you find something?"

Caroline smiled to hide her frustration. "I'm not finding my size. You don't have any out back, do you?"

The young lady shook her head. "I'm sorry, but no". Andrew watched the exchange from the other side of the store.

She leaned in close to Caroline as she looked up at Andrew and smiled. "Maybe we can find you something more suitable. I'm not sure capris are what you need tonight".

Caroline noticed the exchange between the sales associate and Andrew. Andrew looked away immediately. The pretty girl looked back at Caroline and when she realized that her glance was mistaken, she quickly explained shaking her head. "No. No, that look wasn't what you think. I wasn't looking at him that way. I was...I was..."

Caroline laughed out loud. "It's ok. We're not together that way. I get it. He's a movie star. Who wouldn't look at him that way"?

Andrew listened from where he stood. He did his best to keep from laughing and was surprised at Caroline's comment.

The young woman smiled and leaned closer to Caroline. "Don't get me wrong, He's handsome, and I love his movies, but he's kind of old".

Caroline fought to keep from laughing as she watched the girl recover.

She stuttered. "I mean, he's not old, he's just too old for me to consider, even in a dream". She then led Caroline to a rack of sun dresses.

"Plus, He's already in love". She flipped through the dresses and pulled out a simply cut t-length sun dress. "This is perfect for you. It's not overstated. Not dressy, yet classy. If I had to guess, that's how I would describe you." She smiled as she handed the dress to Caroline. "And it's your size, too".

Caroline took the dress from the girl and studied it. She did like the dress. The girl was right, it was simple. Caroline then looked at the tag and was surprised to see it was her size. She looked at the sales associate and smiled. "I do like it".

"Good. I can see you both had a mishap in the water so I imagine you will need more than the dress. She discreetly led her, to the back of the store, where Caroline found what she needed.

Caroline placed her hand on the young woman's arm before they returned to the register. "I think you may have the wrong idea about Andrew and me. We're friends. That's all".

The girl smiled and placed her hand over Caroline's and gave it a pat. "You don't have to worry about me. I'm very discreet. Andrew Roberts isn't the only celebrity to patronize this store. I respect the privacy of everyone who come in".

Caroline tried to explain.

"Whatever you think, he is in love. Anyone who looks at him will see it". She dismissed Caroline's statement and led her to the front, where they met Andrew.

The sales associate rang up the purchases and wished them a fine evening as they walked out the door. Caroline looked back one last time, as the young woman smiled and nodded, believing what she said earlier to be the truth.

ELEVEN

Caroline turned her attention to Andrew while she dismissed the sales associate and her observation. She knew Andrew was developing feelings for her, he said so himself. However, he in no way made a proclamation of love. How could he, he barely knew her.

"What were you two talking about?" Andrew intruded on Caroline's silence.

"Nothing. Nothing significant". Caroline paused to come up with an answer. "She's young. I think she was star struck."

"That's odd. She said celebrities frequent the shop. You'd think she'd be used to it."

Caroline had all she could do to keep from laughing. She cleared her throat and tried to change the subject. "I have to say, she's good at her job. She had no trouble guessing my size".

"Caroline, you're avoiding the question. What's so funny? I can tell you're trying not to laugh". He stopped walking and turned to her. "Tell me, tell me so I can enjoy the joke".

"I can't. They're only words from the mouth of a child. Really". Caroline looked at Andrew who stood staunchly on the sidewalk, refusing to budge.

She started to walk, but Andrew reached out and grabbed her arm, pulling her back to face him. "Okay. If you insist". She started to giggle. "She said you were old. I'm sorry. I tried to spare you, but you forced me".

Caroline watched as the smile on Andrew's face disappeared. "She said what"?

Caroline nodded. "I know. Old. She said, old". Caroline continued the charade, making fun for a moment longer. "I think she meant you were too old for her". Caroline started to walk again. Andrew moved to match her stride.

"Okay, why would she say that? What would prompt that conversation"? Andrew was curious, now.

Caroline did her best to change the subject. "You said we were going to get a room". She looked ahead at the two hotels she saw as they got closer to them. "Do you know which one, I mean have you stayed on the coast before"?

"We're not finished with this conversation". They walked in silence until they stopped at the entrance of the "Sands" hotel. Andrew lifted his hand signaling Caroline to enter first.

They approached the counter and Andrew asked if they had an available room. The attendant nodded and they prepared the paperwork while Caroline moved to the large glass windows that faced the ocean. She watched the ocean dance as waves bowed in, making a dramatic foaming entrance, then retreating. She followed the rhythm as the water ebbed and flowed, never skipping a beat.

Andrew walked up behind her and placed his hand on her shoulder. "Okay. We're all set. Let's get out of these clothes and into something more comfortable".

Caroline turned to him her eyes wide with shock. "Andrew, lower your voice. People can hear you".

125

A broad grin passed across his face as he watched Caroline fidget. "What's wrong Caroline? Can't handle it can you"?

"You'd be surprised at what I can handle". Caroline said as she walked toward the elevator chuckling.

"Oh, really? I hope that's not a challenge, because you'll lose".

Caroline laughed as she stepped into the elevator. "I haven't known you that long, but I've known you long enough to know that I'm smart enough not to take the bait".

Andrew reached over and pushed the button and the elevator door closed. "I think you're a chicken." He continued to bait.

By now Caroline was laughing and couldn't respond. She leaned against the wall of the elevator and watched the numbers three, four, five, six... The elevator stopped on the seventh floor and the doors opened to a corridor dimly lit. They stepped out of the elevator and Caroline followed Andrew until he stopped in front of their door, room 715.

Andrew fumbled with the card as he shifted the bag from one hand to the other. The door opened and he stepped aside so Caroline could enter first. "Ladies before gentlemen".

He placed the bag on one of the queen-sized beds and kicked of his shoes. "Why don't you shower first. You really should clean that shoulder, before it gets infected".

Caroline started to argue as she removed her sandals, but when she looked at the sand embedded in the wound, she thought better. She nodded and took the bag into the bathroom.

Andrew retreated to the balcony while he waited. He stood looking out at the sea, wondering what Caroline saw earlier, when she fell. It didn't make sense to him that she would slip into shock when, really the fall was minor. He took a deep breath taking in the smell of fried fish, sea air, and the smell of seaweed. He stood a while longer before retreating to the room, hoping to find water in the small refrigerator.

Caroline came out of the bathroom as he stood and closed the door to the fridge. "That was quick. Wow, you look nice. What's the occasion"?

Woods

Caroline rubbed the towel against her wet hair, to keep it from dripping. She dropped the bag, which held sea water wet clothes, on the floor by the door. "There is no occasion. I was at the mercy of a young woman who for some reason thought I needed a dress". She quickly changed the subject. I'm glad to have the chance to wash away the sea salt. I love the sea, but it dries out my skin. I'm glad you suggested the shower".

"Yes, well it would have been a long drive home in those wet clothes". Caroline stepped back so Andrew could pass. "My turn". He smiled as he went into the bathroom and closed the door.

Caroline took the towel to her head for a moment longer, than looked in the mirror. Her hair was now towel dried, but also uncombed. She didn't have her bag so was unable to properly groom her hair. She ran her fingers through her hair repeatedly until it was free of knots and would lay somewhat flat. Caroline shook her head in dissatisfaction and went to the balcony.

She stood at the rail, leaning forward enough to look to the ground. She briefly watched as people moved in one direction or another, then turned her attention to the sea. She listened to the familiar sound as waves crashed along the shore. Caroline closed her eyes and relaxed as the breeze blew through her hair as she thought, *it will be dry in no time.* The evening air was heavy with humidity, but the wind blew to break up the dampness.

Caroline looked out at the water scanning the beach until her eyes rested on the breaker, where earlier, she fell. She studied the rock from where she stood trying to make sense of the struggle she experienced. She couldn't understand how she could become so disorientated in such a short amount of time. The hair on the back of her neck stood up as the gentle breeze brushed against it. A chill went down her spine as her mind retreated to the scene of earlier in the day.

She focused on the waves, the pulse of the sea, back and forth, up, and down. Something that usually comforted her now caused her distress. She closed her eyes, as she heard the voice, "Julia, Julia." She tried to force a memory. Did she recognize the voice of the man whom she responded to as "Daniel"? *Who are you, Daniel?* She thought.

127

Caroline jumped when Andrew spoke softly from behind her. "Caroline, where are you. Did you leave me again"?

"Andrew. You startled me". She turned to face him. She recognized the scent of soap and shampoo as that provided by the hotel. He was clean and dry in his new cargo shorts and t-shirt. His hair was towel dried and uncombed".

He put his hand to his head and smoothed the free flying hair. "I forgot about a comb".

Caroline nodded. "I know. We're in the same boat". She pointed to her disheveled hair. I guess it's a good thing we're not going anywhere important".

"I know. We must have dinner though. We could order room service. The room is paid for until tomorrow. I know we're not staying, but we could have dinner here before heading back."

Caroline turned to the water one more time before answering. "Sure, why not".

Andrew went to the drawer of the nightstand in search of a menu. "Success". He held up the thin vinyl bound menu. He sat on the bed and Caroline entered from the balcony and sat next to him, looking over his shoulder at the pages.

Caroline expressed concern about ordering fish from a large establishment because she didn't trust it to be fresh. In his desire to please her, Andrew agreed, and they quickly decided on grilled chicken salad and white wine. Andrew called room service, and they returned to the balcony to wait. Caroline leaned on the rail and Andrew in his effort to be close, stood at her elbow while they waited.

Andrew scanned the boulevard below, while Caroline looked up the beach, at the lights that slowly appeared as darkness fell over the coast. They silently stood, each immersed in their own thoughts, neither one intruding on the others quite time, until the silence was interrupted by the car horn from the street below.

Caroline, startled out of her dream state, looked at Andrew who was focused on her. "What were you thinking about, Caroline? You seem so far away".

"I don't know". She shrugged her shoulders. "I guess I was thinking about what happened earlier. I don't understand".

Woods

"Do you want to talk about it"? Andrew asked cautiously.

"I don't know that either. I don't know what to say. I'm a good swimmer. I don't panic. I've been injured before and never reacted that way. I'm confused. It's like some time during the fall I slipped from my life to the life of that of a stranger. I don't think there is anything to talk about".

Andrew placed a hand on Caroline's arm which rested on the rail. "Well, if you change your mind, I'm here to listen. You might be surprised at my ability to make sense of strange situations".

They're conversation was interrupted by a knock on the door. "That will be dinner". Andrew said. He went to the door and a young man wheeled in a cart that carried their evening meal. The man removed a tablecloth from the bottom of the cart and placed it on the table by the window that was next to the door that exited to the balcony. Next, he placed the plates across from each other and removed the cover from the salads.

Caroline watched from the balcony as he returned to the cart to retrieve the bottle of wine, which he opened and poured in each glass before leaving the room. Andrew discreetly handed him a twenty as he closed the door.

Caroline stepped over the threshold from the balcony and walked to the table. She sat down across from Andrew and looked at her salad. Andrew picked up his fork. "What do you say Caroline, is it edible?" He teased.

Caroline smiled as she looked down at her salad. "I think it will be fine".

Andrew lifted his glass. "Here's to you Caroline, the most beautiful woman in the room".

Caroline laughed. "Well, that's difficult. I'm the only woman in the room. I could look like Attila the Hun and I'd still be the winner".

"Except the Hun was a man". Andrew scolded.

"I said I could look like Attila the Hun, not be Attila the Hun". She shook her fork at Andrew and smiled as she corrected him.

He laughed as he held up both hands. "You win Caroline". He then leaned forward. "You need to learn how to take a compliment".

"I guess I never was good at that". She sighed.

"Well, you better practice. After tomorrow, you will be receiving many compliments".

Caroline had forgotten about Peter viewing her paintings. Her stomach turned as she thought of the possibility, that she might not be good enough.

Andrew interrupted her doubtful thoughts. "Thant's enough of that Caroline. Your paintings are beautiful. They each tell a story. And each painting tells a different story to each person looking at them, you wait. You are one of those overnight sensations; a diamond in the rough, a hidden jewel". He paused briefly. "Should I go on"?

Caroline giggled as she shook her head. "No. I get the point. We'll wait to see what Peter says before jumping the gun".

"Yea, okay. We'll see". Andrew looked across the table at Caroline. "But just to keep the record straight, I'm right. You'll see. Cheers". He lifted his glass to meet Caroline's.

"Cheers". Caroline sipped the wine then set the glass on the table in front of her. Andrew followed her lead. "So, Caroline. Now that we are sitting quietly, how about you tell me what was going on at the shop today. I'm old, is that so"?

There was as twinkle in Caroline's eyes as she recalled the conversation, she shared with the shop clerk. She lifted her glass and stalled by sipping her wine. "There wasn't a conversation, not really".

Andrew looked across the table challenging Caroline. "I think there was. And whatever it was you thought it was funny enough to tell me she said I was old. There must be more to it than that. Why on earth would she tell you she thought I was old"?

The moment had come for Caroline to tell Andrew what the young woman said. She wasn't sure she wanted to because it would open up a conversation that Caroline didn't want to have. Not tonight anyway. She gazed across the table into eyes so dark she knew she would get lost if she stared too long. She looked out at the sea as she collected her thoughts.

"Come on Caroline. No secrets". Andrew teased.

"Okay, okay. But remember I'm only repeating what she said. Not what is true. So be still while I talk"'

Andrew laughed while pulling his chair closer to the table so he could study Caroline while she spoke.

Caroline laughed lightly. "Stop that, Andrew. I won't be able to talk with a straight face". She set down her glass and began. "I was looking for capris, you know short pants, and the sales-clerk came to me and asked if she could help me. I thought I caught her looking at you. When I studied her face to see what she was thinking, she looked at me thinking I thought she was staring at you".

She stopped to clarify. "I don't know why she would think that I wouldn't think anyone would be drooling over you or getting excited or whatever it is that young people do". Waving her hands, she returned to her original thought. "Anyway, she misread me and thought I was jealous or territorial or something"

Andrew interrupted. "You were jealous Caroline. Really"?

"Andrew, I'm talking". She scolded.

He nodded and prompted her to continue.

"She looked over at you. A look that I thought was flirtatious. I caught her and she apologized and tried to defend herself by saying she thought you were handsome, but you were old, too old for her to be interested in, 'that way'"".

"She went on to say that even if she did think you were hot, that it would be hopeless because you were in love". Caroline looked straight at Andrew as the words passed over her lips.

Andrew reached for his glass and drank the remaining wine, then returned the glass to the table. "And what do you think Caroline"? He looked into Caroline's eyes challenging her.

"I explained to the young lady that she misread the situation. That we were only friends".

A look of disappointment crossed Andrew's face. "What did she say to that Caroline"?

Caroline softly replied. "She said that while I might believe what I said, she knew better. You were a man in love".

The room grew silent. Andrew stared at Caroline, trying to read her. When she didn't speak, he stood up and turned to look out at the sea.

Remember The Kiss

Caroline was uncomfortable but couldn't find words to break the silence. She wasn't ready for a relationship, but she was afraid Andrew would confirm what she told the pretty young salesclerk. She wasn't ready for rejection. Even though an official offer had not been made or requested.

Andrew returned to the table and sat down. He rested his elbows on the table and leaned forward to look Caroline in the eyes. "How can such a young woman make such an accurate observation. She sees what you are unable or unwilling to see. I never thought I was so transparent. But I guess I do wear my heart on my sleeve". He paused while he searched Caroline's face for a sign. "I guess I'm transparent to everyone, except you. You won't see it. I'm right in front of you and you don't see me".

Caroline twisted the napkin that had rested on her lap, between her fingers. She was becoming increasingly uncomfortable as she tried to find the right words, to respond to Andrew's pleading heart. "Andrew, please. It's not that I don't see, or even that I don't want to see, it's that I'm not ready to see anything beyond the wall that protects me from being hurt. We only met three days ago. You're asking me to risk my heart and soul on a bet, a dare, a whim. I don't know if I can do that".

Caroline knew the moment the words were spoken that she could lose Andrew forever, even though he wasn't hers to lose. He said he wanted to be with her, but how could she know he wouldn't hurt her? In the end she wasn't sure of anything.

"I know you're scared, Caroline. But there are no sure things in life, no guarantees. We win some we lose some, but in the end, we must choose. We must decide if we're going to sit on the sideline or get in the game. You will have to make a choice, Caroline. I'm afraid that either way, you'll be hurt. You'll be hurt because you are choosing with your head, not your heart". Andrew pushed back the chair from the table and stood up. He stood over her as he finished speaking.

"I'm not giving up on you, Caroline. Not now, probably not ever. I may not be here to remind you, but in your heart you'll know. You've been searching for me, like I've been searching for you, two souls wandering this lifetime, looking for that connection, the connection that for many lifetimes came and went, and is presenting itself again. You don't see it, but I do. I'm going to wait, Caroline. Eventually the light will come on. You'll realize what I mean. Until that day, I'll be that friend you think you need or want. Until you remember.

Caroline silently sat waiting for Andrew to finish speaking. She tried to focus on anything but his words, but his words hit her like a ton of bricks. She knew he was right but still she didn't budge. She wasn't ready to forget the lifetime of pain she experienced. She couldn't let go of the feeling that she would only be able to find peace in her loneliness.

Andrew finished talking and walked to the door where he looked out into the evening sky. It wasn't dark, but daylight no longer hung above them. He looked at a sky that hung between day and night, darkness, and light. His heart felt heavy, yet he knew if his heart continued to beat, there was hope.

He turned to Caroline. "Look, it's getting late. At least it is for us. We've been awake too long. We talked through the night last night and we had a long day today. Between the excitement of the party, the incident on the breaker, and now, this deep conversation, I think we're both spent. Let's forget about this for now and check out. I'll take you home so you can get some sleep. We'll both see things clearer in the morning. Plus, we have an appointment in the morning".

Caroline agreed that the day had been long, and she was ready to go home. What started out to be a day filled with excitement, ended on a somewhat disappointing note. She wanted to go home before it got any worse. They collected the few things that they arrived with and left the room. Andrew turned off the light then closed the door.

Andrew left the key at the front desk and they stepped into the evening air and walked back to the car. They walked in silence until they turned down Beach Street. Andrew was first to speak. "Caroline".

"Yes Andrew".

"It's a beautiful evening, don't you think"?

Caroline smiled at Andrew's attempt to make her feel better. "Yes, Andrew. It is. Now the air has cooled a bit, it doesn't feel so humid" Once they turned the corner and left behind the sounds of nightlife on the boulevard, they lowered their voices.

Andrew drew the keys from the side pocket of his new cargo shorts as he shifted the bag in his hands once again. He followed Caroline to the passenger door. He looked down at her and smiled as he unlocked the door for her. He closed the door once she was settled. Then went around the front of the truck and slid in behind the steering wheel.

Caroline clipped the seatbelt in place, flinching as the strap grazed the wound on her shoulder. Concerned that she was in pain, Andrew spoke. "Are you okay? I saw that. I'm sure it didn't feel good".

"No. It didn't". She admitted. "I keep forgetting it's there. That is until I bump into something".

"Maybe we should stop somewhere and get a bandage to protect it. For the first time he looked seriously at the abrasion on Caroline's shoulder. It wasn't worthy of the emergency room, but it probably required more attention than it originally got.

"Caroline, that's pretty deep. It's still oozing a bit. Maybe I should have paid closer attention when it happened. You didn't seem too concerned, so I figured you were fine. But now that I have a chance to look closer, I think you should have it looked at".

She dismissed his attention. "No, its fine. Sure, its sore, but it will be okay in a couple days. I don't want to cover it. Let the air get at it. It will heal sooner".

Andrew wasn't convinced by Caroline's words, but at this point he knew better than to push her. He nodded, started the vehicle, and backed out of the parking space.

The ride home was quiet. Andrew focused on the road, looking over occasionally at Caroline who spoke little, and eventually dozed off. He was content to drive in quiet. It gave him a chance to sort through his feelings and consider all that had happened the last three days. He wasn't sorry he approached her on the boardwalk that first day. He still believed fate would take over and once again reunite them.

Woods

Caroline sat still, her head resting peacefully against the cool window. Occasionally her mind drifted, mulling over past events, working to sort through experiences. Some of which had been helpful, some that brought her pain, and still other she had yet to determine where they fit. The past weekend fit into the latter.

She closed her eyes and let her mind wander as the gentle hum of the engine lulled her into a deep sleep. She rested peacefully at first, recalling the pleasant conversation of recent days. She felt safe and found comfort in Andrew's company. She continued to process the events of his arrival into her life, wondering if it was fate or mere coincidence. His touch was soothing, and his words offered to her a perspective she would never have considered before meeting him.

In her dream, Caroline saw his face smiling down at her. His dark eyes penetrating her soul. She smiled at him in her dream state, until the vision changed.

Once again, she was fighting the waves that were intent on bringing her down. This time though, she wasn't fighting the water of the coast of New England. The sea turned on her as she struggled to keep her head above the surface. It was dark and a storm raged around her, intent on forcing her hand and taking from her, the life she loved. She fought with every ounce of her being to live. She had a reason to fight. She remembered this as she heard him calling her name. "Julia, Julia, where are you". Then silence. Caroline was confused, yet she knew it was her to whom the man called out.

Panic rose in her as she felt her heart being ripped from her chest. Caroline screamed out. "Daniel, I'm here". The waves tossed her around, as she tried to focus. Thunder crashed in her ears and the sky lit up as the storm grew in strength. She was surrounded by debris which she grabbed for, yet she found nothing large enough to hold her to the surface. A barrel passed over her head and disappeared beneath water that was intent on taking her down.

She could hear screaming in the distance. The far-away ship creaked and moaned as the brackets and nails gave way to the force of the storm. Caroline heard a crashing sound as the sail topple over into the water. She watched the boat as the stern came up out of the water then slowly was swallowed up by the sea. She screamed out

"Daniel" one last time before she felt the shearing pain of a plank that struck her across the back of the head. Her voice left her, her limbs went limp, and darkness engulfed her. Her body, heavy now, and lifeless, gave itself up to the abyss that pulled at her. Then darkness.

Caroline woke from what became a nightmare so real that she thought her heart stopped. She thrashed in the seat, screaming out until she heard a man's voice.

"Caroline, Caroline". She felt a hand on her shoulder. Then against her forehead. "Wake up, Caroline". He released the belt that held her prisoner.

She opened her tear-filled eyes and took a deep breath as she focused on Andrew next to her. He had pulled over to save her from her panic and bring her back to the current reality. He sat next to her while she struggled with the abyss that tore her from the one soul that could make her happy. That was another lifetime.

Now he sat next to her, throwing her a lifeline, willing her to return to him, yet again. He reached up and wiped away the tears that stained her sun-drenched cheeks. He pushed back the hair from her forehead then drew her to him. She leaned her head against his shoulder as the tears subsided. He ran his hand through her hair, attempting to soothe her.

Caroline sat for a moment in the safety of Andrew's arms while she recovered from her emotional state. His embrace was comforting and offered to her a peace that she didn't realize was missing in her life. She struggled with her desire to stay where she was and the need to be strong, not dependent on a man. Even Andrew, who somehow, she knew wasn't just any man.

The lights of an oncoming car disrupted the serenity of the moment, bringing Caroline to a decision. She sighed as she gently pulled back from Andrew. He watched her, waiting for a reaction. He wasn't sorry for his reaction. His only desire was to comfort Caroline and help her through a time of change that he hoped would open her eyes to the truth.

She sat an arms-length away, staring into Andrew's eyes. She somehow was lost in the deep pools that drew her to him for some mysterious reason. He sat still, not wanting to frighten her.

Woods

She looked back at him, a deer in headlights. She had many questions that she knew wouldn't be answered as she sat across from this man who appeared in her life only days ago. She cleared her throat as her mind settled.

The nightmare was over. She was on dry land wondering why suddenly, the image of the ocean struggle haunted her. What did it signify? For the first time in her life, she felt free, why would that scene keep repeating itself. She smiled at Andrew, deciding to put it behind her. Hopefully, the nightmare had ended. "I'm sorry about that Andrew. I must have been tired. I had a terrible nightmare. It was so lifelike, it was disturbing. I'm fine now".

Andrew studied Caroline a moment longer, wondering what was really going through her mind. Like Caroline, he decided to put the incident behind him. He nodded and smiled, then turned to face the road. He signaled and pulled out on to the road and picked up speed as he changed the subject. "Are you getting excited about tomorrow"?

Caroline shrugged her shoulders noncommittally. "I don't know. I guess I don't want to get my hopes up, only to be disappointed".

"Well, I'm fairly confident you won't be disappointed. When I look at your work, I feel like I'm being pulled into the painting. It's like I become part of the story you are telling". He shook his head and smiled as he focused on the road. "It's an unusual feeling. You don't find that with many artists".

"I don't know what prompts me to paint the way I do. I don't ever feel like a painting is complete. I stand back and look at it and think I should change something, a color the shading, the whole story. Maybe that's why I don't think I'm good enough". They passed the bridge. They would be home soon.

TWELVE

Andrew signaled and turned. He stopped in front of the garage and looked across the truck at Caroline who again had fallen asleep. This time she slept peacefully without interruption. No storms, no rough seas.

He turned off the engine and sat in the quiet listening to the tick, tick of the engine as it cooled. He didn't want to wake Caroline, but knew she'd sleep better in her bed. He slowly opened his door and stepped out of the truck. He guided the door closed, being sure not to slam it, then walked around the truck and quietly opened the passenger's door.

Caroline woke up as Andrew opened her door. She smiled and stretched as she opened her eyes. "I can't believe I feel asleep again". Puzzled at Andrew's attempt to keep quiet she spoke.

"What? You didn't think you were going to carry me in the house did you"? She started to laugh.

Andrew shrugged his shoulders. "I don't know. You looked so peaceful. I hated to wake you".

"Well, I don't think you would be able to carry me for one. Secondly, you need the key to get in the house. I think your plan was doomed from the start". She joked.

"Well, I tried". He reached in and picked up the bag of wet clothes at her feet as he looked at the fast-moving clouds. "Let's get inside. It looks like rain".

Caroline reached behind the seat and removed her backpack. She opened the bag to find her keys. Success brought her to display them to Andrew and they moved up the dark walkway to the front door. Andrew took the key from her and unlocked the door while Caroline secured the latch on the bag.

Once inside, Caroline flipped on the light switch. She took the bag of wet clothes from Andrew and went to the back side of the kitchen, where she placed them in the washing machine and turned it on.

"What are you doing, Caroline? It's late to be doing laundry, don't you think?" Andrew set the keys on the table by the door.

"If I leave them, they'll stink in the morning. It's a short cycle. It won't take long. By the time I'm ready for bed, the wash cycle will be complete."

When Caroline came around the corner, Andrew noticed the dark circles under Caroline's eyes. "Why don't you go to bed. I can switch over the load when it's done".

Caroline looked at the clock on the stove. "It's quite late. You should go home before the rain starts". The rumble of thunder rolled in and the gentle sound of rain blew against the kitchen window as Caroline's warning became reality. She jumped as a flash lit up the deck. The rain came quickly and grew stronger as the storm got closer. The flash of light was followed by a rumble whose crescendo was a crash that shook the house. Andrew watched as Caroline's demeanor changed. He sensed Caroline's returning anxiety and decided leaving at that moment might not be best idea.

"I don't know, Caroline. That storm sounds like it's getting worse. Do you mind if I stay here? I can sleep on the couch. You won't know I'm here".

Andrew saw the release of tension in Caroline's face. He knew that even if she wouldn't admit it, she was glad for the offer.

"That won't be necessary, Andrew. You can stay in the spare room". She looked out the back door as she drew the drapes across the glass. "There's no sense in going out in the storm if you don't have too".

"Thank you, Caroline. I'd hate to melt out there". He joked, to lighten the mood.

Caroline smiled at Andrew's attempt, she knew what he was doing, and appreciated the effort he made for her comfort. She moved from the door and directed Andrew to follow her. He walked through the living area taking what was now a familiar path to the hall where Caroline stopped in front of the closet door. "There are towels in here". She opened the door to show towels stacked neatly.

She closed the door and turned to face the bathroom. "The bathroom is here. I think you knew that". Another quarter turn. "And the bedroom is here". She reached through the door and found the light switch on the wall to the right of the door.

"I think that's it. You should be all set".

Andrew stepped into the room that he had viewed from the hallway the day before. It was a quiet room, on the back side of the house, with a large window looking out into the woods. A flash lit up the yard, to show the wind blowing through the trees, indicating the storm was still going strong. He stood at the door glancing around the room. There was a small dresser beyond the light switch, on which sat a spider plant and a few photographs. The bed was situated on the back wall with a nightstand at each side of the bed and a reading light strategically placed on each one. The walls were bare, excepting a single painting which hung above the bed.

The framed image caught Andrew's special attention. A chill ran down his spine as another flash of lightening came into the dimly lit room. Andrew moved closer to the bed to get a better look at the picture that sparked a memory to return from the distant past.

Woods

He looked at Caroline curiously, before returning his attention to the painting. "Did you paint that, Caroline"? He asked cautiously.

She nodded in reply as she turned to the image that so many years ago, she set paint on canvas to bring to life an imagined scene. One she wouldn't know the meaning of for years.

Andrew looked at the picture, then at Caroline. He watched as she studied the image that for the first time, she made a connection to. Thunder rolled across the sky and the rain continued to fall, and Caroline became engrossed in the painting.

Andrew watched her expression as the connection came to life. She looked at the storm filled sky hovering above waves that tossed about a sailing ship that was breaking up. The image came to life, as Caroline placed the debris that scattered across the water in her memory. As she looked at the picture, she could hear the rumble of thunder that crashed over waters that rocked the ship back and forth until it broke into pieces and disappeared below the spray that resulted from the wild winds. In her mind she heard him calling her name. "Julia, Julia. Where are you Julia"? Then begging. "Don't leave me Julia".

Andrew watched Caroline as she became more absorbed in the image. He watched until she cried out. "Daniel. Daniel. I can't see you. I'm getting tired. I can't fight anymore". He looked on until he thought if left to her memories, Caroline would disappear into the painting that told a deep seeded story.

Andrew moved to Caroline's side and placed his hand on her elbow. "Caroline". He spoke softly to remind her where her reality lay.

The shock on her face made him anxious to bring her back, but he knew the journey must be in her time, not his. Caroline looked at Andrew and for the first time acknowledged the meaning of the painting.

"I painted that. For all these years I thought I imagined the picture. I had no idea It came from a dream, a nightmare, really". She climbed on the bed and kneeled in front of the painting.

Then turning to Andrew. "What does it mean"? The confused look deepened. The rain grew lighter, and the thunder lessened until the last flash of light carried away with it a storm that had lasted a lifetime.

Andrew stood at the side of the bed looking at Caroline. He wanted to reach out to her, to tell her the truth, a truth that she hadn't really grasped. He struggled between his reality, and hers. His deep connection to her remained strong.

The connection Caroline felt, was to a dream, a nightmare concocted to torture her. To make her crazy. The reality hadn't set in yet.

How could he get through to her, without destroying her? Two hearts that were meant to be one remained divided by time and space. He returned his attention to the painting on the wall. When he looked at it, he heard her. "Daniel. Daniel. Help me". His heart broke for her, the woman in the painting and the woman who kneeled on the bed next to him. One woman, two lifetimes, meant for one man.

He walked out of the room leaving Caroline to struggle with her memories. It was near impossible for him to let her be, but he knew the struggle was internal, and his presence would only make matters worse. He stopped at the door and looked back to where Caroline sat staring, digesting, hopefully understanding the meaning of the last three days.

Time was running out. Tomorrow was his last chance to bring Caroline home. His one hope was that the gift of storytelling through the medium of oil, would set the story straight and bring her back to him.

He left the room knowing he wouldn't sleep this night. He returned to the kitchen and switched out the wash that earlier, Caroline had set to clean. He moved about the kitchen, heating water for tea, and searching for cups and tea bags. It was late for coffee, but he hoped he would find tea to soothe Caroline's nerves when she returned to him. Andrew waited patiently. Walking back to the room occasionally to make sure Caroline was okay.

Andrew turned off the whistling kettle and roamed the house, his effort to remain distracted. He stood in the living room looking at Squam Lake. When he remembered, He moved from the living room through the kitchen, to the room behind closed door, where he found them.

He stepped over the threshold into a Caroline's world. A world she earlier told Andrew, wasn't good enough. The room was dark now, and quiet. He could hear what remained of the rain dripping from the roof. The storm had moved away, and Andrew could only hear a distant rumble that he soon would hear no more. He strained to hear the silence and realized that the crickets were taking their turn at entertaining the night.

He reached up and flipped the switch, turning on the light to bring life to a room that had seen darkness for too long. He looked around quickly, deciding where to start. There were many paintings and he wanted to study all of them. Although he knew realistically, he wouldn't view them all in one night.

Andrew decided he would let his intuition guide him to see the images as he should. The first picture that drew his attention was that of a fox in its den with its cubs. It was a touching scene. The mother coddling her babes, keeping them warm. The expression on her face told him there was a deep love engrained in the animals. He smiled as he moved to the next painting.

The picture before him was one of majestic mountains. The more he looked at it the more he felt he was standing on the mountain, enveloped in the clouds that hovered and weaved their way through peaks and valleys. One minute he felt cold as he imagined reaching out to touch the snow, then a bead of sweat escaped down his forehead as he felt the sun reflecting of the bright snow. He studied the painting long enough to see sitting on a small branch, within a protected valley, a beautiful butterfly. He smiled as he thought of the small details in life that Caroline remembered in her work.

He turned from the mountain top to his right and he stopped in front of a beautiful image of wisdom, old and young alike sharing a special moment. What he saw in the piece was a dance between generations; young and old, strong, and weak, wise, and open to knowing, moving in perfect rhythm through life taking their cues from one another as they navigated the waters of life. A helping hand rested while loving eyes understood, and two hearts enjoyed a love that spanned generations. It was a perfect union of the ages. Caroline hadn't missed a beat.

Andrew couldn't believe the detail in Caroline's work. He was amazed by the depth of life infused in her paintings, and as he stood back and scanned the room, he realized she was a success waiting to happen. He smiled at the realization that she would be an overnight sensation. He longed for her to know success, but at the same time felt a twinge of insecurity, as he wondered if in her success, she would leave him behind. He was shocked by the insecure thought and was about to laugh it off when he heard a noise behind him.

He turned around to find Caroline had entered the room and was watching him. He smiled when he saw her and reached out to take her hands as he met her at the door. "Caroline. I don't know why you would doubt your talent. Your work is amazing. I've been standing here studying some of your paintings and I find myself being drawn to the stories, you tell in oils."

Caroline walked around him and looked at the art hanging across the room. She stopped and looked at a painting here and there, then turned back to Andrew. "You should be careful. What would you do if it happened, if you were sucked in and became part of the story"?

A confused look crossed Andrew's face. When he had time to digest what Caroline said, he shook his head, disagreeing," Caroline. What you're talking about can't happen. You are confusing what you imagine and paint, with what you recall or remember then paint. They are two different experiences".

"I must be going crazy". The pitch in Caroline's voice was alarming. Andrew shook his head to discount her statement. But Caroline continued, ignoring him. "How can I let a painting control my mind like that? I painted that years ago. I can't remember how long ago. But it was a long time ago. Why, now, all these years later would I fabricate a story from that picture? And such a disturbing story".

"Caroline, I can promise that you aren't going crazy. If I explained it to you now, you'd think I was crazy. The correlation between that painting and what you experienced today is not a coincidence. But it is not an indication of insanity either".

"That's easy for you to say"? Caroline interrupted.

'I know exactly how you feel, Caroline. Believe me, I've been there. I remember what it feels like to think I've lost my mind".

"I wish I believed you. But when you asked me if I painted that picture, an alarm went off in my head as I remembered what happened earlier today. When I thought back at what was going through my mind, and then looked at the picture, it's all I could think of was that I created horror through painting".

Caroline stopped and looked around the room. She quickly scanned the artwork on the walls to see if there was anything familiar about the paintings that hung on the wall. "What if my paintings are a premonition of my life"?

Andrew snickered. "Caroline, that's ridiculous. Your work is beautiful. I think you are letting your mind run away with you. I believe there is another explanation. I know there is another explanation".

"How can you possibly explain away the coincidence between that painting and my fall"?

"Caroline, Lets go back to the kitchen. I set water to boil for tea earlier. Why don't we sit down and talk about this where you can relax"?

She looked around the room, and for the first time wished she never started painting. Her eyes were welling with tears and her throat felt constricted. Her heart was heavy with sorrow for the time and patience, she wasted. She turned back to Andrew. "I wasted so much time, in my life. I started painting to fill the hours of time I had when I wasn't socializing".

She lifted her arms gesturing to the walls. "This was my consolation for being kept home, never being introduced to people". She laughed sarcastically. "This. And now, I'm crazy. A recluse who turned art into a curse".

Andrew waited for Caroline to finish, before coming to her defense. "It's not true, Caroline. Your work is brilliant". He approached her and took her hand and gently led her to the door.

"Right now, you need to distance yourself from the doubt you feel because of a recent experience".

He reached up and turned off the light as they left the room. "Why don't you sit on the couch, I'll make some tea". He stopped to explain. "While you were sorting through your feelings related to that painting earlier, I familiarized myself with the kitchen. I love that you grow your herbs and make your own teas".

Andrew turned on the kettle, noting the time on the stove, ten-thirty, then situated the tea-balls in each cup as he waited for the water to boil.

Caroline walked into the living room and stopped in front of the fireplace. She looked above the mantle at Squam Lake, one of her favorite paintings. It was a peaceful scene. Now Caroline looked at it with trepidation. Was there an underlying message in the image that for so long only brought comfort?

"You know, it's a beautiful painting. It's the same piece as when you painted it". Andrew stopped beside Caroline and handed her a steaming cup of tea.

"I don't know if I'll ever look at another of my paintings in the same way, again". She paused as a thought came to mind. "Do you think that there is a dream associated with every painting"?

Andrew shook his head as he placed a hand on Caroline's elbow and directed her to sit on the couch where he sat down, next to her. "Caroline. No. I don't. I think we are all called to process things that we experience, not as they happen, but when we're able. I believe that's what's happening here".

"What do you mean"? Caroline lifted the cup to her lips and blew on the hot liquid, before taking a sip.

"I don't know what to tell you, Caroline. I can explain what happened to me, but I'm not sure you're ready to believe what I say".

Caroline set the cup on the table in front of her. "I think you better try. I don't like this feeling of helplessness. I don't want to walk around thinking I'm crazy, any longer than I must".

Nodding, Andrew continued cautiously. "Okay, but you have to be open minded and be willing to accept the possibility that life is not what you think it is".

Woods

"What do you mean"?

Andrew proceeded with caution. "Well, when I saw you
standing on the boardwalk three days ago, I was drawn to you. At
first, I thought it was curiosity that made me approach you. You
know, the smile. I wondered at that time if you might be, well,
special. You know".

Caroline shook her head. "Special"?

"Yea maybe challenged...you know".

Caroline smiled and nodded. "Oh, okay, I get it".

Andrew continued. "Well, when I stood next to you and
looked into your eyes, I knew why I was prompted to approach
you". He stopped talking and looked into Caroline's eyes. He studied
them, looked deep, as if searching for something or a confirmation
of what he already knew.

"What do you mean"?

"Have you heard the phrase, 'the eyes are the window to the
soul'"? Caroline nodded and he went on. "Well, when I looked in
your eyes, I had a feeling of knowing. I felt a connection to you, one I
couldn't put my finger on. That first day we spent on the sailboat,
brought me to realize there was something familiar about you. Not
the way you looked or talked, but, well, it might sound foolish to
you, but your energy.

I thought I was imagining it, but when we spent the
following day on the trail, I knew it was true. We knew each other".

Caroline interrupted. "That's ridiculous. I'd remember
meeting you". She snickered.

"No". Andrew shook his head impatiently. "We know each
other on another level." He searched her eyes looking for a sign of
understanding.

When she didn't budge, he began again. "What would you
say if I asked you to consider that the dream you had in the car was
not a dream, but a memory"? He stopped to study Caroline while
she digested what he said.

"What would you say if I told you I thought it was a
repressed memory. We all know about PTSD. We hear stories all the
time, about children who repress memories because they are too
painful to remember. They can't understand the memory, don't

know how to process, or what to do with it. Maybe they don't understand what it means. So, they push it back so far in the mind that it stays buried for years, lifetimes. Until something happens to dislodge it and bring it to the forefront of the mind, where the child has grown, or the adult has developed the strength to process and heal from the pain"

Caroline looked at Andrew, confused. "Wait. You think something happened to me and I'm repressing the memory. First, of all, the dream, or memory as you call it can't be real. It takes place probably a couple of hundred years ago". She smiled as the joke came to mind. "I know I look good for my age, but that's impossible".

Andrew smiled and leaned back into the couch cushions. "Okay, let's come at this from a different angle. "Today you fell off the breaker into the ocean. You panicked even though the water wasn't deep. You hit your shoulder, but not your head. Yet for some reason you became disoriented and confused to the point that you were imagining the situation that you've since dreamt about and remembered when you studied the painting in the bedroom. A picture that you painted. Don't you find that odd"?

"I suppose I do. So, what are you saying"?

Andrew wanted her to come to the realization on her own, without prompting. It wasn't happening, though. He couldn't think of another way to put it without bluntly saying it. He leaned forward and took Caroline's hand in his and looked into her eyes.

"Caroline. I'm your Daniel".

She looked at Andrew as the words he spoke settled in her mind. "*I'm your Daniel.*" She looked down at his hand which held hers firmly, then returned to study Andrew's face, as she absorbed what he said.

"You're my Daniel? Who's Daniel? I don't know Daniel. I only know that I dreamt of a man whose name was Daniel. A man I had no connection to except that we shared the same dreadful fate". Caroline fought Andrew, dismissing the idea that he was Daniel.

Andrew held his ground. "It's true, Caroline. Only, you aren't ready to accept it. We have a deep connection that time, and space can't or won't dissolve. Every time, each lifetime, I remember. When I enter a new existence, my soul is missing its second half. For some reason, we come together through each reincarnation. We are reunited to live out the current existence. We pass on when the time comes, only to be reunited again".

He went on. "I don't know why this is. I've thought about it a great deal and the only thing I can come up with is that we have to learn something before we can finally rest in the afterlife, together, peacefully".

Caroline studied Andrew as she thought to herself, *he really believes what he's saying*. "Andrew today has been a difficult one. If you're playing a joke on me now, I have to tell you, I think it's in poor taste".

He shook his head and moved closer to her, caressing her hand. "No. No Caroline. I'm not playing a joke on you. I'm serious, dead serious. We came together at one point in the existence of the universe and that connection was permanent. We keep returning to each other".

Caroline smiled as she considered the possibility of spending eternity with Andrew. And while she liked the idea of being with him, she couldn't believe what he said could be a possibility, not even a remote one. She didn't want to hurt his feelings, but she couldn't fathom the idea. "Andrew. Do you hear what you're saying? We're talking about real life, here. Not one of your movies. What you speak of sounds like something out of the twilight zone. I'm kind of surprised".

"It's okay Caroline. If roles were reversed, I'd probably be reacting as you are now. But I've had a lot of time to consider this theory. I don't know why I remember what I do through each lifetime. I haven't been able to figure out why I remember, but you don't".

He chuckled as he continued. "It seems like we have this conversation regularly. I should be getting better at it. But each time we sit across from one each other, I find myself struggling to explain myself". He lifted his hand to caress the side of Caroline's face.

"Each time we have this conversation I feel like it's the first time. And through each existence, when I see you, find you again, it's like meeting you for the first time. It's like finding the second half of my 'self.' I want to pull you close and hold on and never let go".

Remember The Kiss

Caroline turned from Andrew's touch as she fought between wanting to believe him and knowing that it wasn't possible. "Andrew, how beautiful that sounds. To be able to return to ones' true love outside space and time would be wonderful, but I can't believe what you say. Not now. If it were true, I would think it a cruel joke. To be forced to live a life filled with pain and disappointment for all those years. Why"?

Andrew shook his head. "I ask myself that question too. The only thing I can think of is that we have lessons to learn before we can spend eternity together".

Caroline laughed at the thought. "Yes, but if we can't remember the lives we lived and the mistakes we made while living them, then how are we supposed to learn from them"?

"I suppose we are remembering. Somewhere in our subconscious we remember. I believe one day it will all come together, and like an intricate puzzle, will be complete". He reached out and took her hand again. "And then we can live a peaceful eternal existence".

Cynically, "And where would that be, Andrew? Where would we live out this euphoric life"?

Andrew gazed into her eyes, searching. "I don't know the answer to that question. I was hoping we would discover that together".

Caroline pulled away and stood up. She walked to the fireplace, the image of Squam Lake, capturing her attention. She looked out at the lake from where she stood, remembering the day she painted it. The peaceful moment in a chaotic life. She then turned back to Andrew. "This is too much, Andrew. I think even for you. I think we should put this conversation on hold until we're both rested. Part of me thinks I'm dreaming up this moment". She lifted her hand to her head. "Maybe I did hit my head earlier and don't remember".

She picked up the teacups from the table and went to the kitchen and place them in the sink before going to the dryer to remove the clothes. She leaned in and pulled out the dry clothes, still warm and let them rest over the dryer door. She then returned to the living room to find Andrew still on the couch, his elbows resting on his knees his hands drawn together as though to pray. "Come on Andrew".

He stood and followed Caroline down the hall to his room for the night. Caroline stopped next to him and looked through the door, her eye caught the painting above the bed. She looked at the picture again, focusing on the scene wondering. Her eyes scanned the print as she tried to recall the day, she painted it. She was unsuccessful in her attempt as she took in the scene. The dark sky, the ship being tossed about white foaming waves, debris floating in the water. And then, something she hadn't seen earlier nor remembered painting; a small hand reaching out from the black water. And then she heard the pleading voice. Daniel, Daniel, don't forget me".

She flinched as the voice faded away, and looked up at Andrew, wondering if he heard it too. He looked down at her and smiled. "Goodnight Caroline. I hope you have peaceful dreams". He leaned toward her and gently kissed her on the forehead before entering the room and closing the door.

Caroline stood outside the door, feeling uneasy. She hesitated for a moment, before turning to her room, knowing that she needed to rest if she wanted to be prepared for Peter Carlton. She walked into her bathroom and changed into night clothes, while she considered the possibilities that might be offered to her. Standing in front of the mirror she studied the image that looked back at her. The face was familiar, but as she looked into strained brown eyes, she was surprised to realize the woman that looked back at her was a stranger. What did she really know about her?

She turned from the mirror and moved into the bedroom where she slipped in between soft cool sheets. She rolled on her side, plumping the pillow then settled to look out at into the moonlit sky. The storm had cleared and as Caroline lay still in the night, she could hear the cricket's song. She took a deep breath and sighed as she fell asleep to the gentle sounds of the night.

THIRTEEN

Andrew stood against the closed door looking at the painting the hung above the bed. The moment he hoped for was creeping up on them, and not in the way he hoped it would.

He slowly reached up and turned off the light switch on the wall to his right and walked to the bed where he turned on the reading light. The dim yellow light on the nightstand reflected off the image that hung on the wall in the night. Andrew stood next to the bed staring at the story, he knew all too well.

Turning his back momentarily to the bed, he sat down and removed his shoes. Then, he pulled the shirt over his head and dropped it to the floor, finally realizing how tired he was. His body was screaming for sleep, but his mind wouldn't settle. He turned back to the painting wondering what prompted Caroline to paint it. It seemed clear to him that she had no recollection to the past. Nor did she seem to be drawn to him. His eyes scanned Caroline's work, taking note of the details of the sail as the mast cracked. And the barrels and nets that were thrown from the ship during the storm. But none of it compared to the hand he saw reaching out from the foam filled waves as he remembered her calling out. "Daniel, Daniel, don't forget me".

Andrew's eyes were filled with tears as he stood up and removed his shorts, then pulled back the covers and climbed into bed. He lay on his back staring up at the ceiling where shadows danced in the night. The same moon that Caroline noticed from her room shone light across the lawn outside, the storm having been swept away.

The hour was late, Andrew suspected, and he lifted his arm to confirm the time by the face of the watch on his wrist. It was past the hour of midnight, a new day, yet the feeling of despair hung in the air. Which was cooler now that the storm had cleared away the stagnant humid air of the day before. He smiled as he thought about the temperature change, remembering someone saying, *if you don't like the temperature in New Hampshire, wait a minute, it will change*. He was sure every state claimed that statement, but as he lay still in the early morning hours, he thought for sure it was true here.

His eyes burned, and he blinked away what remained of the tears he shed while recalling Julia's voice, or Caroline's. He tried to forget the words she spoke earlier. Words that pushed him away, denied him and his need to be close to her. He wondered if this would be the end. If this would be the incarnation that would prove to be the final connection between the two. Was it possible that they could meet through the centuries, again and again, reconnect on the deep level that existed in both their souls to have these be their final moment together? He dismissed the words that he didn't want to believe could be true.

Andrew turned over and willed himself to forget. Yet each time he forced Caroline from his mind, it was her face he saw in the night. He saw her on the sailboat in the sun, and walking along the trail of the Basin, and again as she sat on the rocks while the waves broke along the shore. It would be impossible to forget his second self. It would be useless for him to force the memory of her from his mind. Everything about Caroline was imprinted in his subconscious, an indelible mark that would last through eternity. He knew as he thought these things that it wasn't possible. She was part of his soul. He only needed to be patient. She would come to realize the truth, the connection, and they would be together.

Andrew turned once more, to lay on his back where he again watched the shadows as they changed with the breeze. He listened as the wind blew against the side of the house, a gentle *whooshing* sound in the night, keeping time with the crickets whose song continued uninterrupted. He listened intently to the chirping sound, counting as the cricket's songs slowed with the dropping temperature. He counted with each sound, one, two, three, until he dozed off. Falling into a deep sleep.

FOURTEEN

He watched as she ran along the docks looking intently through the crowd. She carried with her a satchel that, though not large, was heavy enough to slow her down. She ran in and out of groups that had gathered, disappearing from his sight occasionally. He watched as the warm sun shone on her hair. There was excitement in the air, and he could tell as he looked up at the clear blue sky that the trip should start out without incident.

"Daniel. Daniel."

He scanned the crowd to find her again as she called out to him. He lifted his arm and waved with excitement. He pushed his way through the people on deck as he ran to meet her. "Julia, I was beginning to worry. I thought you'd changed your mind and weren't coming". He yelled over the throng of people who waited.

"Excuse me. Excuse me". She laughed as she pushed her way through the crowd. "Excuse me, please. I must pass". She looked up as Daniel walked briskly down the gang plank to meet her.

"I'm so happy to see you, Julia". He took the bag from her and grabbed her hand. "Come on. Let's get you aboard so we can relax a bit. I think it's going to be a tight voyage. There are so many people on board".

They walked together up the plank and cautiously stepped on board. Julia took a deep breath, taking in the ocean air and smell of stale wood. She looked up at the sail that appeared to go on forever. "My, it's much larger than it appears from the docks". She turned and smiled up at Daniel, excited to taking such a leap of faith.

"You'll be perfectly safe, my dear". He looked up at the sky again. "It's a beautiful day to journey across the Atlantic. The weather should stay clear for the crossing. We picked the perfect time of the year for this trip. I imagine we will arrive on American soil in six weeks if the weather holds out".

Julia's eyes grew large. "Six weeks? I guess I didn't think about how long a voyage it would be",

"3000 nautical miles at least". Daniel said.

Julia laughed. "I guess I'll have to take your word for it. I have no idea what a nautical mile looks like".

They laughed for a moment then turned their attention to the mass of people that boarded the ship. At first, they were surprised and excited about the journey. But as the boat filed up, excitement turned to concern as they walked past the tiny deck space and were directed down steep stairways into the enclosed lower decks, which was crowded and hot. Daniel smiled at Julia. 'It will be okay, you'll see".

The hours turned to days in the bottom of the ship where the air became stale, and it was more difficult to watch those around them. Mothers and fathers watched as children became sick while others died.

Julia looked around the hull of the boat despairingly. What she saw brought her to tears. The stench and fumes of vomit, the seasickness, scurvy, and mouth rot were enough to make her wish she had never set foot on the ship. She watched as young and old alike were starving. They all suffered from mouth rot a result of old sharply salted food and meat. Many died of dysentery from bad water.

Julia looked despairingly at Daniel. "I don't know how much of this I can take. I can't believe the conditions we must endure. All this sickness and disease is more than I can take. And the poor woman giving birth at the back of the boat didn't have a chance. To be pushed through the loophole and dropped into the sea because she couldn't give birth under these circumstances".

Daniel put his arm around Julia. "I know, Julia. I'm sorry you must endure such conditions. It's the only way we could make the crossing though". The boat rocked and swayed, and Daniel noticed the look of unrest on Julia's face. "Do you think you can follow me? If we can get through all these people, we can take some fresh air on deck".

Julia nodded as Daniel took her hand and led her through the crowd and up the stairs where they took a deep breath and walked to the rail. They no longer celebrated the bright sun, for this day was cloudy and the wind picked up. It didn't matter to them at the moment for they only wanted to breathe in the air that would fill their lungs without making them feel like they wanted to vomit.

She knew she shouldn't, but she reached out to Daniel, who took her in his arms, and she cried. Her hopes for the future were fading as the days passed. She was becoming discouraged and was afraid they wouldn't make it to America. They had seen so much death already.

Daniel looked over Julia's head as the wind gained speed and the clouds rolled in. The sky grew darker, and waves started to swell. He held her tighter not wanting her to panic as the timbers began to creak. She lifted her head from his shoulders as the ship dipped and staggered. The clouds that were pale in the distance turned dark with black and gray streaks across the sky.

Another wave sent them toppling over. A sudden drop of the ship in a trough of a wave and the smack of the impact as it hit the bottom threw Daniel to his knees. They waited feeling as though time was suspended while the world was still.

Then the ship fell quiet. During the calm they heard the sails flap and then hang still. The silence was deafening.

The seas were like glass, not a wave could be seen, the ominous clouds pressed down on the sails, nothing moved, the seagulls had disappeared. Then they heard from a distance. "Dear God, save us. The watchman yelled as he scrambled down the ropes to the deck.

The captain ordered the crew to take down the sails. They heard the feet of the crew running across the deck as they heard "Reef in". The glassy sea began to stir, turning black as it stirred up and started to move.

The wind screamed and howled like a whistle. It poured out of the darkened sky as the boat healed over and the sea suddenly bowed up and threw them toward the clouds that split with a flash of light.

The ship rolled.

Daniel saw nothing but the prow of the boat rising from the sea. The ship was propelled from the sea, and it stood on its stern. They saw only the sky in front of them. Daniel looked beyond and seas, the wave towered high above the ship as it fought its way to the icy white crest of the wave.

He waited for the wave to wash over them. They braced themselves as it crashed down on the deck of the ship. It shuddered and shook as another wave rose and broke against the ship.

Julia screamed as the ship creaked and shook against the extra weight of the water.

Sailors fought for control of the sails clinging to spars, hanging from the ropes as they kicked and screamed, fighting for their lives. The captain shouted commands that no one could hear, and the crew fought to steer the prow into the flailing seas, while the winds blew stronger stirring up more violent waves.

The ship gave a huge heave that sent them across the deck. They struggled to their feet clinging to the sides of the rail as lightning flashed across the sky.

Julia rubbed her hands against her eyes that burned with salt water, and she pulled away as a sudden heave of the ship threw her into the rail, which she clung to as a mighty wall of water stood before the stern then washed down on them with such force, they were lifted off their feet.

Julia snatched at the ropes as the water washed her from the rail. She grabbed at the line, but the water took her. She was airborne before she had time to tighten her grip on the rail or even think about what was happening to her. The wind took her breath away as she was forced into the icy cold water.

The waves swelled and when she tried to scream out, her lungs filled with salt water. Each time she surfaced, she cried out to Daniel as her eyes searched for him. "Daniel! Daniel. Don't leave me, Daniel!" Julia panicked as she was forced below again and again until she had no more energy to fight the stormy seas.

She struggled one last time and as she bobbed to the surface where she was stunned, as a plank, freed from the ship slapped her across the back of the head. She felt a sharp shooting pain searing through her body, and she was no longer able to fight. The heaviness in her heart permeated through her body. She willed herself to kick, to fight her way to the surface, without success. She could feel her body falling, dropping deeper and deeper into the abyss, until there was only darkness and the fight no longer mattered.

Daniel watched her white face in the black water as it stole her from his grasp. She went past him and flew over the rail, turning over and over in the waves, her arms flailing as she tried to keep her pale face above water.

Julia's mouth moved as she screamed violently then disappeared from Daniels's view. He no longer saw her but felt the pounding of the waves against the compromised ship, "Man overboard", he yelled to no avail, his words were carried off in the wind as the storm continued to scream.

The water washed from the deck as Daniel clung to the rail searching in vain. Julia was swallowed up by the sea. "Julia. Julia". He screamed, "Where are you, Julia"? The ship wallowed in the trough of the wave, but not for long. Daniel braced himself and another towering wave swept across the deck and pulled him from the rail. His hand, which up until that moment held tight to the rail, gave

Remember The Kiss

way and pain shot through his arm as his body twisted when he was lifted from the ship.

Daniel hit the water with a force that knocked the wind out of him. He went under, once, twice and a third time before he could push the pain of his arm from his mind and take in a breath of air. The waves dipped and surged pulling and pushing him where he didn't want to go. He turned from the rocking ship and put his attention on the white foaming waves, hoping to find Julia among them.

He cried out to her. "Julia, Julia. Where are you? Julia, hear me, Julia. I will find you. I promise you. I'll find you and bring you home. Hold on, dear." Until his voice was horse and he no longer had the energy to fight the violent waves. He tried to swim from the boat into the blackness of the sea to find Julia. He knew she would be scared and, by now too tired to stay afloat. He knew he had to find her. His mind told him he couldn't lose her. Yet when he tried to fight the waves, his arm wouldn't cooperate. He had broken it at the elbow when he was thrown from the deck. His arm was useless now.

He bobbed up and down with the wave, his head dipping below the surface and forcing icy water into his lungs. He coughed and sputtered each time his head was above the waves. He treed water, trying to remain focused on finding Julia. He watched closely as debris flew past him so he wouldn't be knocked unconscious. Daniel strained to listen, hoping to hear Julia's cries for help but he could only hear the roar of the wave as they forced him below again, until his body gave out. He went down one last time, deeper and deeper into a dark abyss as he heard Julia's voice crying out to him as he lost consciousness.

Woods

FIFTEEN

Andrew sat straight up in bed as he her heard her scream. The sound woke him from a dead sleep, and he was trying to remember where he was. Was that Julia in a dream, or Caroline who cried out to him?

He threw his legs over the side of the bed and grabbed the comforter and wrapped it around his waist as he headed for the door, He stumbled on the blanket as he opened the door and went to Caroline's room where he was sure it was her that screamed.

Andrew opened the door to Caroline's room, to find her sitting up in bed in the early morning light with her head in her hands crying. He was still waking up and was somewhat confused as he set aside his dream to focus on Caroline. He slowly approached the bed   , not wanting to add to what he believed an alr

He went to the opposite side of the bed and gently sat down next to her. He placed a hand on her shoulder. "Caroline. Are you okay"?

Caroline dropped her hands to her lap after wiping the tears from her face. "I'm fine". She sniffled.

"I heard you scream from the other room. What was the nightmare"? Andrew asked, not sure that he heard her scream. The scream could have been part of his nightmare.

Caroline silently nodded as she lifted her hand to catch the final tear that escaped down her face. She looked at Andrew, unsure if she wanted to explain. "Yes. The same one I had in the car on the way home last night, only more vivid".

Andrew nodded, knowing the dream she shared the night before was only the tip of a memory that a lifetime ago, had been her reality, their reality. "I know. I'm sorry".

She turned and studied his face. How could he know, she thought? How could he understand what she felt at that moment? "How can you know my pain"?

He studied her face wondering how he could get through to her, when finally, it dawned on him that her experience was his experience. "Caroline. If I could tell you what your dream, or nightmare rather, was about, would you believe that what I say is true"?

Caroline sat up straight and brushed the hair back from her face. "Andrew, I already told you what the dream was about last night. Of course, you'll know what it's about". She chuckled. "There's a painting above the bed you slept in, depicting it. I've spelled it out for you".

"That's true". Andrew admitted but added something to prompt Caroline to consider his offer. "If I can share more details than what you shared, would that make the difference"?

Caroline shifted in the bed. She pulled the blankets up as she drew her knees to her chest than wrapped her arms around her legs. "I won't promise anything, but if you want to talk, I might consider what you say".

Andrew accepted Caroline's challenge. He too made himself comfortable. He sat back against the pillow and leaned against the headboard, his legs stretched out on the bed. Caroline smiled at the sight. "You look like a caterpillar wrapped up in a cocoon".

"Funny, Caroline. It's nice to see you found that dry sense of humor". He smiled back at her as he searched her eyes for that familiar spark. "Okay, I won't start at the beginning, however, I will start at a time that is close to what you shared with me. Let me see".

He paused to think about where he should begin. "The shipwreck was part of a bigger picture that started in a port in London. The port that docked the ship that would later...well, we know what happened there. Anyway, the ship was docked, and I stood waiting on deck, watching for you. I don't mind saying I was a little nervous thinking you wouldn't show up. But then I saw you running along the docks carrying a bag that held all your belongings".

Caroline noticed a twinkle in his eyes as he recalled vividly what she dreamed about. "My heart skipped a beat when I saw you, I ran to meet you and we boarded together". Andrew looked at Caroline, for approval.

She nodded. "Continue".

The ship was crowded, and everyone was gathered below deck in steerage then we were under way. As the days passed, the conditions grew worse. There was sickness and disease that wouldn't subside. There was a point where we snuck up on deck after you expressed concern about the conditions".

Andrew looked to Caroline. When she didn't budge, he cautiously continued. ""There was a particular circumstance, which caused you much distress. A pregnant woman". He stopped wondering if he should continue.

Caroline's eyes grew large, and she swallowed as she nodded. Andrew continued. "She wasn't able to give birth under the circumstances. They ended up pushing her through a port hole. It was a terrible scene". He shook his head. "We went up on deck to get some fresh air and try to push the image from our minds. While we were on deck the waters began to swell. The wind rose to a gale quickly. The ship rocked and shuttered, and the waves washed across the deck".

Andrew stopped there to assess Caroline's state of mind. Her face was drawn and pale and tears returned. "Should I go on"?

Caroline shook her head and raised her hand to her mouth as she watched Andrew. He looked down, focusing on the pattern on the quilt he was still wrapped in. He cleared his throat. "Do you believe me now"?

Caroline sat staring at Andrew, Not knowing how to respond. "I don't know what to believe. But what you said mirrors the start of what began as a sweet dream. But the journey, it was horrible. the dream was so clear, it's as though it was happening at that moment". She stopped talking and looked at Andrew who sat, contemplating the situation. The last few days were a blessing to her, but now, as she sat next to Andrew, she wondered if she was cursed.

How could such a circumstance occur? How could it be possible that any person could return to life in another form, again and again? Caroline struggled between wanting to believe Andrew, and not being able to trust herself or anyone else. She shifted once again on the bed, and turned to face Andrew, who focused on Caroline's eyes. *The windows to her soul,* he thought.

Caroline rested her hand on Andrew's as she spoke. "Andrew, I don't know what to think. How can any of this be possible? When I listen to what you tell me I can only think we're living an episode of the *Twilight Zone*. What you tell me, isn't possible. We live, we die, and that's the end of it. No do overs or second chances. It's finite".

Andrew challenged Caroline, standing his ground. "Do you know that for a fact? Are you completely certain that there is no possible way that our souls could return, again and again to this plane, this existence"? He watched her as she looked down at his hand, then ran her fingers along his, tracing the lines of his hand.

"Until today, I would have emphatically answered that question with a definite 'no', but sitting here with you, now, I'm left with many questions, that lead me to feel I can no longer be sure in my answer". She looked into Andrew's dark eyes, trying to place him in another lifetime, trying to imagine or "know" him from the past.

      "I can hardly believe any of this. How is it possible, that any of this is true? Maybe we're dreaming it, maybe all of us are living a dream". She tried to lighten the conversation. "Like the character in *Groundhog Day*, who wakes every day, living the same experience over and over". Then she became somber as she looked again at Andrew who listened intently. "Will we ever wake up"?

      "I don't know the answer to your question, Caroline. But it is possible. If you stop to think about quantum physics, and the reality of manifesting, and bending time, and the possibility of time travel, to the scientific community everything is possible. It's all probable. They have the education, background, and experience to provide an educated answer that I'm ill qualified to produce for you".

      Andrew then thought about what many refer to as a higher being. I don't know why life follows the path it does. Maybe it isn't scientific, maybe its faith based. Maybe we are existing in our personal purgatory, we keep coming back until we get it right. I don't know the answers, I only know the experience. I don't know why I remember, and you don't. Sometimes I wonder if it's a promise I made to you. I did tell you I wouldn't leave you, that night when the storm raged around us. I watched as we were torn from one another, separated to fight for our lives alone, until we each, in our time succumbed to the sea. Where we were suspended in time, waiting to find each other, so we could return to one another as the universe intended. I only know that while we were fighting the raging waters, it's all I could think about was rescuing you and saving us. maybe it's a promised unfilled".

      Caroline released Andrew's hand. "Let me ask you a question. Assuming you're not playing a trick on me, do you remember everything about every life you lived? You said you remember this conversation, previously, in another life, and that you'd think you'd get better at it. Do you remember"?

      "I do remember the conversation with you each time. However, it isn't like a memory, it's like a Deja vu moment. It's like 'didn't I just have this conversation'. It's not a pictorial memory of where we were, what we were doing and how the conversation transpired. It's a feeling, a sense a longing to make it real, to bring it back or to make it final, I don't know, I can't explain it. You don't feel anything? I mean for me"?

"I don't know Andrew. I mean, when I saw you on the boardwalk, I thought I recognized you, but then I looked at you and realized, of course I knew you. You're a celebrity everyone knows you. Of course, the more time I spend with you, the more I feel like we've been together forever. But how do I know that's not because I'm comfortable with you? How do I know that it's not that you're a decent person who has a decent heart, which we all desire"?

Andrew smiled down at Caroline, knowing, he couldn't answer her questions. He knew in his soul that Caroline was his second half, the one he was to share his experiences with, in this life and any other life of which he would return.

Caroline listened to Andrew while he discussed the reality of living many lives and living those lives together, and that somehow the universe brings them together through each existence.

Caroline wondered as she listened to Andrew, about their meeting through each lifetime. If what he said is true, is the reason they find each other throughout time, to torture each other, with the knowing they will be ripped apart by death in this life, to be reunited in the next. A cat and mouse game of sorts Caroline thought.

Andrew believed as was evident by his words that the separation and reunion was so they could learn from one another and therefore live a life better each time. Either way there was doubt in Caroline's mind as she listened to Andrew while they sat next to each other.

"Caroline". Andrew sounded somewhat frustrated as he broke into her thoughts. "Are you telling me that you don't know without a doubt that we've been together somewhere in time? You don't feel anything for me"?

"No that's not what I said, Andrew. What I'm saying is I find it difficult to believe that it is possible to come back and fix mistakes that were made during another lifetime. I was raised to believe, you live, you die and if you lived a good life you go to heaven".

She hesitated, not wanting to encourage Andrew. "I'm not saying it isn't possible. I'm saying it's outside my realm of understanding. Yes, sometimes I feel like I've known you forever, but there are other times when I faulter. I remember who I am and the life I've lived. I don't trust my reality. I don't trust that what I feel, or experience is right for me, look at my life, look what I've done to my life, why would anyone choose to live this life"?

Andrew turned to face Caroline. It was his turn to take her hands in his. "I'm not saying I understand completely why the universe works the way it does. I don't know why I've lived the lives I've lived, or why I've chosen the people I have, to live out that experience. I must believe somewhere in my subconscious there is a place where the answers reside. I must trust in the process that will bring us home".

"Look, Caroline. None of us realize what the life we chose will be like once we've chosen. We chose based on a subconscious knowing that we will learn from the experience or will make the existence of those we live with, better. Finally, there is the possibility we have a lesson to learn or feel that particular role will help us meet the challenge to become the person we are supposed to be".

Andrew moved closer to Caroline. He drew her hands to his chest and gazed into her eyes. "I know. I can tell, I can feel it in my bones, I see it in your eyes. Your soul reflecting from the deep recesses of the universe saying, I've been lost for so long, I'm tired, and long to be at peace, and not to run anymore.

You're there Caroline. You're here, you're at that point in this existence where you have experienced what is required. It's now time to take the next step".

What is that step? Caroline's eyes pleaded, unsure of the answer.

Andrew held Caroline's hands close to his heart. He looked into brown eyes that searched the deep pools of his for a sign, for some form of direction or encouragement. What she saw looking back at her left her breathless.

Andrew brought his free hand to Caroline's chin. Something she remembered him doing once before, or maybe twice, she couldn't remember how many times before. Was she becoming confused again? Andrew shook his head slightly, as if he read her mind willing it to be silent. He ran his hand along Caroline's jaw until his hand stopped below her ear, then returned to her chin.

"Caroline, I can think of only one thing I haven't tried to help you realize the truth. To help you see that we are two halves of the same soul. We are meant to be together. We have fought through storms and floods and fires to sit right here, face to face".

Caroline's heart stopped beating, as her breath caught in her throat. She couldn't speak and found she didn't want to as Andrew leaned in and gently kissed her. He rested there waiting for Caroline's response.

Caroline's heart raced then skipped a beat as her lips met Andrew's. She froze as he waited, afraid to move, either forward or back. This was a moment she recalled, a feeling that rose from her soul like the wave of the storm that took him from her all those years ago. She sat now, across from him waiting, and wanting. She pulled her hand back from his chest and lifted it to place it on the back of his head and along his shoulder. Then leaning in she released her doubts and opened herself to him.

Tears streamed down Caroline's face as she realized she had spent her whole life searching for the moment that she now experienced. The kiss was electric, sending charges of energy through her body and brought to her mind, many lifetimes of love and sharing that she didn't realize she missed.

They were suspended outside space and time in an embrace that they both spent a lifetime missing. Andrew drew Caroline closer, and she relented as they left the world behind. Remembering a life that for so many years was non-existent. Until, breathless, they separated, coming up for air.

They sat in silence until the energy subsided, Andrew still holding Caroline in his arms, Caroline relaxed and for the first time in her life, this life, she felt hope.

They enjoyed the peaceful moment until Andrew broke the silence. "Well,"?

"Well. Well, what"? She teased.

"Really, Caroline"? He took the bait. "You can't tell me you don't feel something. There's no way now".

Caroline smiled as Andrew, letting him squirm a little longer. "No, Andrew. I can't. I won't. Now, I know why my life has been such a challenge. How can one accomplish anything with only half a brain, or heart or half of a soul"? Her eyes sparkled as she gazed into his. I've spent my life living in the dark, waiting for you to save me. And I didn't even know it".

Andrew drew her to him once again and held her tight. "I'd like to spend the day here, with you, no interruptions. But we have an appointment. Remember"?

Caroline nodded while still resting against Andrew's shoulder. "I remember. Do you think we could cancel"?

Andrew put his hands, on Caroline's shoulders and moved her an arms-length away. "No. Caroline. As much as I'd like to stay here. You must follow through with this meeting. When he sees your work, your life will change".

Caroline shook her head "I don't want it to change. Now that I found you, I don't want us to be apart".

"Caroline. Be realistic. We can't sit on this bed forever". He paused, not able to resist. "We'd starve".

"Funny Andrew. But we'd be together".

"Don't get sappy on me Caroline. We're not back on that ship. We're living in the twenty-first century. We can be together and still live our lives and grow in our career's. This is your time. You were meant for this. So, let's get up and get ready. It's eight-fifteen. We'll have time for breakfast before Peter arrives".

Caroline smiled at Andrew as she sat back. "I know, I was only giving you a hard time. But I don't know about this whole art thing. I don't know if I'm cut out for the spotlight".

"You'll get used to it. I should know". Andrew pulled the quilt tighter and moved to the edge of the bed. "Why don't you take a shower, and I will find something to make for breakfast".

Caroline agreed, "Okay, but you should shower too. I mean in the other bathroom, alone".

Andrew laughed as Caroline stumbled over her words. "I know what you meant".

Remember The Kiss

"You have a set of clean clothes too. Remember. They're hanging over the dryer". Caroline went on. "I showed you where the towels are".

Andrew nodded as he stood up. Okay, I'll do that first". He leaned over and kissed Caroline gently on the lips.

Caroline smiled as she watched Andrew leave the room. She couldn't believe her life was finally taking a turn for the brighter. She thought back on the moments of her life that challenged her and brought her to her knees, reflecting on the ups and downs to realize that the trials she faced compared in no way to the joy she felt at that moment. She was returning from the dead to experience a renewed existence. She threw back the blankets, realizing that today was her do-over day as headed for the shower.

SIXTEEN

Cambria

Caroline went to the kitchen after a revitalizing shower, to find Andrew standing over the stove. "I'm so glad we live in the twenty-first century. I bet I never would have seen you cooking back in the day".

"Funny, Caroline. You better be careful, or you'll find yourself cleaning up after breakfast by yourself". Andrew waved a spatula in the air as he scolded her.

"It smells good. Where did you find what you needed to cook? I didn't think there was any food left in the house". She scanned the counter to answer her question.

"I found some eggs in the refrigerator. Some tomatoes, spinach, feta cheese, and a little basil, and we have a tasty omelet".

Caroline collected plates and set the table while Andrew finished cooking. "Do you want coffee? I can probably find the coffee pot somewhere in the cabinet".

"No". He chuckled. Water is fine. I put the pot to boil so there's water for tea if you like".

"Thank you". They talked their way through breakfast, then they cleaned up while they waited for Peter to arrive. Caroline stood at the sink cleaning dishes as Andrew cleared them from the table. He walked up behind her and placed a plate in the soapy water, then leaned over and kissed her neck as he ran his hand across her shoulder.

"Andrew. The dishes, please". Caroline giggled. "I hope you don't think I'll let you take advantage of me now that I see things your way"?

"You sure know how to spoil a guy's fun". He teased. "But seriously Caroline". He turned her to face him, her wet soapy hands dripped on the floor. He took her face in his hands and kissed her while she held her hands out to keep from getting wet.

She laughed in between kisses. "Andrew really? I don't want to have to change clothes before Peter arrives".

"It's only water, it will dry". He continued to kiss Caroline while laughing at her response to his antics. "I've waited a long time to be able to kiss those lips again". He pulled her close until their bodies met.

Caroline responded to his advances by placing her wet hands around his neck. She chuckled under her breath as she waited for Andrew to react.

'He jumped back. "Hey, your hands are wet". He laughed as he moved away from her.

"It's only water, it will dry". Caroline mimicked Andrew's words through her laughter.

He reached for the sprayer on the sink, but Caroline intercepted him, anticipating his next move." Okay, mister, that's enough of that. Peter will be her soon. I don't want him arriving to find a flood in my kitchen".

The laughter ceased and Andrew approached Caroline and landed one final kiss before retreating. "You're right. Let's finish up here before he arrives. Are you getting excited"?

Caroline turned back to the sink to wash the final dish, then drained the sink. "I don't think so, maybe a little nervous. It's strange to me, having someone who knows art, want to see my work. I can't imagine anything will come of it. I never dreamed I'd be painting professionally".

"Well, I'll tell you what I think. I believe you will be a hit. He's going to want to see your work on display". Caroline handed the dish to Andrew. He wiped it dry and handed it back to Caroline. "I think your nerves are keeping you from seeing the possibilities. It won't be long before he's standing in that room telling you how talented you are".

Caroline placed the clean dish in the cabinet and was about to reply, when there was a knock at the door. She nervously smiled at Andrew as he went to greet Peter. She walked around the corner as he opened the door.

"Peter, come in". He extended his hand in greeting. "Thank you for taking the time to come out here. I assure you it will be worth your while".

"Andrew". Caroline interrupted. "Why don't you let the man in before you start your sales pitch". She turned to Peter. "I'm sorry for Andrew's over zealousness. I think he's getting a little ahead of himself. As I told you yesterday, I'm not a professional painter""

'Peter chuckled. "No apologies necessary, Caroline. This is how things are done in the creative industries". He looked to Andrew. "Andrew knows this all too well. Seize the moment, we say. When an opportunity arises, you should jump at the chance to have your work assessed. You never know what might come of it, or when the opportunity might come again".

"Well, as Andrew said. "Thank you for taking the time to look. I must tell you I'm a little nervous about having a stranger critique my work. I've never shown it to anyone, until Andrew that is". There was a momentary silence while Caroline considered her next move. "I'd offer you coffee, but I..."

Peter interrupted. "That's not necessary Caroline. How about we cut to the chase and look at your work. He walked from the dining area to the living room where his attention was drawn to the painting of Squam Lake over the fireplace. They stood in silence waiting for Peter's assessment. "Is this one of yours, Caroline"?

Caroline began to stammer. "Yes, this is one of my earlier paintings. I've improved since then".

"Caroline". Peter stopped her from explaining further. "You don't need to defend your work. This is quite good. I like how you captured the light through the trees. If I stood here long enough, I'd think I was standing among the trees. Excellent".

Andrew noticed Peter's eyes wandering. He stepped up and led him down the hall. "Peter, you must see this snow owl. He's quite captivating".

Peter stopped in front of the image and studied the detail. "Those eyes are looking right through me. My God Caroline he's beautiful". He looked at Caroline, who stood blushing, a result of his complements.

Andrew agreed. "Well, you haven't seen anything yet". He was about to direct Pater to the gallery of paintings, when Peter stopped dead, to look at the painting above the bed in the spare room.

Caroline's stomach began to turn. She didn't want to see that painting today. She wanted no memory of that time. She didn't want to remember the pain she suffered through that image. Andrew sensed Caroline's uneasiness and attempted to redirect Peter's attention, but he wouldn't have it.

"Wait, wait, wait." He pulled back his elbow from Andrew who had placed his hand there to coax Peter away from the painting. "What's this, Caroline"? He stepped into the room and approached the foot of the bed, where he looked upon the haunting image on the wall. From there he turned to Caroline and studied her, trying to read her, to understand where the painting came from. What would produce such a scene? "What were you thinking when you painted this picture, Caroline? It's beautiful in a haunting sort of way. When I look at it, I feel all the pain I've experienced in my life being pulled from me, through every pore in my body to be absorbed into that piece. This one is...well, I have no words".

Andrew looked at Caroline as she drew and held the breath that would keep her from coming apart while in the presence of the painting. He quickly responded thinking that Caroline was incapable of doing so at that moment. "She painted that one years ago...".

174

"It's okay, Andrew". She interjected. "That painting came from a very deep painful period in my life. I don't think I realized what I was painting at the time". She looked at Andrew as she continued. "It is a haunting image. However, I believe it's' one that saved my life". Andrew smiled at her, hearing the gratitude in her voice.

"Well, aren't you something Caroline. Surprises come in many ways. You my dear are a breath of fresh air. Do I dare ask if there's more"?

Andrew chuckled under his breath as he nodded, a broad grin passing across his face. "You have no idea, Peter. No idea. If you follow me, I'll show you what I mean".

Andrew stepped into the hallway. Peter followed behind him. Caroline stayed back taking another look at the ship that hung above the bed. The sun peeked through the blinds and left a streak of light above the ship, illuminating the clouds and casting a shadow across the hull of the sinking ship. She watched as the storm raged on perpetually, in the image that haunted her mind for the last few days.

For years, the painting hung on her wall without connection, without causing any emotional disturbance. Until Andrew returned her to herself, until he helped her realize that for years, she hid behind pain that held her in bondage. Thanks to Andrew, she was now free from that pain. She knew who she was and where she was going. She turned from the painting and left the room, following the voices that were now passing through the kitchen.

"Caroline, are you coming?" I'd like you to see the look on Peter's face when I open this door". He joked.

Caroline walked around the corner. "I'm right here. And stop teasing me. And don't mislead this poor man. You're not leading him to a gold mine you know".

"Let him be the judge of that. "Andrew opened the door and stepped into the room first. Peter followed immediately his mouth dropped open as Andrew turned on the light.

"Oh, my God Caroline, why are these paintings hiding in the dark"? He walked to the center of the room and stared at the wall where hung, many paintings. He looked back at Caroline waiting for an answer.

She shrugged her shoulders not knowing how to reply. "I don't know. I didn't have any place to put them. The room was vacant, so here they are".

"That's not what I mean. Why aren't these on exhibit somewhere"? He walked toward the wall to get a better look. He stopped in front of the portrait that the day before, Andrew admired. "Who are these two beautiful ladies? There is clearly a connection between the two. They cling to each other so lovingly. Is the older woman dying"? He looked back at Caroline, waiting for an answer.

Caroline walked from the door to where Peter stood. "Well, I suppose, in a way yes. We all will die eventually". She gazed at the picture, studying the young woman's smile, the curve of her face, the sparkle in her eye, the strength in her body. She then shifted her glance to the elderly woman whose eyes searched the face of the young lady at her side. Caroline followed every crease in her skin and the frailness of her body. She focused on her gaze, knowing she searched for the youth that was lost to years of struggle and pain. She knew their story.

"Can you tell me about that piece, Caroline? It's beautiful. The eyes remind me of yours". Peter waited for Caroline to answer.

"You're quite perceptive Peter. It is me".

Peter looked confused. "Which one is you"?

Caroline stared at the image, knowing its secret. "They're both me; me in my youth, looking forward to the experience of life. And the excitement that comes with age and knowledge". She paused as though she remembered a time before living those experiences. "And me in my old age, looking back at my innocence, my youth while mourning that which was lost through pain and suffering and missed opportunities".

Andrew crossed the room and placed a hand on Caroline's waist. "Oh my God Caroline that's beautiful. I didn't know that. Why didn't you share that with me earlier"?

Caroline looked up at Andrew and smiled. "You didn't ask".

The three stood in silence waiting for someone to speak. Peter turned to Caroline and shook his head. "Amazing. I love that painting, the idea of you assessing your existence globally through an image so touching. To look at yourself objectively through the eyes of time and space and conclude that many of us never realize". He paused to contemplate his final word. "Love".

"Caroline, I'd like to spend some time in here, do you mind? I want to study your work. Look at the world through your eyes. You have a unique way of seeing things, and a very real way of portraying it on canvas. I'd like to take my time, really digest what I see here. Do you mind"?

"No, of course not. Take your time. I'm sure we can find something to occupy ourselves with while you...". Caroline paused to think of the words. "While you do what you do".

"There is no need to keep you in suspense of my opinion of your work. "From what I see, your work should be on exhibit somewhere. The public should be able to enjoy your perspective of life. I think the only problem will be deciding which ones to exhibit first".

Andrew looked at Caroline who stood, speechless. She looked up at him and smiled, then she looked around the room, at the art she created. For the first time she really looked at what she accomplished. She finally was able to value herself through her work. Her ideas, her joy, her pain, her love, all portrayed in oil and it was good enough. It was more than good enough. It was worthy of exhibit.

Andrew stood next to Caroline while Peter sang her praises. Andrew knew he was right and was proud of Caroline's accomplishments. He turned his focus from Caroline to Peter, to the paintings displayed on the wall, then back to Caroline. He then leaned closer to her. "Caroline, how do you feel"? He whispered.

'I think I'm in shock. I don't know how much more excitement I can take today. I never thought anyone would be standing here telling me my hobby was worthy of exhibit." She smiled up at Andrew as she wondered what she did to deserve this shift in her life.

Andrew leaned closer and spoke. "You're worthy of much, much more. Why don't we leave Peter to his work and find something to occupy ourselves with until he's finished here"? He then gently kissed her as he whispered. "I think we're almost home".

The two left the room arm in arm, leaving Peter to explore Caroline's world. Hoping he would be able to find the right paintings to exhibit. They knew today was only the beginning for Caroline, but they had no idea where this beginning would take her. Caroline hoped it would be to new and exciting places to meet wonderful people. While Andrew hoped the opportunity would be to her advantage, and there would be no pain involved in the new adventure. For the time being, they would enjoy imagining the possibilities while becoming reacquainted with whom each of them had become.

SEVENTEEN

Peter watched as Caroline and Andrew left the room. He waited for them to close the door then stepped forward once again to study the image of the ladies, which spoke to his heart. He couldn't believe such a painting existed, that Caroline created such a perspective of life, in a compact scene. He looked again at the eyes as he smiled while thinking, *the windows of the soul.* And those eyes captured her likeness in a way that captivated him.

He decided to title the image *Lady of Love,* before moving on.

He moved in the direction of the door so he could begin his journey from that point to be sure he wouldn't miss a single painting. Peter stopped to look at the fox in the den with her babies and moved on quickly, impressed by the detail of the animal. Before moving on, he noted the auburn eyes of the mother fox. It was as though they were looking through him. A chill went down his spine as he moved on.

He passed nature scenes that both warmed and chilled his senses. He was impressed with the detail she put into each piece. At that time, he thought he might like to exhibit Caroline's work in stages, maybe a show with nature scene only. He would think more about it as he had a chance to see more of her work.

He passed by a field of deer, that portrayed a place of great peace. As he looked at the painting, he swore he could hear crickets chirping. It was almost as though he saw the grass swaying in the breeze. He smiled as he moved on.

He passed by the *Lady of Love* and stopped in front of a bird suspended in flight. The painting caught him off guard. He was about to duck, thinking the bird would fly over his head. He chuckled as he stood straight, admiring how the colors blended, together to create a beautiful creature. Another very real portrayal.

Peter continued to walk around the room, moving from one painting to another. He often returned to a painting to revisit the senses it revealed in him. He'd stand immersed in the piece, wondering how she was able to draw from a stranger, the feelings that would be present in real life. Peter felt a connection to her through her work.

Each time he walked across the room he saw something in a painting he hadn't seen the first time. He stopped in front of a child playing in the sand, the sun reflecting of his golden hair. His dog lying on the grass watching and waiting. The dog looked upon the child with what appeared to be love in its eyes. It was obvious the child was the dog's best friend. One could tell by the intent look on the animal's face.

It was getting more difficult for Peter to remove himself from the painting in which he stood before. He was becoming more apart of each piece as he continued through the room.

Next, he stopped in front of an image of a great oak tree. The roots embedded in the soil while the branches stretched out toward the sky, reaching for the heavens. The leaves hung from branches that rustled in the wind, with an occasional escapee, falling to the ground. He was impressed with the majesty of the presentation, a proud, old oak tree, standing tall through the ages. He could feel its life force.

Peter backed away from the painting to get a better sense of its existence, when he backed into the doorknob of what he believed to be a closet. When the door opened, he turned to pull it closed.

180

When he reached out to the doorknob, he glanced in the room, to find it wasn't a closet, at all.

His jaw dropped when he saw the treasure before him, another wall of artwork. He was puzzled though, at this room, closed off from the rest of the space. It was absent of furnishings and had a faint musty odor. It was clear the room was unkept, by the cobwebs that hung from the corners of the room, and those suspended across the art that hung on the wall.

Peter carefully stepped into the room, not only afraid to disturb the dust, but also fearful that someone would find him there in a place that was so intentionally closed off. He looked around in amazement, wondering why. The work was beautiful. He was beginning to doubt that Caroline was a novice, who painted only as a hobby.

The room, he guessed was ten feet long and probably as wide. A small window covered by a dusty blind kept the bright light of the sun at bay but allowed in enough light for him to see the beauty that hung in front of him.

What he saw was from another time, another place, far removed from the present day. At first, he thought there was a theme associated with the artwork, but further investigation revealed paintings portraying different time periods in history. He noticed first a painting like the ship that hung in the house, not only a ship, but a harbor scene. It was a panoramic image of a busy port. People hustling about, dust flying as a horse drawn carriage passed. Smiling faces as people waved from the deck of a small ship, merchants selling their wares to people in need or want. He guessed the scene painted to be a period sometime during the 1700s. It must have been a happy time because the painting was bright and cheery.

Peter's eyes traveled to his left to study the next painting. One he guessed to be painted around the same time. This scene, however, was perplexing. The space was dark and dirty and packed with people who looked hungry and sick. He was witnessing some struggle for life, while others mourned the loss of a child, husband, or parent. He focused on a woman who lamented a child who, by appearances, died in his mother's arms. Tears streamed down her dirty face as she looked around for someone to help her or at least validate her pain.

His eyes wandered from the crying woman to a lifeless man propped up on the hull of the boat. He sat with his legs out straight, his head hanging, his body leaning. He would have fallen over were it not for the body next to him. He too was dirty and covered with lice. Peter looked back at the mourning mother, then scanned the painting. They were all covered with boils, lice, or both, with greasy hair clinging to sweaty heads. What a disturbing image, his stomach turned as he stepped back from the wall. He moved on to the next piece while feeling sad and depressed.

The next picture was brilliant but was as sad as the last. Peter thought as he stopped in front of an image that continued the theme of death in the prior picture. He saw an image of a hand coming up out of the dark water, eerie, as if it were crying out for help. The hand was that of a young woman. The hand stretched out from the water. He could almost hear the person screaming out in pain as the black waves forced the person further, deeper, into the abyss that would become her final resting place.

 Peter reached up to wipe away a tear that escaped down his face. He was surprised at the emotion the paintings were stirring in him. He took a deep breath as he moved on.

He continued exploring what he decided was a goldmine of oil paintings. He studied images that moved him into the nineteenth century and early twentieth century. He stopped in front of an image of a man working in a field cutting wheat as the hot sun beating down on his shoulder wet with perspiration. His hair was wet and clung to his head. He looked intently at the man's face, noting the lines around the eyes and mouth. His skin had a leathery texture from working in the sun. The muscles in the man's arms were defined. Peter followed the length of his arm to where his hands held to the scythe, as he moved back and forth cutting the wheat. In the distance Peter could see the uncut wheat waving in the hot summer breeze.

Peter moved on, viewing other scenes like the farm scene. A woman working in a garden, children running around a cabin, and a woman cradling a baby, as she looked at it lovingly.

When he reached the end of the room, He turned to the wall adjacent to the paintings he had been studying, to find a lonely painting on the wall in front of him. It was the only painting on the wall, and he suspected it was because it held a special place in the heart of the creator.

What he saw was a young woman embracing a man who looked down at her lovingly. The two were clearly in love. They gazed into each other's eyes noticing no one else. They could have been the only ones in the room. They floated across the floor, she in a wide hooped skirt, he in his waistcoat and breeches.

Peter studied the painting sensing there was something familiar about it, yet he couldn't picture what that was. He gazed upon the couple dancing, as they came to life in the painting, swaying to the music that was playing silently in his head. Clearly a picture of a couple in love. He wondered why it hung alone on this wall.

He turned from the picture as something on the opposite far wall caught his attention. It was an eerie picture he couldn't take his eyes from. He approached it, almost in shock as he looked, into a sea of darkness, water, whose current held a secret. As he got closer, he could see the silhouette of two images floating in the darkness. He moved closer and the silhouettes became clearer. They were two bodies hidden in the darkness. Erie, it's all he could think of was death as he focused on the images revealing themselves in the darkness. The young woman's hair had escaped its restraints, her loose skirts weighed her down, pulling her into the abyss. Her hands reached out through the darkness to a man who fell not far from her in waistcoat floating in the darkness his hair flowing with the current that carried them to their death. The man reached out to the woman who reached out to him. They were sinking yet suspended in an eternity of death.

He couldn't help but stare at the image even as he felt the disturbing presence. It was like a dance with death, beautiful yet sad. When he was finally able to take his eyes from the image, he realized there were tears falling down his cheek for the second time in only minutes. He lifted his hand to wipe away the tears. He thought if the paintings brought so much emotion from him, one who rarely was moved by anything, he couldn't imagine what the art would bring up for others.

He turned, looking around the room one more time, taking in the remaining oils that hung in the darkness, all of which had their own meaning. He glanced back at them as he turned and walked to the door where he stood scanning the room one last time before he stepped back and closed the door.

EIGHTEEN

Peter opened the door to the deck to find Andrew and Caroline reclining in the sun, laughing. He recognized the twinge of jealousy as he realized that through Caroline's work, he felt an attachment to her. He felt that he knew her from seeing her work.

"I'm somewhat perplexed and wonder if you might explain to me why you only made some of your work available today"? Peter shrugged of the jealous feeling. He knew it would be temporary. It usually was.

Caroline looked up at Peter, confused. "I'm sorry, I don't understand".

"I backed up into what I thought was a closet door while studying the painting of the Oak tree. Which by the way was beautiful, how do you do it"? He then shook his head to dismiss the second question. "

I went to close the door when I realized there were more paintings in that room. I hope you weren't keeping those hidden for a reason. Because I must show those pieces. They are...well, they take the breath away".

Andrew looked at Caroline suspiciously. "What is he talking about, Caroline"?

Caroline shyly looked at Andrew. "I guess I forgot they were there. It wasn't intentional. I haven't been in that room in years. It must be full of cobwebs by now. I'm embarrassed that you would see the space like that."

Peter looked intently at Caroline, so much so that she became uncomfortable. Andrew watched as Peter studied Caroline and knew right away that Peter was interested in her for more than the art she created. Andrew became jealous, which surprised him. And he interrupted the conversation.

"Peter, I'm sure it wasn't intentional. The idea of having someone look at her work came on suddenly, and when I saw you yesterday, it made sense to get you over here while you were still here".

"I really did forget about them. I haven't been in that room in years". She chuckled. "I'm sure you can tell that by the dust that probably covers everything".

"I'm not accusing you of anything Caroline". He was looking intently at her again. "I was surprised to find such expression hidden. There was a moment that I thought that maybe you had professional training or education. Maybe you weren't being truthful with me about painting being a hobby".

"No. Truly, I've never had any training". She stopped to think. "Do you really think they are that good"? Her face lit up at the prospect.

Peter smiled at Caroline's expression. "Yes. I think your work is wonderful". He stopped to decide whether to share with them how her work affected him. "I have to tell you that I was surprised to realize the emotion I felt after studying some of those paintings".

Andrew became more curious but remained silent until Peter finished talking. He was proud of Caroline. He wasn't surprised that Peter found her work intriguing. He watched Peter with concern though. He couldn't help but think that Peter was interested in more than her talent as a painter. He set aside his suspicion for the time being so he could focus on Caroline and her reaction to Peter's opinion.

Peter walked to the table and sat down across from Caroline. He sat back in the chair and studied her. "What goes on in that mind of yours? When I study your work, I become lost in it. It's as if I'm being drawn into the scene. I'm not saying as a player, but as though I'm taking on a role of one who you've painted into the scene. It's like I feel the pain, or joy," He sat up and placed his elbows on the table and leaned toward Caroline. "Or love". He paused. "That you've painted into each piece. It's almost eerie".

Andrew cleared his throat to break whatever spell Peter appeared to be under. Caroline looked at Andrew questioning him with her eyes. "I feel the same way, Peter. That's why I knew someone needed to see her work". He looked to Caroline and smiled. "She's a natural".

Caroline gazed back at Andrew, blushing as he paid compliment to her again. She then looked across the table at Peter, who she noticed was watching her. It made her uncomfortable, but she remained still, hoping it would pass.

"I'd like to know what the story is behind the ocean paintings that appear to be part of a theme".

Caroline's heart skipped a beat as she realized the paintings, he referred to were created years ago while she struggled to figure out where she fit in in the life, she had made for herself. She knew he was talking about the paintings that paid tribute to another lifetime. She quickly looked to Andrew, who knew nothing of the paintings, so he was of little help.

"Do you know which ones I'm speaking about"? He studied her face, looking for answers in eyes that were far from revealing. "I'm talking about the painting of the port, and what appears to be a death sentence for all those people in the hull of the ship you painted them into. I'm talking about the hand reaching out from the depths of despair, portrayed as a black sea. And about the silhouettes sinking, suspended in an eternity of death. Where did that come from"?

Caroline recovered quickly from her shock. She laughed lightly. "I'm not sure where they came from". She gave Andrew a quick glance, but he was no help, because he didn't know what they were talking about. "I painted them years ago. I guess, I was going through a time in my life when things weren't going well", She laughed again. "No, I wasn't having a nervous breakdown. I don't know, maybe I had a dream about the images, I don't recall".

Andrew sat up in his chair as he began to understand what they were talking about. He looked at Caroline while she brushed off the history of the paintings as a mere dream. He was even more curious than ever to get a look at the art she had hidden away in the dusty corner of the house. He would bide his time. Peter wouldn't be there forever.

"Okay, you don't want to share. I get it. We all have secrets we want to keep".

"Peter, it's no secret. There is no story associated with the paintings, that's all".

He watched as she dismissed his questions. "I understand. No problem. How about the couple in love"? He sat back in his chair again to observe her reaction.

Andrew watched the interaction between Caroline and Peter with some discomfort. He knew Peter was playing a game that he thought he would win. But he wasn't sure if Caroline would give in to him. He hoped she wouldn't.

"I'm assuming you're referring to the Waltz". Her eyes lit up as she looked from Andrew to Peter. "That painting has a story".

Andrew looked on curious about the painting that brought such animation to Caroline's face. He focused on her as she told the story.

"Many years ago, I met a young man. I hadn't been out of school long when I met him. Obviously, we were still young and innocent". She looked at Andrew and smiled. "It was the summer after graduation, and I was still unsure of what my future held. I often would walk out to the docks and watch the boats coming and going, wishing I could be on one of them.

Woods

I wanted so desperately to get away but being young and not knowing what I wanted to be when I grew up, I struggled to stay home". She looked to Andrew again before continuing. "Then one day this young man backed into me on the dock where I was daydreaming. He almost knocked me in the water. But thankfully he had quick reflexes and grabbed me before I went over the edge. When he put his arms around me, I thought I had died and gone to heaven. He looked into my eyes and that was that.

We spent the summer together, making plans, for the future, our future. We were going to float across the water and live happily ever after".

Andrew listened to Caroline's story sensing something familiar about the tale. It wasn't until she mentioned floating across the water, that he realized what she was saying. He smiled to himself as she finished the story.

Peter was intrigued by that time. "What happened"?

The smile left Caroline's face as she finished the story. "Life. He died, and I died inside. Death of the worst kind. Anyway, somehow I found my way back to life". She looked at Andrew and smiled. "And I painted the picture".

"Why the period clothing"? Peter looked confused.

"I don't know. I guess I'm a romantic at heart. Sometime when I think of romance, I picture that time in history as chivalric. Chivalry might be dead, but when you paint you can bring anything to life".

Peter nodded. "When I look at your work, I believe that".

"That's all there is to tell". Andrew thought Caroline seemed proud of herself and her ability to spin a story. He knew the truth, and while the story was true, she omitted a few details, he thought, to protect the innocent.

"Well, I guess I have to be satisfied with that". Peter said. "So, I guess now would be the time to discuss organizing an exhibit".

Caroline's eyes lit up as she looked to Andrew, then Peter. "You're serious? You're not kidding around, right?"

Peter laughed. "No, Caroline. I'm not kidding. Your work is exceptional. I took pictures". He held up his phone. "So, I could start planning. When I return to New York, I'll review my schedule and

189

determine what date would work best. I could schedule based on my calendar, but I don't like to do that. Sometimes my assistant double books my time. It's easier to verify the schedule then it is to move things around later. I definitely want to exhibit Lady Love. I knew that as soon as I saw it. And I'd like the Shipwreck too. I'd like to show all of them, but one show at a time. Well chose a few pieces for this one and save some jewels for the next one".

"The next one"? Caroline looked surprised.

"Yes, the next one. Once people visit the first exhibit, they will be screaming for more. You should be prepared to sell them too".

Caroline's eyes grew large as she realized that she would be parting with paintings she put her heart and soul in to. She wasn't sure she was ready for that. She glanced over at Andrew, knowing he read her mind. "Caroline, it's all part of growing up".

"I know, Andrew. I need some time to get used to it, though".

Peter shifted his weight in the chair, crossing one leg over another. "Well, I don't know what you're talking about, but you don't have much time to get used to anything. These things happen quicker than you think it will. I'm hoping to make this exhibit happen sooner than later".

Peter smiled and nodded at Caroline. "I want you in New York right away".

Andrew's radar went up immediately. He looked in Peter's direction, watching his demeanor change. Andrew became increasingly uncomfortable as the silence grew and wondered if he misjudged him. Caroline didn't have time to respond, before Andrew spoke up.

"So, Peter". Andrew broke the uncomfortable silence. "What's the plan, moving forward? We should take some time today to go over the process involved in putting together an exhibit. Caroline doesn't want any surprises. This being her first exhibit, we want to make sure everything goes smoothly".

Peter nodded as he looked across the table at Caroline. Caroline squinted. The sun rose in the sky indicating the morning would soon pass. It was getting too warm to sit at the table in the hot sun. Caroline stood and reached up to open the umbrella, to busy herself as she shrugged of the uncomfortable feeling.

"Yes". Peter gazed across the table at Caroline. "There is a lot to consider as we prepare for the show. I will take care of most of the work, of course, but before I move forward with the exhibit, I need to know Caroline, how serious are you about your work. Earlier you said painting was a hobby. If I'm going to invest in the time and effort to get you into the gallery, I need to know if you are serious".

Caroline looked to Andrew who sat smiling back at her, before responding to Peter's question. "Well, I have to be honest with you. I never considered the possibility of anyone seeing my paintings, let alone having them on display in a gallery. But now that you've seen my work, and think it's good enough, I feel encouraged. The more time I think about it, the more excited I feel about moving forward with the exhibit".

"I understand that, but what are your long-term goals regarding your work. If offered, would you want to exhibit again"? Peter asked.

"Well, I'd like to spend more time on my craft. I suppose as I have more time available, I'll be able to produce more art".

Andrew chimed in. "Well, Caroline, you have one clear advantage going into the exhibit. You have many paintings, so you will have time to create more great paintings while your other work is shown". Andrew studied Peter while he spoke about Caroline's work. Then testing him. "Caroline will need to spend more time here in order to create, I would imagine".

Caroline listened to Andrew, wondering why he thought it necessary to remind Peter of such a necessity. "Of course, I will. I'm sure it won't be necessary to stay in the city for long. I'd like to go so I can see what's involved in the process".

Peter shifted in his seat. "Well, you will need to be in New York for a while. There will be people to meet. You're entering an entirely new world, Caroline. It may take some getting used to". He reached across the table and placed his hand over Caroline's as he finished. "You don't need to worry though I'll be there to help you through the process".

Remember The Kiss

Caroline smiled at Peter as she withdrew her hand and placed it in her lap. She then looked to Andrew, a curious look on her face.

Andrew quickly changed the direction of the conversation. Bringing more focus on preparing for and understanding the process that was involved in a successful exhibit. They spent the remainder of the morning and part of the afternoon discussing what Caroline should expect.

They sat at the table as a light breeze blew across the back yard, discussing certain paintings and what they meant to Caroline. They talked about the experience that brought her to paint. The noon hour approached as they discussed the history that might be associated with each piece. Peter told her she would need to be prepared for interviews by ruthless journalists, so she would need to have her stories straight before being put on the spot.

Caroline wasn't sure she was ready for interviews and quickly changed the subject. "I don't know where my manners are, would you like something cold to drink? Maybe I should prepare lunch, it is after noon". She stood and stepped back from the table.

Peter followed her example. "No, thank you, Caroline. I think I've stayed long enough. I have a plane to catch this afternoon and there are a few things I need to finish before I leave. Thank you for allowing me to see your work. I'm impressed and am looking forward to working with you".

Andrew stood up as Peter reached across the table and shook Caroline's hand. He then offered Peter his as he said good-bye. "Thank you, Peter, for coming out. I knew her work was good". He turned his attention to Caroline. "I told you Caroline, you would be a success".

"Well, don't go patting yourself on the back. I haven't had a successful exhibit yet". Caroline glanced at Andrew.

"Okay, then. I will be going. Caroline, I will let you know when we will be ready to move your work. Then shortly after that we can arrange for you to join me in New York". He took her hand in his. "We will have a wonderful time".

Andrew studied Peter as he made his final plea to Caroline. "I can't wait to show you around". He released her hand and nodded in Andrew's direction. "Thank you, Andrew, for introducing me to this beauty. She certainly is a goldmine".

Caroline and Andrew stood together watching as Peter stepped up on the deck and went through the house.

When he closed the door, Caroline turned to Andrew. "Andrew, I don't know about this. He's a little too friendly for my liking".

"Well, I think you'll have to remain on guard when he's around. I don't think I trust him. I'm almost sorry I asked him to review your work".

"It's okay Andrew. I can take care of myself. He can't be that bad".

"I hope you're right". He smiled as he put an arm around her waist. "Now let's go take a look at the secret paintings. I'm dying to see them".

NINETEEN

Caroline stood in front of Andrew as she slowly opened the door to the room she hadn't visited in many years. They stood together in the doorway as their eyes adjusted to the dimly lit room. The afternoon sun creeped in through the dusty blinds to illuminate the particles of dust suspended in air and reflected off cobwebs that looked like spun silk in the shadows of the room.

Andrew looked around, noting the dust and cobwebs. "You weren't kidding when you said you hadn't been in here in years. It truly is a mess". He teased.

"I know Andrew. I don't know why I never come in here. It's almost as if I wanted to eliminate the images from my mind, forget a time that I didn't remember living".

"I could accept that reason if that ship wasn't hanging above the bed in your spare room". Andrew noted.

Woods

"I don't have a reason, then". Caroline stopped in the center of the room and looked along the wall. She glanced at the paintings as a stranger initially, until she stepped closer to the wall. She reached up her left hand and placed it on the canvas of the harbor scene disturbing dust that had been still for years. She smiled in wonderment at the painting, then looked up at Andrew. "My dream, I remember this from my dream".

Andrew moved next to Caroline and placed a hand at her waist. "Yes, Caroline. Your dream. Your life, my life, our life from another time. I can't believe how you captured it. Your subconscious is amazing. I never could have imagined something so detailed". He leaned forward and kissed her on the forehead. "I wonder how true a likeness it is".

Caroline studied the painting closely. She followed the people who walked along the dock, with her hand, tracing a path in the dust as she imagined walking, just, there. She turned back to Andrew. "Do you remember any of this? I look at this painting now and wonder which one came first. Did I dream the dream or paint the picture first? Which one prompted the other? Was any of it real? I stand here now talking to you and wonder if I'm crazy".

"Caroline, you're not crazy. For some reason you are now able to remember another lifetime, one you lived, even if it was briefly".

"Well, I'm beginning to think none of it was real". Caroline returned her attention to the harbor. "Maybe I'm confusing dream with reality".

Andrew placed a hand on Caroline's shoulder. "Caroline. Don't torture yourself. I know what you're experiencing. You'll feel confused for a while. But it will pass".

"What if it doesn't? What if I dreamed you up? Maybe I'll wake up and none of this will be real". Caroline moved her focus to the image next to the harbor. She felt disturbed by the painting that portrayed the death that seemed so real to her. A chill went down her spine as the words rang in her ears. *I don't know how much more of this I can take.* Then she thought of the pregnant woman who centuries ago, was pushed to her death.

She quickly moved on to see the piece that was the woman's hand reaching out from the black water, with waves foaming as they rocked and swayed. An eerie feeling passed through Caroline as she studied the hand that reached out for a lifeline.

Andrew sensed her discomfort but felt helpless in his effort to console her. He looked around the room at the other paintings until his eyes settled on the painting, that earlier, Peter had praised. He stopped where he stood and stared. What he saw filled his heart with an unmentionable pain, then love, then sadness. He approached the piece and looked at it closer. The young woman, whose eyes twinkled as she smiled up at the man who held her, as they glided across the floor. The dress was a pale blue, with white lace hanging from the sleeves. Her partner in his trousers and dark waist coat, looked deep into her eyes as he smiled, Andrew imagined the man smiled at his good fortune to be holding such a woman in his arms.

He returned his attention to the young lady's eyes. Brown eyes that he would have drowned in had he been the man dancing across the floor. He stared at the eyes in the painting until it dawned on him, that he knew those eyes. He turned to Caroline, who stood watching him, and spoke. "The eyes, that must be what Peter thought was familiar in the painting". He looked at Caroline intently. "Those are your eyes".

Caroline approached Andrew and stood next to him as he turned to face the painting. "Yes, they are. And I believe the young man she dances with is you. You know, I didn't make up the story I told Peter about this painting. I used to dream about it often. I don't know when the dream stopped, but it was many years ago. I'm afraid this is another of those situations when I can't find the line, between dream and reality".

Andrew still faced the artwork that pulled at his heart strings. "I believe you. When I look at the two of them dancing, I feel happy, then sadness and loss. I wonder if it's because of a real connection". He looked down at Caroline in search of an answer. But a painting across the room caught his attention.

He felt as though his heart dropped to his feet when he saw it. He slowly walked across the room to, where hung, on the opposite wall, the lovers, another dance. He stood stunned to find a sea of darkness that flowed or moved to its own rhythm. His breath was caught in his throat, he couldn't move. Embedded within the water was a young woman with hair, free flowing as it moved with the current. Her heavy wet skirt pulled her down into a deep darkness that Andrew couldn't imagine. He watched as she reached out, his eyes following the path of her longing, where he saw him, a young man falling deeper, as his hand searched for hers. It's all he could think was this is a dance with death.

He turned around to find Caroline still standing on the other side of the room watching him. Wondering what he was thinking. He looked at her, stunned. "Caroline, is this what I think it is"?

Caroline nodded as she walked to him. "Yes, the shipwreck. I know I went down, sinking to an abyss of darkness, and I believed you did too. I couldn't imagine anything different. It seemed fitting to place the paintings opposite each other. One a dance of life, a new life, just beginning. Our lives in front of us, where we hoped to make all our dreams come true. And the second, a dance with death, where we swayed with the current, going with the flow as we fell deeper into the dark water until we met death together, yet separately".

She looked at the painting somehow soothed, to know they were together in the end. "It's a terrible thing to die like that, but at least they, or we, died together".

Andrew couldn't take his eyes off Caroline. Her face was serine, accepting of a fate that tore apart two people in love. He thought it strange that one could die such a death, and still find peace in remembering it but now he thought it was time to let go of that pain, that memory. It was time to make new memories. They were given another gift, another chance to get it right.

Caroline was the first to speak. "I think we've been in here long enough. At some point I'll have to come in here and clean this room. I'll need to take down the paintings Peter wants to put in the exhibit, but I can do that later".

"Do you want me to help you, Caroline"? Andrew was concerned.

"No, Andrew. This is something I must do myself. Plus, you can't stay here forever.

Andrew nodded as they walked out of the small room. "I know. I hated think about it. The weekend went too fast".

Caroline tried not to think about Andrew's leaving. She closed the door and the two of them walked through the room where hung, the remaining paintings. Andrew stopped to take another look. "Caroline, I can't believe you have kept this talent hidden for all these years. I'm glad you're going to take a chance. I think it will be good for you".

He paused to think a moment. "I think you should be careful, though. Watch out for Peter. I know he wants to show your work, but while we were outside talking, I couldn't help feeling he had an ulterior motive. He is much too anxious to get you to New York. Just be careful when you get out there"

"I think you have a wonderful imagination, Andrew. I'm sure he only wants my work. But I'll be careful".

"I'm not as confident as you are. However, I'll give him the benefit of the doubt for now". He turned to Caroline and placed his hands on her shoulders as he looked into her eyes. "I mean it Caroline. Don't be blindsided by him while you're in New York. Don't let him dazzle you with the excitement of the city. That kind of excitement doesn't last".

"Andrew, I have no intention of letting anyone dazzling me. I am my own person. I am excited about the prospect of new experiences, but I'm not sixteen years old. I am a responsible adult. I can take care of myself". She paused to think. "Plus, what would he want with me. I'm sure he's used to more sophisticated women than me".

"Yes Caroline, but some men are challenged by the pursuit with no intention of committing to anything beyond a little fun. I know you can take care of yourself. I'm only asking you to be on your guard with him". He lifted a hand to her chin. Then took her hand in his. "He's a nice guy. I've never had reason not to like him. But today I believe I saw a different side of Peter and I feel it necessary to tell you to pay attention. If I'm being honest, I have to say that I'm concerned because I don't want him to do anything that could interfere with our solidifying a relationship". He paused to choose his words carefully. "Caroline, I know you're still on the fence about this whole 'other life' thing. And I understand when you say you're not ready for a relationship. I only want to make sure that when you're ready, that you chose me. I want to be the one that spends what remains of this life with you".

"Andrew, I believe you're a wonderful person. And yes, you're right, I'm still not reconciled to the idea of reincarnation, but you paint a pretty picture. It would be wonderful to finally be with the man who I'm destined to spend eternity with. And to trust that person. I promise you I won't run off with another man until I consult with you first".

"Thank you. Now let me take you out for a late lunch. We can enjoy what remains of the afternoon before I have to leave".

TWENTY

Caroline sat across the table from Andrew for the last time, during the weekend visit, enjoying a light meal. They ate lunch on the pier, in the heat of the afternoon. The umbrella shaded them from the hot sun and a light breeze occasionally blew across the lake to cool the air under the umbrella. They both enjoyed the warm weather, so the heat wasn't oppressive to them.

"So, Caroline, tell me how you feel about embarking on a new life. I know you said you're excited, but how do you feel about a long-time career as an artist? Not just an artist, but one who is admired by thousands, maybe millions of people."

Caroline laughed out loud. "Andrew, I think you're exaggerating. Millions of people, really? I think you give me too much credit."

Andrew pointed his fork in her direction. "That's what you said about your painting in the beginning. Let me see, how did you put it. 'I'm not very good. It's only a hobby'. Well, I think it's time you pull your head out of the sand. When you get to New York I think you'll find many people will want to own a piece of your work. Mark my words".

"Okay, mister smarty pants. We'll see". Caroline leaned across the table. "Either way I'm who I am, no amount of exposure will change that".

Andrew smiled as he reached across the table and lifted Caroline's hair from the ketchup next to her fries on her plate. "Well, I think we may have to teach you some table etiquette". He took his napkin in his other hand and wiped the tomato sauce from the ends of her hair. "We can't have you embarrassing yourself in public".

Caroline laughed at herself as she leaned against the back of the chair. "Well, I'll try not to eat in public without you. Although I think that might be a challenge in New York. I will have to, at the very least, eat in the hotel restaurant if I don't want to starve".

Andrew wiped his hands on his napkin as he smiled. "I'm sure you'll be fine. I don't imagine you'll be eating too many burgers with fries. You will probably be eating more refined meals out there".

Caroline looked out across the lake as she considered the possibilities in front of her. She would meet new people while exposing her soul, through her art, to complete strangers. Her heart skipped a beat as she wondered if she really was good enough. She didn't think she could stand to be humiliated by thousands of people. She looked out over the water at boats moored as they rolled with the waves.

"Earth to Caroline".

Caroline smiled, as she dismissed her insecurity. "I'm sorry, what"?

Andrew leaned his elbows on the table, then picked up a fry and popped it in his mouth. "Caroline, it's going to be fine. I know you think your work is amateur, but when I look at it, I'd swear you were trained by the best. You have nothing to worry about. You need to enjoy this time. Relax and enjoy the excitement". He hesitated briefly. "I wish I could be there with you. I'd love to see the expression on your face when you realize your work is accepted by your peers".

Caroline nodded as she shifted in her chair. "Yes, I think the whole thing would be a little easier if there was someone, I knew there to support me". She studied Andrew's face, wondering if she truly knew him from another life. Yes, the kiss was familiar. When he kissed her, it felt like she was returning home.

"I'll tell you what". Andrew reached across the table and Caroline responded in kind. He took her hand in his. "I'll meet you in New York when we're done filming. I'm sure we'll be finished before the exhibit ends. Then we can explore the city together".

Caroline nodded, as she squeezed his hand. "Do you think you'll really be finished by then? I would love to have you meet me there". The excitement rose in her voice. "You can see me in my new element". She joked. "I hope I survive until then". The familiar tone returned to her voice.

"I'm pretty sure we will be finished. We only have a few scenes left to film. I won't promise, in case. But I'll do my best to be there".

"That's good enough for me, Andrew. I know you have prior commitments, and don't want you to feel obligated. I'll be fine in New York. Once I get there, and I am settled, I'll be fine. It would be great to see you though".

"Okay, we'll leave it an open-ended date. I'll do my best to be there before you return home". Andrew agreed.

They finished their lunch and then took a walk along the pier. It was a beautiful afternoon, and by the time they started out on their walk, the sun was fading west. The air cooled some-what and the breeze picked up along the water. Caroline heard the familiar sound as the waves slapped along the posts that held the pier six feet from the water.

Andrew reached out and took her hand in his, as his eyes warned her that he would not be denied the slight pleasure. She relented *this one time* she told herself as she smiled up at him. They removed from the pier and walked down to the beach where, because it was late afternoon, there remained only a few families enjoying the water. Most had retreated to their camps and hotels for dinner. Caroline was thankful for space.

They talked about the movie Andrew was finishing, as they walked in the sand. Caroline pulled on her hand and Andrew released easily waiting to see what she intended. She kneeled and removed her shoes to walk along the water's edge. The water was cool and tickled her arches as it rolled into the shore, then receded. They continued to walk hand in hand once again.

Andrew stopped to look out over the lake. "Caroline, you won't forget me will you"?

Caroline laughed lightly. "No. Of course not'. She turned to face him. "You sounded like a lost little boy, just then. Have you becomes so attached in the few days we've spent together"?

"Don't laugh at me, Caroline". Andrew turned the tables and now teased her. "I was lost, until the day I saw you standing at the rail on the boulevard, with the ridiculous smile on your face. I knew at that moment I was in for it. I don't think I knew why at the time, but now, it all makes sense".

He searched Caroline's eyes. "I wonder if you realize the importance of our meeting. I hope while you're in New York, you have time to consider the situation, and that you finally give up the ridiculous idea that you will only have peace if you remain alone. I won't push, but we belong together. The sooner you realize it, the more time we will have to enjoy each other".

Caroline stood gazing into Andrew's eyes. *His voice seems a thousand miles away*, she though as she continued to listen to his words. The more she listened to him, the more she felt, the familiarity of him, his voice, his touch, his kiss. She was confident that what he had been telling her was true, but she wasn't ready to admit it, to herself or him. "I hear you, Andrew. But I'm not sure. I mean It's true, I feel like I've known you all my life, but that doesn't mean in another lifetime. I will consider what you've said. In the meantime, let's enjoy the remainder of our visit.

The sun burned a deep orange as it receded behind the tree line, and reflected off the water, displaying deep oranges within the toughs of the waves, and erupting into a pale pink spray as they broke against the rocks along the shore. Caroline pointed to toward the trees. "It's going to be another hot day tomorrow".

"One of many more before the summer ends". Andrew agreed. The two stopped and watched until the sun disappeared. They then turned and walked back toward the pier.

"I've enjoyed the last few days. I think I've been more places and seen more things during our visit, than I have in many years. I'm glad you had the nerve to approach me". Caroline stopped at the edge of the grass and brushed the sand from her feet. She put on her shoes, and they walked across the grass to the sidewalk, where they headed for the truck.

Caroline noticed the sound of crickets as early evening approached. She knew they wouldn't be sharing dinner together. The hour of leaving was fast approaching, and she knew it would be a while before they would meet again. Caroline thought it odd that she would feel such loss when she only met him three days ago. She smiled as Andrew's words rang in her ears. *I won't push, but we belong together. The sooner you realize it, the more time we will have to enjoy each other.*

The drive back to Caroline's house was a quiet one. Andrew now, drove the route efficiently. Caroline was happy to have someone else drive. She wasn't afraid of the road, but to Caroline, driving only delayed the amount of time one had to spend enjoying life. A necessary evil, she thought.

They pulled into the driveway one last time. Caroline opened the door and stepped onto the gravel driveway. Andrew was at her side before her feet hit the ground. They silently stood next to each other listening as the creatures of the night made their evening debut. Caroline recognized the gentle hum of insects in concert, with the crickets leading the show.

A chill ran up Caroline's spine as the leaves rustled in the breeze. "It's so peaceful here at night. I enjoy listening to the sounds out there, the insects, the owl that hoots in the night, and the and the gentle sound of the mourning doves as they sing each other to sleep. It's soothing". She looked up at Andrew who hung on her every word.

He placed an arm around her shoulder. "Yes, well, it's getting late, and I'm afraid you'll be listening to them alone tonight". They moved up the walkway to the front door where they stood, each minute, the sky fading a little closer to darkness.

They stopped at the door and Andrew took the key from Caroline, which she dug out of her purse while the walked to the door. He unlocked the door and pushed it open but stood steadfast at the threshold.

He turned and took Caroline's hands in his. "I don't think I can recall a time when my heart felt so heavy". He drew her hands to his chest. "I've found my second self, the best half of my soul, and I hate to leave you".

Caroline swallowed hard as his words echoed in her mind. She fought back emotions that she didn't know still existed inside her. "I don't know what to say Andrew. This has been among the best days of my life. If I never see you again, I'll remember you with fondness and...love. You've touched my heart and you showed me that there is kindness among men".

Andrew pulled Caroline closer to himself and whispered. "Caroline, it isn't fondness that I desire from you. I'm glad I've touched your heart, but I didn't come here to touch your heart. I came here to find my soul mate, my second self. I didn't realize it at first, but soon after I saw you, I understood why our paths crossed. I might be leaving tonight, but it's not forever. I will see you in New York. And when I do, you need to be prepared to make some plans, because I want us to be together, Whatever, that looks like, however we work it out, we will be together".

"Andrew, I'll take time while in New York to work through all this and what it means to me, to us. I'm still trying to digest the idea you have about our being soul mates. Regardless of whether, or not it's true, I've developed feelings for you that I can't ignore". Caroline paused to collect herself while looking into Andrew's dark eyes. "I will miss you greatly, Andrew".

They silently stood as the sound of the night serenaded them while they gazed into each other's eyes. Andrew leaned in to meet Caroline and their lips met. They stood embracing as the evening turned to night. The breeze picked up and it began to rain.

Andrew held Caroline tight as the rain grew more intense. He knew it was time to go yet neither one of them was ready for the weekend to end. Caroline rested her head on Andrew's chest waiting for him to break away. For the next few minutes, he held her, while they listened to the rain fall.

The time had come, and Andrew drew back from the woman he knew, the woman he had known for many lifetimes. The woman he would spend eternity with. "I have to go Caroline".

Are you sure you can't come in for just a little while"?

"No Caroline. I'm afraid if I come in, I won't leave, and I'll miss my flight. A lot of people are counting on me. We will see each other in New York in a few weeks". Andrew was trying to convince both Caroline and him.

"I understand. You're right. The next few weeks will fly by". She was trying to sound convincing. "You will be busy with the movie, and I will be busy getting together paintings and preparing for an exhibit. We will be distracted with our work. Our meeting again, will come soon enough".

Andrew looked down at Caroline once again and kissed her gently on the lips. "Remember the kiss, Caroline". He whispered.

Caroline nodded as Andrew released her and stepped back. He turned to walk away and stopped at the end of the walkway. He looked back at Caroline, smiling. "I'll see you soon".

Caroline smiled through misty eyes. She waved and nodded, unable to respond. She stood in the doorway watching Andrew as he backed out of the yard and drove up the street. When she could no longer see the truck, she turned back to the door where she crossed over the threshold and closed the door.

TWENTY-ONE

Caroline walked up the concourse and through the door, arriving at La Guardia Airport with little fanfare. She walked through the crowd of people hugging, and welcoming their loved ones, while she scanned the area for a familiar face. Peter was meeting her at the gate to take her to her hotel before discussing further the exhibit that would take up the next three months of her time.

She couldn't believe that the time had come where she would be mingling with strangers who would hopefully become acquaintance, and for a select few, even friends.

It was almost a month since Andrew said goodbye to her on that warm summer night. She spent most of the past month preparing for the exhibit. The first and most difficult thing she did was prepare her Curriculum Vitae. She never liked talking about herself and found the CV task daunting. It wasn't easy to come up with a resume when she only painted as a hobby for the past thirty years. Once the resume was complete, she needed to prepare and artist statement.

There were paintings to select and to title. Caroline needed to inspect each of the thirty paintings and frame the ones that she hadn't in the past. She needed to take pictures of each painting. Then she had to pack them carefully and send them to Peter at the gallery. Once her art was packed up, she created a certificate of authenticity for each one and put them in a manila envelope to take with her to New York.

After she shipped the paintings, Caroline took time to pick out a few outfits to wear while she was in New York. It was then, that she realized how much time she spent working on the exhibit. So much so, that she barely had a moment to dedicate to wondering how Andrew was doing. When she stopped to rest, Caroline found that she missed Andrew terribly, which surprised her. How could she know someone for three days and form such and attachment? She knew how Andrew would answer that question and she smiled as she remembered his parting words. 'Remember the kiss, Caroline'.

Now, Caroline stood at LaGuardia, remembering that kiss as she tried to focus on the task at hand. She scanned the crowd looking for Peter. She had only seen him a couple of times and worried now, that she might not remember what he looked like. She wasn't as observant as she should be at times and scolded herself for not paying attention.

"Caroline". Peter waved and smiled as he walked to Caroline. "How was your flight? Do you have additional luggage, or is that all you brought"?

"Hello, Peter. It's good to see you". She lifted the carryon. "This is all I brought with me. I sent my clothes to the hotel a few days ago. I made arrangements for them to set aside the box for me so I wouldn't have to worry about lost luggage".

"Good idea, Caroline". He stopped to study her. "You look as beautiful as you did the last time, I saw you. Are you excited about the exhibit"?

Caroline ignored Peter's compliment as she replied. "I am excited and a little nervous too. I can't believe I'm going to be exhibiting paintings that I never thought were good enough to see the light of day. Sometimes I wonder if I'm dreaming and will wake to find it's all a big mistake".

"Far from it, Caroline, you're definitely not dreaming". Peter led Caroline through the airport to a limousine that waited along the curb outside the door. "Let's get you to the hotel so you can get settled in". He opened the car door, took Caroline's bag, and placed it in the trunk before walking around the car. He slid in next to her and smiled. "You can relax for a while before I take you to dinner. Then we can go over a few last-minute details before tomorrow. In the morning we'll go to the gallery, and I'll show you the exhibit. You'll see your work as it will be displayed before the exhibit opens and I'll introduce you to a few key people, people that could be important in furthering your career as an artist".

"Sounds like you have everything under control". Caroline looked out the window and watched as they left the airport. She looked around as she tried to get her bearings.

"The hotel is only a block from the gallery. I wish you would have let me make hotel arrangements for you. You could have stayed at one of the best hotels in New York. You're certainly close to the Gallery, maybe two or three minutes and we're in a safe neighborhood so there is that". He leaned closer to Caroline which made her uneasy. "It will be convenient to be so close to your room. You never know when it might come in handy". He placed a hand on the seat between Caroline and him, close enough that he touched Caroline's thigh.

She slid to the right enough to put space between them. Caroline remembered what Andrew said about Peter. She hoped he had been wrong, but now feared she would have to keep up her guard throughout the trip. "I appreciate you're offer, but I like the idea of being close to the gallery. Plus, I prefer to take care of myself. I can't wait to see the exhibit". She tried to clear the air by changing the subject. "How many artists have work at the gallery this season?"

Peter smiled as he replied. "The Gallery covers about five thousand square feet. We have anywhere between fifty and seventy-five artists showing a season. It's pretty impressive".

"I'm sure it is"'. Caroline agreed. "I'm thankful that my work will be among them".

"Yes, and if you play your cards right, your art will remain part of the exhibit for as long as you wish". Peter watched Caroline, waiting to see how she responded.

She wasn't sure how to take Peter's comment but was sure there was a sacrifice somewhere there in what he said. She chose not to take the bait and played a hand of her own. "As with anything, before I commit to an agreement, I must see how the trial period pans out, before solidifying any arrangement".

"I see". Peter digested Caroline's words, deciding to take things slow. 'Well, let's get you to your room so you can relax". The car stopped in front of the hotel and Peter signaled to the driver, that he might remain in the car. He then got out, hurried around the back of the car, and opened Caroline's door.

He reached out and offered his hand to Caroline, which she took cautious of its meaning. She exited the car and followed Peter to the back of the car where he removed her carryon from the trunk. He placed it on the ground and pulled up the handle and handed it to Caroline. "You have plenty of time to relax before dinner. I made reservations for dinner at seven o'clock. I'll pick you up around six-thirty"

Caroline nodded as she took the bag from Peter. "Thank you, Peter. I'm grateful for your help. I'll see you at six-thirty".

"Caroline".

"Yes, Peter".

"Welcome to New York".

"Thank you, Peter. I look forward to the adventure".

Peter nodded and smiled. "As you should".

A chill went down Caroline's spine as Peter's words settled in her mind. She smiled and walked through the door, happy to have some distance between her and Peter. She went to the front desk and collected the key to her room. The concierge advised her that the luggage she sent ahead was in her room. She thanked him and walked to the elevator and finally to her room where she was happy to find a temporary escape from Peter. She went to the bed and sat down at the foot before stretching out to relax as she thought, *this trip is going to be more of a challenge than I thought.*

Caroline stared above the bed, following a small crack from the light hanging from the ceiling above her, until it disappeared. She wondered how a hotel on the scale as this one would allow for such a flaw.

She stayed still a moment longer before rising from the bed. Then she walked to the window and looked down on the activity ten stories below. Taxi's stopping and going, people crossing traffic, and entering and exiting buildings, going about their afternoon business. Caroline wondered about the lives of those that hustled along the street. What were their struggles, who did they love, were they happy? She smiled to herself, knowing the questions weren't easy ones to answer for anyone.

The smile disappeared from her face as she turned back to the room, where she focused on her struggles. Finally set free from her internal demons, Caroline was moving in a direction of positivity and growth. Then there was Peter. She couldn't help but remember, the law of relativity; for every action is a reaction. The action she took to move forward and test her talent, had caused a reaction that she was sure would test her in ways she hoped she could avoid.

The tug of war between the joy of knowing her talents would be celebrated, and the damper that Peter could cause, were only a few thoughts that went through her mind as she unpacked her bag and went to the bathroom to freshen up. Peter would be returning shortly, and she didn't want to keep him waiting. She would clean up, change, and sit reading while she waited. There would be no surprises tonight.

Caroline sat flipping through a magazine when the phone rang. "Hello? Thank you I'll be right down".

She placed the book on the chair and remembered to take the light sweater she brought in case the evening grew cool. She closed the door and headed for the elevator, making the short ride to the main floor, where Peter waited, smiling as though he hid a deep secret.

"Hello Peter. I hope I dressed properly for dinner".

He looked at her, his eyes moving from head to toe. "You look perfect. The good thing about New York is no matter what you wear, your dressed for the occasion". He took Caroline's arm and placed it in the crook of his elbow. Now, it's time to dine".

They walked out the main entrance into the still warm evening air. "I thought we would try Armani Ristorante tonight. They have a wonderful Agnello, lamb with sweetbread stuffed artichokes. I thought you might try the Polpo, it's quite good. It's been a while since I've been there'. He looked over at Caroline before continuing. "A good meal is always better when the company is pleasant".

Caroline ignored Peter's advances. "I can't say I've ever been to Armani. But it will be good to try something new. I'm not fond of octopus, so I think I'll pass on the Polpo. Maybe you can tell me a bit more about what I should expect when the exhibit opens. The whole idea of showcasing my art still seems foreign to me. I'm not sure how well received it will be".

They continued the conversation once they arrived and were seated. Peter tried to get Caroline to think about something other than the exhibit. Caroline wanted to learn all she could about the art world. She didn't want to be ignorant of what went on around her as she became familiar with her new role. Peter on the other hand had other ideas of which Caroline had no interest. She was quickly learning that Peter was more interested in her than in her work.

They scanned the menu and Caroline settled on the Spinaci Novelli to start. And for the main course, the Ippoglosso; buttered poached halibut fillet with fermented broccoli and clam foam. She would be brave tonight with the food at least. Peter settled on the Agnello he spoke of when they arrived. Then ordered a bottle of wine and sat back to look across the table at Caroline.

The sever brought the wine to the table and poured it for them, leaving the bottle at table side then took their order.

Woods

The discussion continued until their meal was placed in front of them. Caroline studied her meal briefly, before sampling her halibut. Peter leaned over his plate and dug in as though it would be his last meal. "Caroline. Why don't you relax tonight? Enjoy your meal, have a couple of drinks, forget about the exhibit. Tomorrow will come soon enough. Let's make this night one to remember". Peter smiled and reached across the table to place a hand on Caroline's arm. "We are becoming acquainted tonight. I want to know more about you, what are your likes and dislikes, your dreams and aspirations, and what you're willing to do to accomplish them".

"I suppose I'll do what's in my power to be successful. I don't object to hard work and discipline. After all, these are things that help us meet our goals. Right"? Caroline shifted in her chair, removing her arm from the table, thence from Peter's reach. She lifted the napkin from her lap and dabbed the corner of her mouth, buying some time while she considered what she should say next.

Peter sat back in his seat and lifted his wine glass to Caroline as a sly smile crossed his face. "Here's to hard work, discipline, and the joy that comes when one realizes there is an easier way to get what you want".

"The wine is excellent, Peter". Once again, Caroline attempted to distract Peter. "I try not to drink too much though. Even a good wine, often gives me a headache. It's quite good, though".

Peter lifted his glass as he smiled. "Maybe I should get you something stronger".

Caroline shook her head politely refusing his offer. She tried to remain pleasant and made many attempts to redirect their conversation to the exhibit, the gallery, and his expertise in the field. She tried to focus on her meal, but it was becoming more difficult for Caroline to dissuade Peter. He wanted to talk about her personal life, which she wasn't comfortable with. She spent the last year trying to heal from past hurt and didn't want to discuss her past with him.

She sat across from the man who was supposed to help her grow into a new career. Where she would meet new people and learn more about the world of which she was about to become part. She thought about Andrew and how different he was from Peter. What she would give to have Andrew sitting here with her instead of Peter. She remembered Andrew's words. *I mean it Caroline. Don't be blindsided by him while you're in New York. Don't let him dazzle you with the excitement of the city. That kind of excitement doesn't last.*

At that moment Caroline became determined. She wasn't going to let anyone sabotage her in the new life she was making and wouldn't let Peter blindside her. She would remain on guard and would play his game to her benefit. She only needed to hold out for another week, then Andrew would be here.

Caroline managed to make it through the evening and when Peter dropped her off at the hotel, he did his best to suggest she invite him up to her room. "Peter, I think I should turn in...alone. I believe that wine has gone to my head. If I can get a good night's rest, I should be able to avoid a headache tomorrow. I wouldn't want to spoil my fist day in New York because of a migraine".

Peter took the hint. And much better than Caroline thought he would. She thanked him for a wonderful evening and went inside, making her way to her room while congratulating herself on avoiding his advances. She only hoped she could find enough excuses so she could keep her distance while still being able to work with him. She was excited about her new career and didn't want anything to spoil the opportunity she had in the exhibit.

Caroline stepped into her room and walked to the window where she looked down at the street below, the same street where she earlier watched the afternoon activity. What she looked down on was the same street, however, what she saw was a much different view. The Avenue was lit up like Christmas, with signs blinking and traffic coming and going. She smiled as she realized that the city was as alive now as it had been earlier in the day. New York never sleeps.

She turned from the window and prepared for bed. She went to her carryon and pulled out a bottle of water. She didn't want to have a headache in the morning so she was sure to drink what she could to cancel out the alcohol she drank at dinner. When she was settled, she pulled up the covers as she sunk into the soft mattress. She lay for a moment in the dark watching the shadows dance on the ceiling over her head and listened to the sounds of the night which were almost so distant she could barely hear the traffic below. She took a moment to think about Andrew and smiled as she faded into a deep sleep.

TWENTY-TWO

T he days that followed proved to be as challenging as the evening of Caroline's arrival. She showed up at the gallery for the first time and was amazed to see her art displayed and ready for the viewing public. She almost didn't recognize her work as it hung on expansive walls.

Peter worked hard to prepare for the exhibit and Caroline was grateful to him for taking the time to work with her. He spent the first three days making sure everything went off well. He had a business to run and that was his first, priority. Even Caroline would take the back seat when it came to money. She was impressed by Peter's ability to take control and bring the dreams of others to life. She saw a different side of him when he walked the length of his gallery.

Caroline preferred that side to the person she saw at dinner each night. It was always the same. He'd look at her and smile while he would tell her what she wanted, when he didn't know her well enough to make such assumptions. Caroline was glad for the long days of preparation which made real, a dream she never knew she had, until she met Andrew.

The day finally came when Caroline would be in the spotlight. She woke early and showered while she tried to talk herself down from the anxious fit she felt coming on. She wasn't prone to anxiety attacks, so she knew the feeling she experienced would pass. It was only a matter of when.

Caroline called room service, so she could enjoy a quiet breakfast. She wasn't ready to be around people yet, so she took her time getting ready. Although, she kept her eye on the clock that sat on the nightstand, so she wouldn't be late for her debut. She laid out her dress across the bed and stared at it wondering if it was the right choice for the occasion. She wiped her clammy hands on her robe as she willed the butterflies in her stomach to calm down. It was too late to change her mind now. And she settled on the fact that the simple black dress would have to do, as she dressed and stood in front of the mirror.

The image that looked back at Caroline seemed like a stranger to her. She studied herself while she adjusted the strand of pearls around her neck that went well with earrings that hung from her small lobes. She smoothed the front of her dress and tucked a stray hair into the pin that held back her bronze hair.

One final look in the mirror was all she had time for now. She checked her hemline before moving her focus to the black sandals that adorned one rhinestone along the strap of each shoe that hugged her feet. It was time. The phone rang and Caroline took a deep breath before answering. 'Hello, yes, tell him I will be right down".

There was no turning back now, Peter met Caroline in the lobby where they exchanged morning greetings before leaving for the gallery. Then Peter apologized. "I know we could have walked from here, but I thought it might be nice to arrive at the gallery on the opening day of your exhibit, in style". He opened the door and waited while Caroline slid in across the seat. He then ducked in and sat next to her as he signaled to the driver.

Caroline watched as they pulled away from the curb. She thought it seemed senseless to hire a car to drive them halfway around the block but was too preoccupied to argue, so, this one time, Peter got his way. There was barely enough time to finish her thought when they arrived at the gallery. The car stopped in front of the main entrance and Peter and Caroline performed the dance of which they'd become accustomed. Peter exited the car, walking around the back to meet Caroline at her door.

Peter reached out to take Caroline's hand as she stepped out of the vehicle. The building loomed up in front of her, larger than life, as the reality of the moment hit her. Today was the first day of a new life. It was the day Caroline would step into a new role. If everything went according to plan, she would be changing careers. Her stomach started to turn again as she followed the path to that led to the door. On her way her eye was caught by the sign. *Caroline – a Life in Pictures, an Exhibit.* Her heart leapt as she read the words that solidified the idea that was now coming to life. Caroline wished Andrew could be there to share in this joy. She wouldn't be there if it wasn't for him.

Caroline felt a hand on the small of her waist. "Are you ready"? Peter stood next to her, ready to walk at her side as they approached the door. He reached out and opened it then stepped aside so she could pass through first. The sly smile reappeared as they entered the room.

But Caroline's attention was no longer focused on Peter. She scanned the room, shocked to find it filled with many people. Music played softly in the background beneath the low murmur of voices exchanging opinions and sharing conversation. In the center of the main room stood a long, elegant table displaying hor dourves, and she caught a glimpse of a young man as he passed by with a tray on which sat glasses of champagne. Caroline smiled trying to picture herself in the center of that which was in front of her.

Peter placed a hand on her elbow. "Caroline, you haven't said a word. What do you think"?

She turned to him, seeing him for the first time since they walked into the room. "I think I'm in shock. I didn't realize there would be so many people here…at one time. And champagne, really Peter? Isn't that going too far? I'm a no body".

Peter lifted his finger to her lips as the muscles in her face became tense. "Shhh, Caroline. Don't talk like that, especially here. You're not a no body, not anymore. As soon as your art was placed on those walls, you became the most important person in the art world. People have been talking about this exhibit for weeks. We built up a buzz so irresistible that wild horses couldn't keep them away".

Caroline relaxed as she looked at Peter and smiled. "I can't believe this. You did all this, for me. Why? You barely know me. Even if my work is good, how much could you really benefit from it"?

Peter led Caroline to a quiet corner before answering her question. At which time he spoke softly. "Yes. I did this for you. I also did it for me, for us".

Caroline looked confused. "Us? What do you mean us"? Panic rose from the pit of her stomach as she stared into the face of the man who was about to make her famous.

"I find it hard to believe that you are unfamiliar with the idea, you scratch my back, I'll scratch yours. It's the way things get done. No one climbs the rungs of success without someone holding the ladder steady. I got you here, but it will be up to you to decide whether you stay here".

Caroline's heart sunk to the depths of her rhinestone sandals. "I don't think I understand what you're saying. I hope you're not saying what I think you're saying".

"I don't think there is any mistaking it. I got you here. Now I want something in return. I've been patient these last few days. I haven't pushed you. I've wined and dined you and dropped you off at the hotel without forcing myself on you. But now it's time to pay up. I want you, Caroline. I want you at my side, in my bed, and working with me here. We will support each other". Peter placed his arm around Caroline and pulled her to him.

She could feel his breath on her neck as he finished speaking, and her heart stopped beating. Her breath drew shallow as she tried to remain calm, and not allow her words get ahead of mind. She knew very well what men like Peter were about, although, she's hoped he would prove both her and Andrew wrong.

"What do you say Caroline"? He whispered in her ear.

The burning in Caroline's stomach moved into her esophagus, and she fought against the urge to vomit. She saw her dream pass in front of her then disappear. Knowing there was no way she would sacrifice herself to a man ever again. Whatever she agreed to would be driven by her hearts-desire. Not ploys and plots or the games others played to amuse themselves.

It was then she heard the words as they slipped past her lips. "I'm sorry Peter, I can't agree to such an arrangement. It's not moral or just. I wouldn't be able to live with myself. I won't make a deal with the devil to get ahead. I'd rather pack up those paintings and return them to the dark space they've occupied for the last twenty years. For the first time in my life, I'm happy, truly happy. I can't let you take from me".

Peter released her and took a step back as he stared into Caroline's eyes. The sly smile passed across his lips before he struck. "You give yourself too much credit Caroline. Do you think that I'm going to stand here, after all the work I've done, and let you walk away? No. We made a deal. You owe me".

Caroline met his stare while she stood her ground. "I read that contract Peter. There is nothing in it that says I must give myself to you, or anyone else. The first week is a trial period. At the end of the week one or the other of us can terminate the contract. There is nothing in the fine print. You can't force me to do anything I don't want to do".

"What's he trying to make you do"? Caroline jumped when she heard Andrew's voice. She turned around, shocked, and happy to see him. Yet she remained composed so as not to let either one knows how upset she was.

"Andrew, it's wonderful to see you. I wasn't expecting you to be here today". She wanted to throw her arms around his neck, but there were things more important that needed her attention right now so any reunion would have to wait.

Andrew felt disappointed by Caroline's response, but smiled at her, as he turned to look at Peter. "What's going on here, Peter?

Did I hear correctly, are you trying to force Caroline to do something she doesn't want to"?

Peter glared at Caroline then looked at Andrew. "I was explaining to Caroline that her work was not as good as I originally thought. Once I saw her work in the light of the gallery, I noticed many flaws, the work of an amateur".

Caroline's heart broke as she listened to Peter rip apart her work. Now it was displayed for all to see. There would be art collectors and dealers at the gallery who would laugh at the work she tried to pass off as professional art. She fought back tears. There was no way she would let Peter see her cry.

"I'm surprised to hear that, Peter. You were so confident when you first viewed her work. It seems strange that you would wait until this moment to tell Caroline she painted like an amateur. I don't believe it. I don't think you do either. Why don't we take a stroll around the gallery, together, all three of us"? Andrew smiled at Caroline before continuing.

"Peter, you can show us how you placed Caroline's art strategically in certain light to bring to life the images that each tell their own story". Andrew tried to soothe Peter by boosting his ego.

Peter glared at Caroline, then turned to Andrew. "I don't think I have time to devote to such a trivial task. I need to do damage control today. Tomorrow I will arrange to terminate the contract. At the end of the week, I'll pack up Caroline's work and she can return it to its dark corner". He sneered at Caroline as he finished speaking. "Never to see the light of day, I'm sure".

Andrew slipped his arm through Caroline's and walked with her to the open area of the gallery. "Don't listen to him. What happened back there"?

Caroline lifted her free hand to wipe a tear that escaped down her cheek. "It's as you suspected, he said he only helped me to get me into bed. He wants me in his bed and working in this gallery where we will live happily ever after". She turned to face Andrew. "What am I going to do? He humiliated me. I suppose it won't matter. I mean when I take my work down and return home no one will ever remember I was here".

Andrew took Caroline's hand and kissed it. "Don't you worry about your art. And don't believe what he said about your work being amateur. We both know that's not true. Now, why don't you walk around with me, and we can view your work in a new light. We'll worry about the rest tomorrow".

"It's a good thing you showed up when you did, Andrew. I don't know what I would have done if I had to spend another moment with that man". Caroline took Andrew's arm once more and they walked the length of the wall that displayed her work.

They stopped when they reached the shipwreck painting that Andrew saw for the first time on the wall in Caroline's spare room. "It looks different here, don't you think"? He paused while he recalled the catalyst for the image that had haunted her. "How are the nightmares, Caroline"?

"Surprisingly, they've subsided. I barely remember the dream. Except when I look at this painting. But even then, it's like a distant memory, something to recall with little emotion. I don't know what changed. But I'm glad it did". Caroline stepped back from the painting to make room for the couple that stopped to study the image.

Andrew took Caroline's hand to stop her from moving on. He leaned in and whispered in her ear. "Wait, let's see if they express an opinion about this one". Caroline nodded and they stood silently a few feet from the couple. "I'm not sure I want to hear what anyone might have to say after listening to Peter".

"Peter only said that because he got caught in his deception. Now, be quiet and listen". He whispered.

The two stood side by side, looking around on occasion to avoid suspicion, while straining to hear. The strangers stood for many minutes looking at the picture. It was the woman who spoke first. Caroline couldn't help but notice the commanding presence of the dark-haired woman whose bright blue eyes concentrated on the picture. "What do you think of this one"?

Her partner, a tall middle-aged man, with sandy blond hair, took a step back and studied the piece. Caroline held her breath, afraid to know what he was thinking. "I like it. It shows great depth, and an introspection that draws in the viewer. The more I look at it, the more I feel a part of the story the artist is telling".

"I think you're right. When I look at it, I can almost feel the wind on my face. And my stomach turns as I imagine the ship dipping and swaying as the waves surge. It's very good". A small smile passed across the lips of the woman as she turned and looked up at her friend. "Peter was lucky to stumble on Caroline, whoever she is. I think she's going to be a goldmine".

Caroline looked up at Andrew as her eyes grew wide, expressing the excitement she couldn't speak at the moment. Andrew lifted his finger to his lips to caution her to remain quiet.

"I wonder where he found her. I see an unbridled passion in each stroke of the brush. She is quite expressive. When I look at her work, each piece, I see more than a picture, I see a lifetime of struggle or joy, depending on the painting. How does she do that"?

"I don't know what makes painters good at what they do. I imagine she must be drawing from some experience. Although I don't know how that could be. Her work spans many generations. Whatever her secret is, that is what will make her successful. Great even". He paused as he stepped forward to get a better look at the brush strokes. "I wish we would have found her first. I mean, Peter is good at what he does, but he lacks the commitment to push his clients to greatness".

Andrew squeezed Caroline's hand cautioning her again to remain quiet. The couple stood for a moment longer before moving on to the next painting. Andrew turned to face Caroline. "Do you know who they were, Caroline"?

Caroline shook her head. "No, I don't. I wonder if they have connections that would help me"? Her voice gave away the discouragement she felt.

"That was Rebecca and Gerald Hanson. They own *New York Galleria*. Its world renowned, they're famous for finding and displaying unique art. They have connections. They are the connection". Andrew watched as the two disappeared in the crowd. "We need to talk to them before they find Peter".

Caroline looked confused. "Why. Peter so much as said my work is amateur. He doesn't think my work is worthy of his time or the space it occupies in his gallery".

"That may be true, but if they find him and congratulate him on finding such a gem, he surely will want to keep your art here. You won't ever get away from him. He will haunt you, like the nightmare you have been haunted by for years".

Andrew looked around the space for Peter. "I have a plan. You need to find Peter and distract him. Find a way to keep him busy for a while. I'm going to find the Hanson's".

"Andrew, no. That can't be a good idea".

Caroline. Didn't you hear them? Gerald said he wished they found you first. You find Peter. I'll talk to the Hanson's, the worst they will do is say no. You won't be any worse for the asking. Now, go".

Caroline sighed as she thought about what Andrew said. She then shrugged her shoulders, and without another word, left Andrew's side and disappeared in the crowd.

Andrew looked in the direction that the Hanson's moved, only moments earlier. He scanned the crowd hoping to see them from where he stood. When he didn't recognize any sign of the pair, he followed the direction they took, hoping to find them. He made his way through the crowd, occasionally looking at Caroline's work as he passed. He smiled as he remembered the day they first met, not knowing at the time, the talent she kept hidden.

He studied faces and listened to conversations as he made his way through the gallery. He heard nothing but positive comments about Caroline's work from people who enjoyed their time at the gallery. It was those comments the fueled Andrew's desire to give Caroline a fighting chance. He knew now that Peter wasn't the best option for Caroline. She wouldn't soar under Peters' watchful eye. He would clip her wings and keep her locked up in his gallery. She would be like a caged bird singing a sad song while missing out on life. Andrew knew he couldn't let that happen.

Andrew caught his breath as his eye was drawn to the couple, tall and short, dark hair, and light. He heard Rebecca laugh as she conversed with another couple in front of the *Loving Ladies*, the painting that reflected Caroline's life. He approached the small group cautiously. He waited for a break in the conversation before speaking. "Excuse me, Ms. Hanson".

The small woman turned to Andrew, her bright eyes recognizing him instantly. "Oh, my. What have I done to deserve to be approached by Andrew Roberts? Please, call me Rebecca".

Andrew nodded and smiled. "Okay, Rebecca. May I speak to you and Gerald for a moment"?

"Of course,". Rebecca rested her hand on Gerald's arm and winked at him. "Gerald, Andrew Roberts would like to speak to us". She looked at the couple that stood next to Gerald. "Would you excuse us for a minute? I promise we will continue the conversation shortly".

Rebecca and Gerald followed Andrew to a quiet spot near a tall sculpture of what appeared to be the Tree of Life. "Thank you for allowing me to take a few minutes of your time. I overheard you talking a while ago. You were in front of Caroline's *Shipwreck*. Did you mean what you said about wishing you found her first"?

Gerald looked down at Rebecca and smiled then focused on Andrew. "Are you kidding. I like Peter, and I think he has a good thing going here, but I think we could have offered her a better option. Rebecca has an eye for art and a heart of gold. She would have nurtured the girl and guided her to greatness. I'm afraid Peter will only sell her".

Andrew nodded. "I agree, completely. What would you say if I told you, the contract between Caroline and Peter is only temporary? They signed on a trial basis. Either of them has the option after seven days to terminate or renew the contract". Rebecca's eyebrows went up as she looked at Gerald, waiting for a reaction.

Gerald proceeded cautiously. "Are you sure about that? And how do you have access to the information"?

Andrew told them the story about how he met Caroline, and how when he stumbled on her paintings, he thought she was a natural. He went on to explain how he knew Peter and though he might be able to help Caroline find her way in the art world. Unfortunately, Peter was more interested in Caroline, then in her

225

work. Caroline found out that day he expected something in trade for his helping her. He further explained how Caroline stood up to Peter, telling him she'd take home her work and return it to the dark forever before she'd agree to his terms.

He continued to explain that Caroline was distraught and disappointed but wasn't willing to compromise. Peter went on to tell her she was an amateur and would never amount to anything without his guidance. So, by the end of the week Caroline would be free to move her art elsewhere.

"So, you're the one who found her". Rebecca studied Andrew. "You're in love with her, aren't you"?

"Rebecca, that's not our business". Gerald interrupted.

A slight smile passed across Andrew's lips. "I'm not afraid to answer Rebecca's question, Gerald". He looked directly at Rebecca. "Yes, I'm in love with her. I'd do anything for her. She is a special woman and deserves a chance to realize her dream. I don't want to see her get hurt. So, if you think you can help her, and are willing to guide her, I think you better do it soon. If Peter gets wind of the comments you made in front of the *Shipwreck*, he will bully Caroline into extending the contract". He paused briefly before finishing. "Are you interested"?

"Are we interested"? Rebecca looked up at Gerald waiting for his response. "What do you think Gerald"?

"I think we should meet her and ask her what she wants. Then we decide. Why don't we have dinner tonight, the four of us? We can discuss it then. The gallery closes in an hour. Do you think you can keep Caroline away from Peter until tomorrow"?

Andrew nodded. "I'll keep her away from him".

"Okay then, it's settled. We have reservations at Le Bernardin, tonight at seven. Meet us there. We can discuss Caroline's options then". Rebecca smiled up at Andrew. "Bring a copy of her current contract with you if you can get a copy. I want to see it".

"We'll be there". Andrew was preparing to leave but turned back to Gerald. "Promise me you will do what's in Caroline's best interest, not for your agenda".

Woods

Rebecca answered as she lightly laughed. "Andrew, Caroline's best interest is our best interest. We have all we will ever need in this lifetime. We are concerned with the best interest of all our clients. We will guide her well. But let's wait until we see what she wants to do. I know you want what's best for her, but we want to hear from her mouth, what she wants. We'll see you at seven tonight".

Andrew nodded and smiled. "That's all I can ask. We'll see you at seven". He watched the Hanson's return to their prior conversation before turning back to the gallery, which he scanned looking for either Caroline or Peter. He walked through the crowd listening to comments about art that hung on expansive walls. He paid special attention to those that studied Caroline's work. Andrew was happy to hear the positive comments made about the many pictures that Andrew knew were Caroline's.

He continued his search for Caroline. The longer he looked the more worried he became. When he saw a server walking toward him, he smiled nervously and stopped him. "Excuse me, have you seen Peter Carlton? I wanted to congratulate him on his success with this exhibit, but I can't seem to find him".

The man nodded as he moved the tray from one hand to another so he could address Andrew properly. "I believe he's in his office. I saw him walking that way with Caroline earlier. I had a chance to look at her work when I came to work this morning. She's good. Peter got lucky when he found her".

Andrew tried not to let the server see his impatience. "Could you point me in the direction of his office? I don't mean to be rude, but I don't have much time for my visit. I'd like to see him before I leave".

"No problem." The man pointed in the direction of Peter's office. "His office is that way. When you reach the corner take a left. His office is at the end of the hall".

Andrew thanked the server then quickly walked in the direction of Peter's office. His mind raced as he reached the corner where the walls met that created the hallway. He kept his eyes on the door as he picked up his pace and approached it. Andrew stopped in front of the door, listening to voices on the other side as

227

they escalated. He recognized Peter's voice immediately, wondering if his harsh words were directed at Caroline.

When he heard her reply he quickly reached for the doorknob and entered the room. The door opened into a large space, where stood, in its center a desk of steel and wood. Andrew focused immediately on Peter, who stood with his right hand over his eye. Caroline had backed away from Peter and leaned against the desk, breathing heavily while she massaged her right arm.

Andrew knew there had been some sort of altercation. He could tell from the conversation he overheard from behind the closed door. He went to Caroline, right away. "What's going on here"?

Peter removed his hand from his face and pointed at Caroline. "Her. She's what happened. Your girlfriend is crazy"!

Caroline pushed herself from the desk and stood straight, ready to defend herself. "He's not my boyfriend". She looked quickly at Andrew before focusing on Peter. "And you deserved what you got. You can't bully people and get away with it".

Andrew focused on Caroline's arm. There was a large bruise on her right upper arm. Her hair had come lose from its clip and she was visibly shaken. He approached her somewhat hurt by her response to Peter's insult. For the moment he let it pass because of his concern for her wellbeing. He stopped in front of her and looked at her arm. It was clear to him what happened. Andrew knew at once that the bruise was the result of Peter's forceful hand. He reached up and brushed the hair from Caroline's face. "Are you okay, Caroline"?

She nodded as she looked in Peter's direction. "I'm okay. He didn't hurt me".

Andrew lifted Caroline's arm as he spoke. "It looks to me as though he did. This is quite a bruise, Caroline."

Peter interrupted Andrew as he addressed Caroline. "Is she hurt? Are you kidding me? I'm the one you should be concerned about. She's an animal".

Andrew looked in Pete's direction, noticing for the first time, the blood that ran from his eye. It wasn't extreme, but it appeared to Andrew that Caroline did the best she could to defend herself. He looked at Caroline, and she looked up at him as she confirmed Peter's accusation.

"I had no choice, Andrew. It was the only way I could get him to let go. I'm not going to be the victim of any man, ever again". She looked directly at Peter. "I told you 'no'. I'm not interested in you that way. I thought you were the person who would help me with my art. I never agreed to become anything beyond a client. If you thought otherwise, that's your mistake, not mine".

Andrew moved to the desk where he picked up the phone. Peter quickly moved in his direction and placed his hand over Andrew's so he wouldn't lift the receiver. "What are you doing"?

"I'm calling the police. What do you think I'm doing? It looks to me as though you tried to force yourself on Caroline. Rape, even attempted rape is against the law, no matter who you are". Andrew stood his ground.

"What? No. My career will be ruined. The publicity will ruin my reputation. Even if I prove her wrong in court". Peter glared at Caroline. "Even if I make it look like her fault, it will be too late".

"I guess you should have thought about that before you forced yourself on her".

Caroline stepped forward. "Andrew, wait".

"What do you mean wait? After what he tried to do to you. He could have…well, it could have been a lot worse if I hadn't shown up. He should pay for what he did".

"I know. You're right, but I don't know if I want my career in the art world to start out this way. I don't want my success coming on the heels of pity. I don't want to be a martyr. Then I'll never know if my work is really good". Caroline looked at Peter before continuing.

"Peter. I don't want to work with you. I don't want to sleep with you or do anything else with you. Neither do I want you to destroy my reputation in the art world before I get started". She looked to Andrew who stood waiting to make the call. "Andrew, I want to report this, but I will agree not to press charges as long as Peter agrees to leave me alone. That means he agrees not to say anything negative about my work to anyone, publicly or privately. If he agrees to these terms, I will agree not to press charges".

Andrew studied Caroline for a moment. He looked down at the bruise, knowing the inner strength she would draw from no matter what was decided. He then looked at Peter, who stood next to him, the small drops of blood drying as they spoke. "Peter, will you agree to the terms Caroline suggested"?

Peter nodded as he glared at Caroline. "I suppose I have no other option".

"Okay, then. The agreement will be as follows. Peter you will agree not to see Caroline. You won't say anything derogatory about her person or her work to anyone, publicly or privately. You will return all artwork to her in the condition it is in right now. All her work. Caroline, you will file a police report and get a restraining order on Peter, to include his seeing you, calling you, saying anything about you or your work. The restraining order will remain in effect until any statute of limitation to prosecute Peter, runs out".

Caroline stood determined not to break down. She nodded in agreement but remained silent.

Andrew looked at Peter, wishing he hadn't introduced him to Caroline. He couldn't believe a man could be so changeable. The person he thought he knew never would have done what he did. He then turned to Caroline, who stood steadfast, ready to take on the world. Andrew knew she was hurt, but she would never admit it. He wanted to go to her, take her in his arms, and protect her from the Peter's of the world. But he remained where he stood, knowing she would turn him away. He felt helpless as he lifted the receiver and dialed, hoping he was making the right choice.

TWENTY-THREE

Caroline and Andrew walked into the restaurant side by side. Caroline was glad for the opportunity to dine with someone other than Peter. A chill went down her spine at the thought of his name. The dull pain in her right arm was a constant reminder of the close call she survived that afternoon. She looked up at Andrew who stood next to her talking to the hostess. She studied his face wondering if she misjudged him the way she did Peter. Could she trust him? She knew now wasn't the time or the place to be contemplating such a question. She would save her doubts for when she was alone in her room later. Tonight, she would focus on the reason she came to New York for in the first place. She only hoped the people she met next would provide her a better opportunity.

Andrew placed a hand on Caroline's elbow, bringing her back to his side. They walked through the restaurant until they stood at the table where Andrew introduced Caroline. Gerald invited them to sit and asked what they were drinking. Caroline was too nervous to consider drinking. She wanted to be on her game as she discussed her future with these two strangers.

Rebecca smiled at Caroline as she sat down. "So, I understand you're not planning to renew your contract with Peter Carlton, is that true?"

Caroline nodded. "Yes, that's true. After working with him over the last week, I realize we view the world of art differently. If you don't mind, I'd rather not go into detail about the arrangement, but would like to look forward to better opportunities".

Rebecca reached out and placed her hand over Caroline's briefly. "I understand, Caroline. I appreciate your wanting to remain professional. I'd like to say, I think you're making the right choice. I mean, Peter is good at selling art, but if you want to grow, he may not be the best choice for representation".

Gerald chimed in. "We're not saying you will have us represent you. We want you to know that we appreciate the fact that you realized sooner than later that Peter wasn't the right fit for you. You should take your time making that choice. We thought it would be good to get together tonight to discuss your options, get to know each other, so all of us have the opportunity to see if we would be a good match". He picked up the menu from the table. "Why don't we order, so we can talk, uninterrupted. I'm fascinated by your work and would like to know what motivates you to paint the subjects you do".

They all followed Gerald's lead, and perused their menus then, when the server arrived at the table, he answered their questions and left the table with their order.

The group sat together talking about how tough it could be to break into the industry. Rebecca spoke specifically to Caroline. "I can't believe you hid away those paintings. Their beautiful. I think it's criminal to hold them hostage, when so many could be enjoying them".

Andrew interjected. "When I saw them, I was floored. Caroline said she didn't believe they were good enough to be seen in public. I asked her why she kept them the way she did if they weren't good enough. She said, for her painting was like raising a child. You wouldn't throw out a child because they didn't turn out perfect. She couldn't throw out the paintings either".

Gerald leaned forward, to pick up his glass as he addressed Caroline. "I think subconsciously you knew they were good enough but consciously were afraid to hope".

Caroline lightly laughed. "I guess I never thought of it that way. Truly, I started painting as a hobby. It was something I could do in the evenings when the children were young. It was relaxing. I certainly never thought I'd be sitting here talking to you about the industry".

"So, you have children"? Rebecca asked.

"Well, yes. They're grown and on their own now. I miss having them around, and realize I need to find something to do with my time now that my parenting days are behind me. Actually, I never would have considered exhibiting my work if Andrew hadn't pushed me".

Rebecca looked to Gerald as she took his hand from the table. "Gerald and I would have loved to have the opportunity to be parents".

They smiled at each other as Gerald squeezed her hand then explained. "It wasn't to be for some reason, so we devote our time to our clients. In a way they are our children. We take them under our wing, nurture them in their craft, and watch them grow, until they are confident in their work, and are able to sell or display what they create anywhere in the world".

Caroline studied Gerald as he spoke. "That's beautiful. I don't think I've ever heard anyone speak about anyone so genuinely before. I think your clients are probably lucky to have you work with them".

Rebecca sat back in her chair waiting for Caroline to finish talking. "You know, you could be one of them if you choose. I like you. I think you'd be a good addition to the family".

"Rebecca". Gerald warned. "We agreed. No pushing". He turned to Caroline. "We agreed tonight we would get to know each other. We'd take our queue from you. I understand your experience with Peter wasn't a pleasant one. We don't want you to feel pressured or obligated in any way, to work with us.

The server arrived at the table and placed their meals in front of them. "So, please, relax, enjoy your dinner, and we'll continue the conversation. Right, Rebecca".

"Of course, Gerald". She turned to Caroline. "I'm sorry, Caroline. I get excited when I see great art and know it deserves to be shared. Gerald says I'm too passionate about art. I don't believe there is such a thing. In any case, he is right. Ignore my over zealousness. Let's enjoy the evening and what is meant to will be".

Andrew sat back and watched the interaction between Caroline and the Hanson's. He listened to the exchange sensing a connection between them. Caroline seemed at ease, even as Rebecca pushed her, in her loving way. Gerald and Rebecca worked on Caroline gently. It was obvious the Hanson's were meant for each other. They worked together well. Watching them was almost like watching a dance. Gerald releasing Rebecca only to reel her back in.

Andrew was jealous of the connection they shared. He longed to be part of something, someone who would respond in kind. He watched Caroline as she laughed at the Hanson's, and the quirky way, they read each other, completed one another. He knew she was enjoying the evening. He did his best to sit back and let the conversation flow, without his input. It was enough for him to be near Caroline. He knew his time would come. He would wait patiently. Peter made Caroline doubt herself and her abilities to trust. Andrew only hoped the Hanson's could repair the damage Peter had done. He hoped it would be during that meal. Caroline shouldn't lose momentum.

They continued the conversation as they worked on the meal in front of them until, finally their plates were clean. Gerald ordered dessert, swearing they had the best "Truffle Vacherin' he ever had. It was the intermission between dinner and Dessert that Rebecca reluctantly asked Caroline if she could read the contract she signed for Peter. She didn't want to scare off Caroline, but the evening was coming to an end and she wanted to take any opportunity to get Caroline to consider letting them exhibit her work.

Caroline reached for her purse which hung on the back of her chair. She removed the folded paper and handed it to Rebecca. The table was silent while She read the words that had committed Caroline to the week of discomfort, she currently endured.

Rebecca handed back the contract. "I only wanted to read it to be sure Peter couldn't come back on you later. I always want to be sure the cord is cut before beginning a relationship with new clients. I'm not saying you are agreeing to let us represent you, but I thought it would be a good idea to get it out of the way in case down the road, you decide to work with us".

The server placed a Truffle in front of Gerald as he spoke. "What do you think, Rebecca? Do you think there will be any hurdles to deal with"?

Rebecca watched Caroline place the folded pages in her bag. "No. Surprisingly, the contract is pretty clear. It secures Caroline for seven days. At the end of seven days, they can renegotiate. It doesn't make sense to me. Caroline's good. Her work is exceptional. I don't understand why there isn't a noncompete clause. Usually, the agent will state, the client can't sign with another agent for amount of time. He must have been pretty sure Caroline would resign. I can't imagine he really believes her work is amateur. You're fortunate, Caroline. You could have been stuck".

Caroline looked at Andrew securing the secret that set her free. Andrew was impressed with Caroline's quick thinking, even though he wanted Peter to pay for his behavior. But they agreed, so he did as she wished, hoping Peter would keep quiet.

"Yes, I am. I guess it's a good thing Peter believes I can't paint. Now I can decide what I want to do without being coerced. I think I knew Peter wouldn't be good for me, but I wanted to believe that he truly thought my painting was worth his time. Well, it doesn't matter anymore. I'd like to forget the whole thing".

"I can understand that Caroline". Gerald paused to choose his words carefully. "But please don't sit idle because of one bad experience. There are many galleries out there that would do right by you, including ours. There's nothing we'd like more than to be able to help you find your way in this industry. We wouldn't force you to do anything you weren't comfortable with. Having said that I want you to know that we would love to work with you. We believe we could help you get the exposure that would set you on the road to success". He looked at Rebecca and nodded.

Rebecca reached in her purse and removed a folded document. "Caroline, we don't want this to scare you off. But we don't want to waste time either. You're here in New York for a short time. We only have tonight to convince you that we would work in your best interest. We drew up a contract, for you. It doesn't commit you to sign it. We want you to take it home and read it. Study it. Have your attorney review it. If it works for you, then you can sign it and send it to us. I know were in a bit of a time crunch as relates to the work you already have here in New York. My hope is that by the time you must remove your art from Peter's gallery, you will decide to sign the contract. If you do, we will, on your behalf, arrange to remove your work from Peter's gallery. We will then store them only until we can prepare an exhibit for you. That way you don't have to have them shipped back to your home".

Rebecca looked at Gerald before continuing. "If you decide to sign the contract, I'd like to come to your home and see the remainder of your work. We can spend some time together to decide how to best display what you have. We can also determine which pieces you'd like to sell and how much they might be worth".

Gerald chimed in. "All that can come later though. So, please put the contract in your purse and read it later. The remainder of the evening is dedicated to dessert".

Caroline took the contract offered by Rebecca. She did as she was asked and placed it in her bag before the server placed a Truffle in front of her. Her eyes grew wide, her reaction to the cake she knew she didn't have room for.

Andrew laughed as he replied. "Don't worry Caroline, you can take home what you don't finish. Truffles make a great breakfast".

TWENTY-FOUR

The car pulled up to the door and stopped in front of the hotel. Andrew quietly sat waiting for Caroline to speak. When the words didn't come, Andrew started. "I think that went well. What do you think"?

Caroline's head was spinning as her mind jumped from Peter to the Hanson's, to Andrew. The day was long and the energy of unsurety pulsed in her veins. She thought about all that happened that day, wondering if she would be able to keep up the pace. "I think I'm in a fast-paced city, where I'm finding if I blink, I might miss something important. I've been living in a quiet town for many years, Andrew. I don't know if I'm ready for this".

Andrew turned to Caroline. "Caroline today wasn't a good day for you on one level, but it was a great day on many others. You found out today that Peter is a jerk and can't be trusted. We both knew that was a possibility. But you also met the Hanson's who are genuine, and I feel, want the best for you. I know I introduced you to Peter, and I'm sorry for that. Somehow, we knew going in that he might be a problem. But you were willing to take the risk. I didn't think he would go to the extent he did to bully you, and I'm sorry for it. But I hate to see you give up because of one bad experience.

I think you should read through the contract. Have your attorney review it. Then decide. I know you don't want to sit idle. You said yourself, that you wanted a new life. This is that life. I won't force you to do what you don't want to do, but I want what's best for you. The real you. The woman who is scratching at the lid.

You've been buried too long. A diamond in the rough. It's time for you to shine. You've put in your time. You've been forced, driven and pressured. All that heat has formed a beautiful diamond, ready to be pulled from the earth to shine like no other. I believe in you. I trust your ability and know that you're ready. Now is the time.

When Andrew paused, the driver cleared his throat, breaking the temporary silence. Andrew took Caroline's hand and smiled. "The clock is ticking. What do you say about having a drink with me? I know the lounge inside is still open. We have some catching up to do". He looked out the window into the twilight. The sun was gone, but it was still early enough that the sky appeared more of a deep blue, than the dark of night.

Caroline noticed the numbers changing on the meter. She wasn't sure she felt like visiting, but at the same time she hadn't had a chance to talk to Andrew alone since his arrival. "I think I'd like that. I've missed you".

Andrew opened his door and Caroline followed suite, picking up the bag which held her breakfast, chocolate cake. He stopped at the driver's door and paid the fare before taking Caroline's arm. "I was hoping you would say that. I've missed you too. You're right, we do have some catching up to do. I want to hear all about your visit to the Big Apple".

"Well, Andrew. There isn't much to tell".

"Let's go inside and get a table, so we can talk". Andrew opened the door and let Caroline pass through. They walked past the concierge and into the lounge. They looked around and simultaneously pointed to a table tucked away in the corner. Caroline lightly laughed as they crossed the room and sat down. Andrew signaled to the server, who quickly arrived at the table. Caroline agreed to share a bottle of wine with Andrew to celebrate her upcoming success.

"I don't know how much I feel like celebrating. I feel like I'm no better than Peter, bribing him to keep quiet, so I can get ahead". Caroline shifted as she got comfortable in her chair.

"Caroline, you didn't do anything wrong. It was quick thinking on your part. He never would have stopped bullying you. He would have spread rumors and destroyed your career before you had a fighting chance. Let that go". He paused to take a drink of water from the glass the server placed in front of him. "What do you think of Rebecca and Gerald"?

"They seem like nice people. From what I understand they are quite successful".

"Are you going to consider their offer"?

"I think so. I mean, they said some pretty nice things about my work, when they didn't know I was listening. And Rebecca appears to be knowledgeable about the industry. I got the impression the Gerald is a straight shooter. He seems concerned about the opinion of whom he's dealing. I want to sleep on it, though. Tomorrow I'll read the contract and email it to my attorney so she can review it. Then I'll decide". Caroline thanked the server who placed the glass of red wine on the table in front of her.

"I think that's the sensible thing to do". Andrew reached across the table, taking Caroline's hand in his. "I've missed you, a great deal. I found myself often wondering what you might be doing. And thinking about the time we spent together. This is like coming home after wandering the desert". He squeezed her hand gently.

"Who would have thought two people could form a connection so quickly". Caroline said.

"Connections continue through time and space, even in love". Andrew's eyes met Caroline's.

She dismissed Andrew's claim. "I have to admit, in the past I never would have gone sailing with a stranger, even a celebrity stranger ". She joked.

"Are you glad you did"? Andrew gazed into Caroline's eyes hoping they would reveal what her lips wouldn't.

Caroline's breath caught in her throat as Andrew's eyes bore into her soul. She knew what he was doing, and she wanted to look away, but she couldn't break his spell. She enjoyed being with him. While in New York, she found her thoughts turning to Andrew when she had a free moment. Caroline struggled with what she wanted and what she had committed to. She promised herself she wouldn't turn to a man again for happiness. Finally, she was finding herself, and realizing a dream that was buried so deep she never realized it existed.

It was her final thought that made her realize, that Andrew wasn't like any man she was tied to in the past. He is the one person who encouraged her to dream. He convinced her to take a chance, to grow. She wouldn't be sitting across the table from Andrew Roberts if he hadn't talked her into it.

Her heart beat deep in her chest, as Andrew studied her. He leaned over the table. "Dance with me". It wasn't a question, but a statement.

Caroline found she couldn't say no. "I haven't danced in a long time, Andrew. I'm not sure I'm the best dance partner".

Before she knew what was happening, she was standing on the small dance floor, in Andrew's arms. The pianoplayer, watched as Andrew drew Caroline to him. She took her queue from the pair, that she observed, were one. She slowed the pace and as her fingers caressed the keys and she started to sing *Come Away with Me*.

Andrew swayed back and forth, holding Caroline, as they glided across the floor. He held her close, taking in the scent of her hair as one hand rested on the small of her back.

Caroline smiled up at Andrew, then looked away. She was determined to keep her cool, promising never to give in to the feelings she so desperately wanted to ignore. They danced arm in arm as the music continued. Andrew drew Caroline closer and held her tight, so tight that she had no option, other than to rest her head against his chest. She leaned in, and relaxed, as the scent of Andrew's cologne filled her senses. Caroline closed her eyes and focused on the gentle beat of Andrew's heart.

Her pulse quickened as she recalled the moment they first met, in this lifetime. She remembered sailing, hiking, and finally, the kiss. The electric kiss that brought her to her senses, returned her to her true self. A tear escaped down her cheek as she fought against fate and the inevitable. The dream she desired as she stood on the boardwalk was no longer the dream that was her reality. She knew now her fate lay in another direction.

Andrew relaxed his hold, as Caroline rested against his chest. The music played softly, and the world was right for the moment. Andrew listened to the lyrics, humming along until unconsciously, he softly sang, "Come away with me and we'll kiss, on a mountaintop, come away with me, and I'll never stop loving you".

Caroline pulled back from Andrew, far enough so she could look, into the deep dark pools that, she now believed, for many lifetimes, had captivated her. Andrew gazed into her eyes, searching for the woman he knew as his soul mate. On a subconscious level they returned to a time of young love, remembering each other and what they meant to one another. Their minds met as they remembered an existence that cemented a love that time itself couldn't erase.

Caroline could feel her heart beating in her chest forcing the blood to her temples as Andrew consumed her with his gaze. Her stomach fluttered and she became weak in the knees. She lost all sense of who she had been for the many years that she fought to create a life that now, meant nothing. That life was slipping away. It was slowly disappearing, as it lost all meaning, and the connection to that life shrank as they moved across the floor, together.

Andrew felt himself drowning in Caroline's gaze. He drew her hand close and lowered it to her side where he released it, only to gently glide his hand along her bare arm, over her shoulder, until it stopped to caress her neck.

Caroline caught her breath as his hand lightly touched her ear. She brought her free hand around his waist, as she realized there wasn't a place she'd rather be, than in Andrew's arms. She shivered as he ran his hand along her arm one more time before slipping his hand around her waist.

The dance was timeless. For the moment they were lost to the world. They were consumed with one another, seeing only each other as the music hypnotized them. Caroline's throat felt constricted when she realized she couldn't speak, or swallow. For the first time in her life, she realized what real, true love was. In her heart she knew this was it. Andrew was the man she was meant to spend her life with. The realization brought tears to her eyes. She smiled at Andrew, who looked worried about her tears. Caroline shook her head, dismissing the need for concern.

The final verse of the song prompted Andrew to draw Caroline closer. He knew the music would soon end and he would have to release her. Determined to make the most of the opportunity to hold Caroline without her fleeing, he removed one hand from her waist. The music was coming to an end as he returned his hand to her arm where he retraced his earlier path, up her arm until his hand rested on the back of her neck.

Caroline sighed as Andrew leaned in, and with the final words of the song whispered. "Caroline. Come away with me". He then turned her face toward him and gently kissed her waiting lips.

About the Author

Lee Woods was born in Concord, New Hampshire and raised in Soldotna, Alaska. She currently lives in New Hampshire where she raised her two daughters. Lee holds a degree in Early Childhood Education and Business Administration. She worked as a Web Administrator and Benefits Administrator until turning to a writing career. She is the Author of a "The War Within", "A Dangerous Truth" and of the blog site Authorleewoods.com (www.authorleewoods.com).

Lightning Source UK Ltd.
Milton Keynes UK
UKHW020115111022
410273UK00021B/216